THE HIGHBORN LONGWALKER

THRICE NINE LEGENDS

Joshua Robertson

Copyright © 2018 by Joshua Robertson

Published by Crimson Edge Press
www.robertsonwrites.com

All rights reserved. This book or any portion thereof may not be reproduced or used in any manner whatsoever without the express written permission of the publisher except for the use of brief quotations in a book review.

Printed in the United States of America

First Printing, 2018

Paperback ISBN: 978-1-945397-82-0
Hardback ISBN: 978-1-945397-83-7

Cover and typography completed by Venkatesh Sekar.
Cover art used with permission by Joakim Olofsson.

Acknowledgement

In the last days, you will look behind and reflect on what you have done and what you have not. Pray, in that moment, your heart knows peace.

There once was a time when the gods were gods without question. When men were men without example. When heroes were only the frivolous dreams of lurid mortality. It was a time when truths and untruths were indistinguishable, hatred and love were equally excusable, and life and death regaled all of humanity in the same breath. Myths of old were realized and legends were born from the very dust man was formed of, to be told and retold until the grace of time altered them beyond knowing or forgot them completely. Still, some tales were preserved deep within the hearts of mankind, for reasons that could not be fathomed. Perhaps bearing the fruit of some profound truth or kept alive merely by the strength of the men who lived them. Some tales would never be forgotten.

Table of Contents

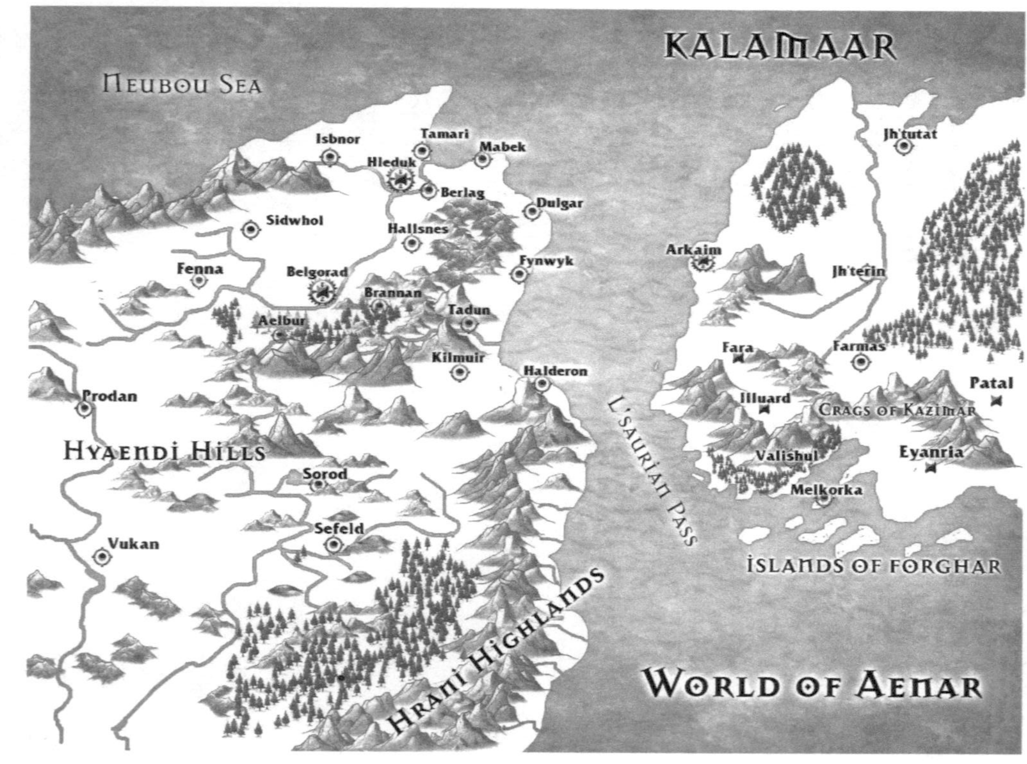

KALAMAAR
NEUBOU SEA
Isbnor
Tamari
Hleduk
Mabek
Berlag
Dulgar
Sidwhol
Hallsnes
Fenna
Belgorad
Fynwyk
Brannan
Aelbur
Tadun
Kilmuir
Halderon
Prodan
HYAENDI HILLS
Sorod
Sefeld
Vukan
HRANI HIGHLANDS
L'SAURIAN PASS
Arkaim
Jh'tutat
Jh'terin
Fara
Farmas
Illuard
Patal
CRAGS OF KAZIMAR
Valishul
Eyanria
Melkorka
ISLANDS OF FORGHAR
WORLD OF AENAR

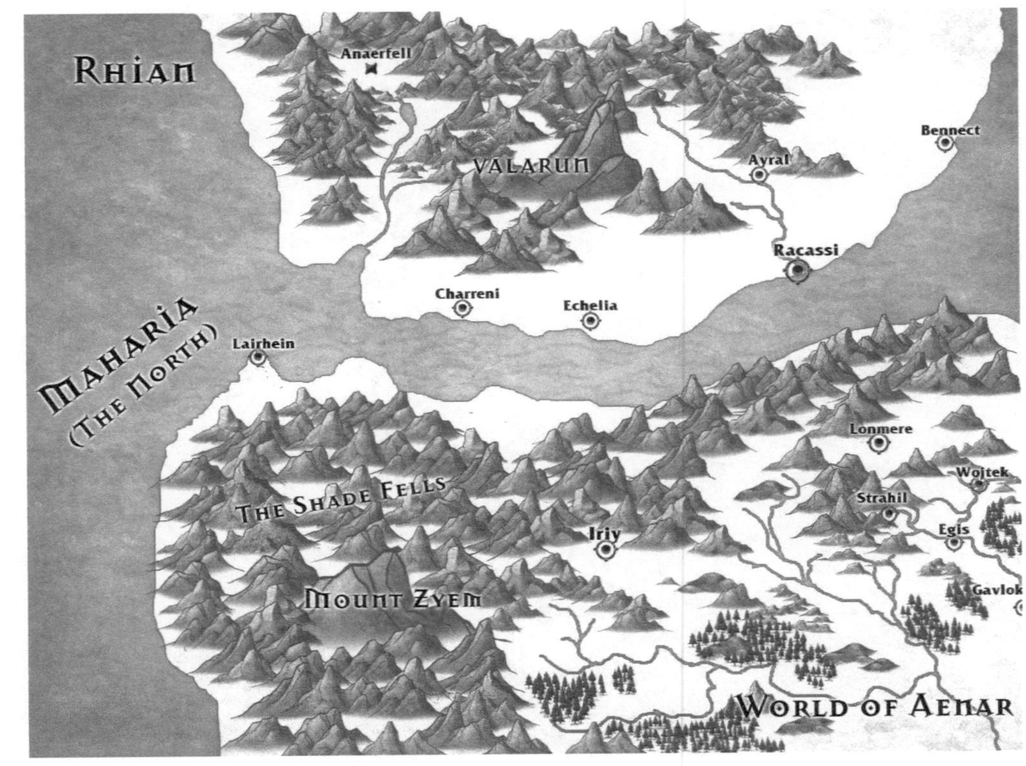

Rhian
Anaerfell
VALARUN
Bennect
Ayral
Racassi
MAHARIA
(The North)
Charreni
Echelia
Lairhein
Lonmere
Wojtek
Strahil
The Shade Fells
Egis
Iriy
Gavlok
Mount Zyem
World of Aenar

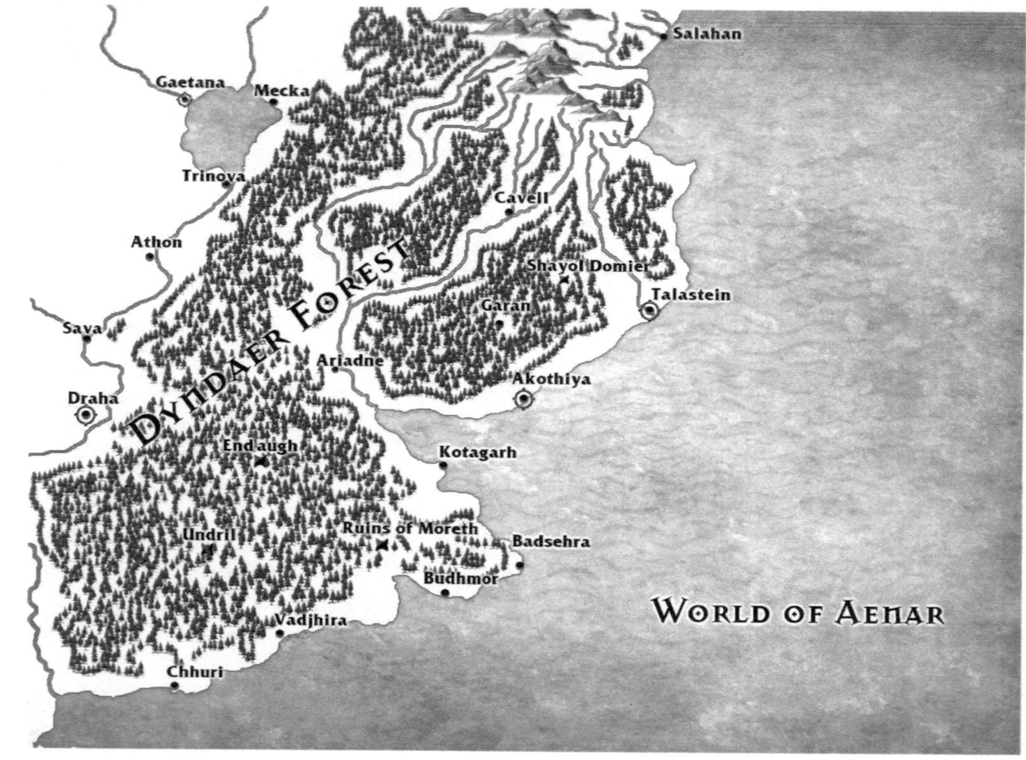
DYNDAER FOREST
WORLD OF AENAR
Salahan
Gaetana
Mecka
Trinova
Cavell
Athon
Shayol Domier
Garan
Talastein
Sava
Ariadne
Akothiya
Draha
Endaugh
Kotagarh
Undril
Ruins of Moreth
Badsehra
Budhmor
Vadjhira
Chhuri

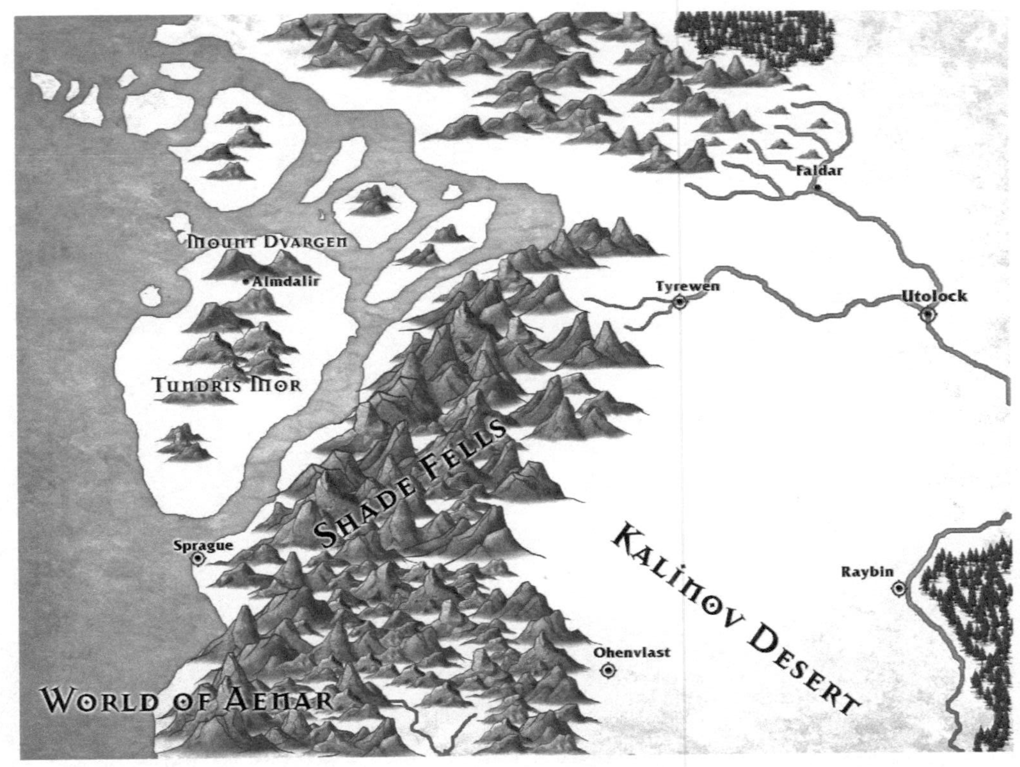

World of Aenar
Mount Dvargen
Almdalir
Tundris Mor
Shade Fells
Sprague
Ohenvlast
Kalinov Desert
Tyrewen
Utolock
Faldar
Raybin

Thrice Nine Legends Saga

The Blood of Dragons by Joshua Robertson & J.C. Boyd
ANAERFELL*
HESHAYOL*

The Kaelandur Series by Joshua Robertson
MELKORKA*
DYNDAER*
MAHARIA*

Other Thrice Nine Legends Saga by Joshua Robertson & J.C. Boyd
STRONG ARMED*
WHEN BLOOD FALLS*
THE NAME OF DEATH*
WARDEN OF THE ASH TREE*
THE HIGHBORN LONGWALKER*
DEATH AT DUSK**

Additional Works

Legacy Series by Joshua Robertson & J.C.Boyd
BLOOD & BILE*

THE HAWKHURST SAGA*
GRIMSDALR*
THE PRINCE'S PARISH*
JACK SPRATT*

**Published by Crimson Edge*
***Forthcoming by Crimson Edge*

THE HIGHBORN LONGWALKER

THRICE NINE LEGENDS

Month of Ripening
Fifth of Warmth
118 CE

Prologue
FALMAGON

"Where did he go?" A strong gust nearly stole the question from Falmagon Sej's lips. He faced the wind, adjusting the wickerwork basket of freshly caught fish that hung over his shoulder. The figure looked to have been far enough from the beach to have saltwater washing over his boots; now, nothing stirred except the wind. His ankle-length brown cloak vacillated, confined beneath the weighted basket.

He caught his breath. The air was filled with the taste of salt.

Jhar Gurov took his time to reply. "A trick of the eyes is all." The fellow Highborn, twice his elder, stood to Falmagon's left, scuffing his boot against the sand. The small movement suggested his eagerness to retreat from the sea and return home.

Falmagon combed the loose strands of his russet-colored hair from his eyes. The northern airstream pestered him since midday, intent on keeping his frayed wisps flogging his cheeks. With a heavy breath, he knotted his hair back with a thin leather cord for what felt like the hundredth time. Then, lifting his hand to shield his eyes from the wind, Falmagon peered through the waning rays of the western sun.

The familiar coastline of his home island, Folkmar, stretched north and south as far as he could see. Besides the waves slapping against the light sands and a few scattered seagulls squawking raucously, the shore appeared barren. Yet he swore he saw a figure standing a hundred paces behind them a moment before.

"I know what I saw, Jhar." He repeated his question. "Where did he go?"

"Come on," Jhar said. "It is high time we return to Melkorka with these fish. They need to be cleaned and salted."

"You saw him too," Falmagon insisted.

Jhar snorted. "I see you, the fish on your back, and nothing more."

Falmagon turned to Jhar, slipping the holder off his back and balancing it against the ground. The fish at the top of the pile flopped and twitched, threatening to offset the weight and knock the container over.

He overlooked the fish, catching sight of the silhouette of their home, the castle called Melkorka, looming on the horizon. Most travelers, whether journeying by foot or sea, would miss the four walls and trifling assembly of stone towers in the array of uneven hills. Nonetheless, if he and Jhar continued their trek, they were guaranteed to walk through the rickety gates before eventide. Falmagon had never known another place to be called home, even though he was not born at Melkorka. He hated venturing too far from the walls. So it was no surprise that the thought warmed him—that is, being behind the castle walls and safe from the wind—yet whoever he saw could not be ignored.

He dipped his gaze from the spectacle of the castle to his fellow Highborn. "No Anshedar travels this far south unless they have a message for us."

"Might not have been an Anshedar," Jhar said in a clipped tone, narrowing his gaze. The mage's black hair rustled in the wind. "You forget your place, Falmagon Sej. We are not Longwalkers like Nedezhda, so leave the adventuring to her. Now, pick up your fish."

Falmagon frowned.

As an apprentice, he was expected to listen to the wisdom of the senior Highborn, but Jhar did not make a lick of sense. They were the Protectors of the Seven Islands and, as such, were responsible for keeping the realm of men safe. Nedezhda Mager being the only Highborn with permission from the Spearhead to travel off the island was irrelevant. Falmagon was talking about walking a hundred paces up the coastline to investigate, not sprinting across Folkmar to chase a ghost. Moreover, the nearest settlement to Melkorka was a fishing village called Narthwich, which was only inhabited by the weaker humans called Northmen or Anshedar. Therefore, it came to reason that whoever they saw walking along the coastline could only be a human.

He grimaced, a curse slipping through his lips. "By *Mulafell*, Jhar! Who else do you think is out here?"

"Watch your language," the Highborn replied.

"Well, you act as though we are in danger." Falmagon dropped his arms to catch his cloak from whipping up over his shoulder. The oversized hood pressed against the back of his skull, threatening to loosen his hair from its binding again.

"Who is to say we are not?" Jhar challenged. His grey tunic rippled against the outline of muscle in his chest and arms, providing a subtle hint of how outmatched Falmagon might be if he engaged in hand-to-hand combat with the older man. Jhar ranted, "You forget these islands were once swarming with demons, and the gods only know what monsters live in the sea. Magic may be in my blood, but I am not stupid enough to go looking for a reason to sling spells. *Koldovstvo* is not a kind mistress. The simplest speck of magic can steal years from your—"

"Life," Falmagon snipped. "I know."

"Clearly not," Jhar said, "or you would be satisfied with a shadow on the horizon staying a shadow."

"A shadow that might be capable of stealing the fish from our nets come morning," Falmagon said, gesturing to the basket at their feet.

"If a man is hungry, let him eat," Jhar retorted.

Falmagon went on, scowling. "Or the shadow could be one of the very men we have sworn to protect. Would you let him be taken by the sea?"

"By the gods, nothing has been taken by the sea," Jhar scowled, his black beard smashing against his mustache. He lifted a finger at Falmagon. "Now listen to me and pick up the fish. Do not forget I am your better."

Scoffing, Falmagon turned away to face the water. His feet were trudging through the soft sands to where he spotted the figure before he consciously made the decision to defy the older Highborn. "You are far from being better than me," he muttered under his breath.

"Falmagon!" Jhar yelled. "Turn your arrogant ass around, or the Spearhead will hear of this."

"Tell him, then!" Falmagon shouted over his shoulder while keeping his eyes forward. His cloak thrashed behind him so violently, he would not be able to see beyond the thick fabric anyway. The sand crunched beneath his boots as he stormed to the water's edge.

He was not surprised to learn of Jhar's cowardice. The Highborn spent most of his time in a rickety cottage within the walls of Melkorka with Dorofej, a timeworn Highborn with as much purpose as a pile of sheepdip. The two either made demands of the apprentices, like Falmagon, or made the enslaved Kras do their bidding while neither of them so much as lifted a finger. The only reason Jhar accompanied him to check the fishing nets today was because Nedezhda had been called by the Spearhead to finish some other mundane chore.

Falmagon would have preferred to come alone.

Reaching his target on the shore, Falmagon squatted to the sand. He was not certain what he expected to find, but his heart raced when he noticed the impressions of footprints in the sand. He reached out and touched the imprint as broken waves washed up over his fingers.

What little evidence remained would soon be washed away. He followed the trajectory of prints with his eyes, leading from the north—the same direction from where he and Jhar had come.

By Mulafell! Someone was following them!

"Jhar!" Falmagon yelled, looking up and down the coast for any sign of life. "Come look! Hurry!"

Whatever reply came was muffled in the wind, but then again, Falmagon did not care to hear it.

He shifted his gaze. The roiling seawater near his fingers parted like the water was being diverged by a rock or some lone piece of driftwood. Yet he saw nothing in the fading light.

He blinked.

The pinpointed area appeared blurry, as though he were looking through a thin veil of fabric or a thin fog. He reached out.

The air in front of him shimmered just before a foot materialized from nothing and struck him squarely in the forehead. He cried out, the force of the kick popping his head to the rear. Pain shot from the top of his head to his shoulders, leaving his vision colored with spots.

Trying to regain his senses, he guessed himself to be sprawled out on the wet sand. The seawater splashed over his legs, soaking the bottom fringes of his wool cloak.

Daring to tilt his head, he saw a middle-aged man in front of him, standing rigid in the shallow water, holding a crooked wooden staff. The medium-length red hair blotched with grey strands caused Falmagon to wrinkle his brow in greater confusion. He only knew a few folks with fire-colored hair among the Highborn and absolutely none among the Anshedar.

"Wait!" Falmagon forced himself to say, which came out at a higher pitch than he intended. He scrambled to get his elbows underneath himself.

"Stay down." The outsider's accent was odd and thick. His blue eyes squinted in a silent challenge, his lips tightening with lines of shadowed wrinkles.

Falmagon lifted himself up a hair more, looking for something else to say. The staff rotated in the man's right hand quicker than he could track, striking him across the side of the head.

His body twisted with the momentum and his face slammed into the sand with a grunt; the side of his head instantly began throbbing. He would not have been surprised if blood was already seeping from a numb wound.

Falmagon angrily gripped a handful of sand in his fist, reaching beyond the physical world to touch the Highborn's magic, Koldovstvo. He could fight if the stranger wanted to fight.

Whatever power the stranger held would be nothing in comparison to that of the Highborn.

His mind vibrated with energy, feeling the earth in his hand, until he sensed a low echo in his chest. With a roar, he whipped around and flung the sand at the stranger. At his command, every grain straightaway expanded mid-air to the size of boulders, blotting out the sun's light and the space in front of him. The oversized rocks should have smashed into the man, crushing him or at least propelling him back into the sea. But the man disappeared again, leaving the rocks to splash into the ocean harmlessly before returning to their normal state.

Falmagon's fury faded to fear. He shifted to get his feet underneath him, twisting his neck to look for Jhar or—

The staff hit him again across the face, snapping his head sideways. He returned to the wet sand with a belated moan, spitting blood from his lips.

"I said stay down," the stranger ordered. "Where did you get this power? You do not deserve it. You do not deserve life."

Falmagon clung to the sandy earth once more. Though this time, his muscles beckoned him to do as he was instructed. A ringing echoed in his ears.

"How many of you exist?" the stranger stooped over, pressing the butt of the staff against his face. "Answer me!"

Darkness gripped at the corners of Falmagon's vision, the sands disappearing momentarily. The northern wind blustered over him, cooling his burning injuries for a moment.

He could not say how much time passed before Jhar reached him, shaking him lightly by the arm. His head spun like he was waking from a dream. "Falmagon," the Highborn whispered. "Are you okay?"

"No. I am not," Falmagon choked.

"Can you walk?" he asked.

Falmagon grunted.

Jhar grasped his shoulder in a meaty grip, helping him roll over and sit up. "Be careful now. I cannot say where he has gone."

"What?" Falmagon held his sore jaw with an elongated moan. He tried to focus on the bare beach. "You did not stop him?"

Jhar angled his thick eyebrows and shook his head. "He was gone before I reached you. Some magic carried him away down the beach, swifter than anything I have ever seen."

"Magic? Koldovstvo? How?" Falmagon coughed, suddenly thinking of the Kras slaves back at Melkorka and their ability to vanish at will. He cleared his throat. "He somehow hid himself from us against the sea. He disappeared and reappeared like one of the little red broods."

"I saw," Jhar said, standing up. "Though I cannot be sure what I saw exactly, outside of you getting the snot beaten out of you."

"No thanks to you," Falmagon said.

Jhar harrumphed with a chortle in his throat, regarding Falmagon. "One look at you and I'm rather glad to have let shadows stay shadows. Next time, you might be wise to do the same."

Chapter I

FALMAGON

The slave bled well. Lying flat on his back with his willowy legs kicking over the edge of the table, the sunbeams glinted off his crimson skin from the northern window. The slave's blood, a shade darker than his skin, pooled in the socket where his eye had darted back and forth only moments before.

Falmagon gripped the faded rags around the slave's chest, securing his hold on the little beast. "That will teach you to spy on your masters, Kras!" With a vigorous jolt, he lifted and slammed the slave against the splintering wood of the table. The few remaining papers rustled with the sudden force, threatening to spin off to the dusty floor or fall to the nearby hearthfire.

The red brood—hardly half the size of a human—struggled uselessly against Falmagon's flexed muscles, gasping for breath. His action caused a ruddy river of blood to course down the side of the slave's face, over his temple and off his earlobe, staining the wood beneath him.

The Kras looked like demons with their pointed ears, crooked teeth, hooked noses, and black-filled eyes. Falmagon curled his lip at the Kras's missing eye, thinking the yawning pit was an improvement to the slave's already gruesome features.

"Hold him and I will seal the wound," Kinhar Sayan, his mentor, hissed from the other side of the table. He leaned his walking stick, a thick ash branch, against the table and hobbled to the hearthfire behind him.

"He is not going anywhere." Falmagon did not bother to look at the wrinkled man, the established Spearhead of the Highborn. Instead, he sneered at the slave. Solidifying his hold with a single hand, Falmagon scooped up the removed eyeball with his fingers. The remnant slowly dripped blood from the dangling nerves. He squished it between his finger and thumb, hanging it over the Kras with a sneer. "How do you like that, spy?"

"My lord," the Kras garbled, his good eye fixated on the lifeless piece cut from his face. Snot puddled at the Kras's nostrils; tears, clear and bloodied, dribbled down either side of his disgusting face. The slave's high-pitched tone reminded Falmagon of a nasally child. "I was not spyi—"

"Go ahead and lie to me, Kras," Falmagon growled, baring his teeth at the underling. "By Mulafell, I dare you to finish the sentence and I will rip your snake tongue from your devilish mouth."

The Kras blinked, causing the pool of blood to pour over the edge of the socket once more. His lips clamped shut with a whimper.

"That is enough, Falmagon," Kinhar said, returning to the table with a simple stick lit with flame. "Hold him still."

Falmagon did as he was instructed, despite the shrill cries of the Kras wriggling beneath his arms. He put his forearm over the chest of the red brood and used his other hand to hold the eyelid open. Blood gushed. He huffed under his breath. "I should let you thrash about and let Kinhar burn more than your wound." The Kras trembled at his words, but immediately stopped thrashing, closing his good eye in fear.

Kinhar raised the stick carefully in his shaking, craggy hands. His long white hair was tied in knots down his back. His colorless, limp beard and mustache covered most of his wrinkled face, allowing Falmagon to see little besides the man's bright blue eyes, flashing in the firelight. The Spearhead was old, more hair than man.

With a grimace, Kinhar lowered the flame to the wound, holding fast with what strength he could muster. Falmagon prepared to have the slave rear up against him, but the creature hardly budged. Instead, the Kras squealed in agony, his lithe body becoming rigid against the table, clearly afraid of moving too much and burning the side of his face.

Kinhar threw the stick back toward the hearthfire, turning his head slightly to the window carved out of the northern wall of his study. Falmagon turned his ear, hearing the shouts coming from the courtyard, announcing a courier's arrival.

"Open the gates," a woman shouted from below.

As though recognizing the voice, Kinhar whipped his head back to the Kras. "You will say nothing to Nedezhda about what transpired here. Say anything to anyone, and I will take more than an eye."

"My lord." The Kras's chin shook in equal rhythm to his head.

"Be gone," Kinhar said, gesturing to Falmagon.

Falmagon pulled the Kras off Kinhar's desk and pushed him toward the door that would lead down a flight of stairs and into Melkorka's courtyard. The slave fell in a heap but swiftly returned to his feet and hurried from the room.

Falmagon pushed his long hair from his eyes, watching the Kras exit from the wobbly door sitting in upper and lower pivots. He waited until the door shut and then addressed Kinhar. "Why not kill him? His life is not worth—"

"You have never held love for the Kras," Kinhar interrupted him, reaching for the scattered parchment on his desk before they became soaked in blood, "or anything. Yet all things have purpose. Few Kras remain at Melkorka, but they have talents that may serve the Highborn in upcoming years. I fear killing them may leave us at a disadvantage."

Falmagon scoffed. "I have found nothing of use in the red broods. Look how they sneak about, hiding in the shadows and whispering behind our backs. Instead of capturing them, they should have been killed during the mountain raids. They may be linked to the stranger Jhar and I ran into on the coast two weeks back. They could be spying for him."

"The Kras have served the Highborn for more than a century. They are not conspiring against us," Kinhar said.

Falmagon grunted, helping Kinhar tidy the desk while ignoring the dark blood seeping into the wood. His face had healed within days of battling the redhead carrying the staff, but no more had come from the incident. Kinhar certainly had been concerned when he and Jhar first returned to the castle, but beyond telling Nedezhda to keep her eyes and ears open when traveling, nothing more was done.

Falmagon could not say what needed doing, but he did not like doing nothing.

"Do not let your concern for the stranger consume you, Falmagon," Kinhar said.

"He vanished from sight right in front of me," said Falmagon. "No Highborn wields magic outside the elements, save Dorofej, who could heal the injured in his youth."

Kinhar snorted, squinting his eyes at nothing in particular. "Hmm. He is the only one I have met with such a gift, but I doubt he could mend a scratch these days without killing himself."

Falmagon frowned. "That is not my point. This stranger did not use elemental magic."

"Everything is connected, but often not in the ways we presume them to be. I suspect the staff you mentioned was magical in nature and gave him some ability to trick your mind," Kinhar said. "I have heard of magical artifacts before."

"Then we should retrieve it for the Highborn."

"If we come across him again, Falmagon, we certainly will want this staff," Kinhar agreed, "but first we must find a way to contend with such power."

"I suppose," Falmagon said.

Kinhar waved him off, changing the topic back to the Kras slave. "Regardless, I assure you, whatever Mojmir heard us say has likely been forgotten already, if he understood anything at all. Believe me, the Kras are no danger to us. They know the history of this castle and little else."

Falmagon frowned. "Why cut out his eye, then?"

"To guarantee they remain harmless. We are master and they are slave, as it has been for a thousand years. A bit of intemperance now and again reminds them of their lowly place," Kinhar replied. He carefully stacked his papers and weighed them down with red rock, no doubt gathered from the Crags of Kazimir.

"As you say," Falmagon said, picking up several books from the floor. "Should we continue our lesson?"

"We should."

"I am eager to learn more of the *Kadari*."

"Do not speak so freely," Kinhar warned. Before the Spearhead could say more, a courier burst through the door of the upstairs study, nearly knocking the hanging door from the wooden pivots. The impulsive entry caused Falmagon to whip around, nearly dropping the books.

Kinhar gasped loudly from behind the desk. He slammed his wrinkled hands down on the papers beneath the rock as though the sudden current could sweep them away.

"By Mulafell!" Falmagon cursed, widening his eyes at the harried courier. He had already forgotten someone announcing a rider at the gates. The Anshedar fell to a knee, crunching his fist against one of the worn timber panels barely holding the eroded flooring together.

"My apologies," the man sputtered, his black bangs bouncing over his light eyes. "The message is urgent."

Before they could say more, a scuffling sounded as another one of the Highborn slaves lurched through the door behind the courier.

"My lords," the Kras wheezed through its offset teeth, raising its pale eyes to Kinhar and then Falmagon. He ran a hand through his long black hair and twitched his pointed ears.

The courier fell to his side at the sight of the Kras, scooting backwards as though he might be eaten by the mangy beast.

The Kras widened the smoky orbs filling his wrinkled sockets but went on with little pause, indicating the courier with his hand. "Leon Lyda from Narthwich has come to deliver an urgent message from Jarl Likshol Avar."

"How in the Nine Lands did you know that?" the courier, Leon, gaped with frightened eyes.

"Lord Dorofej instructed me to properly introduce you to Lord Kinhar," the Kras started, attempting to twist its face innocently. If anything, it made the red brood look more repulsive.

Falmagon glowered at the Kras. He never rightly remembered all their names—especially Mojmir, who Kinhar mentioned moments ago—but this one he knew as Branimir Baran, son of Hrani. The red brood was always clutching to Dorofej's robes like a child would his mother's skirts.

His frown deepened, thinking again of Dorofej, the healing Highborn with no last name. Falmagon never liked him much. When he was not sleeping, he was meddling. He doubted Dorofej knew how to do little else. Since Falmagon had come to Melkorka fifteen years ago, Dorofej had been the bane of his existence, forcing him to complete odd chores or run errands better suited for the measly Kras. And anytime Falmagon attempted to duck the steaming pile of sheepdip, Dorofej would suddenly pop over his shoulder again like a relentless driveling hound.

Falmagon clung to hope, knowing Kinhar would soon advance him from apprentice, giving him equal standing among the Highborn; then Dorofej could pester him no more.

Kinhar spoke, his voice eerily calm and deep. "Be gone, Kras, so we may hear the courier's message."

"As you wish, my lord," Branimir replied, bowing his little body in half and exiting the room with as much haste as he'd entered.

Falmagon followed Kinhar's eager gaze to the courier, who watched the Kras exit the room. The worried look stayed on his face with an open mouth and paled cheeks.

"The beast is a Kras and not to be feared," Falmagon offered, rubbing the stubble on his upper lip. "We watch them well."

"A demon?" Leon trembled, twisting his neck to look at Falmagon. His body soon followed into an awkward half-poised kneel.

"More or less," Falmagon muttered with a snort, despite the knowledge that the red broods were anything but devils from the Netherworld. "Tell us why Jarl Avar sent you to Melkorka."

"Yes, my lord. A stranger…" Leon started with hesitation. Falmagon's heart skipped and fell as the courier continued. "A woman arrived on the island of Cyreus with a message for you, Lord Sayan." He stretched out an open hand to review a crumpled piece of paper with the seal already broken.

"Read it, did you?" Falmagon scorned. He itched to open the folds of the parchment and recite its contents to Kinhar so he might know the message too, but he knew his duty and his place. With two long steps, he bounded past the hearthfire and loomed over the courier. The Northman winced, his hand quivering in anticipation. Falmagon snatched the letter from his open hand, maintaining the glare until Leon looked away.

"No, my lord." Leon quivered, eyes widening as though he realized the error in lying to a Highborn. "I mean yes, but everyone read…er…the Jarl opened the letter and…" His voice trailed off into an unintelligible babble.

Falmagon stepped back, handing the letter to the Spearhead. "A Jarl should know better."

"He meant no harm by it," Leon said. "His duty—"

"Stop talking already," Falmagon ordered. He gulped and shifted his gaze to Kinhar, who studied the letter with a blank expression. Falmagon muttered to his mentor, hoping to elicit some hint of what would cause such disarray among the Northmen. Though in truth, he expected the answer to highlight the redheaded stranger with the staff. Any man who could make himself disappear might also be capable of making himself appear as a woman. "An age has come where Jarls involve themselves in the affairs of Highborn, and messengers speak the minds of Jarls."

"Indeed," Kinhar whispered. He returned his attention to the courier. "That will be all. You may return to Narthwich."

"My lord, what should I tell Jarl Avar? The message was unclear in its warning. What is coming?" Leon asked.

Falmagon's skin crawled as he watched Kinhar grab his walking stick from where it sat perched against his desk and wobble over to the open hearthfire without a word. The hairs of his mustache trembled under his breath as he tossed the letter into the flames. Falmagon watched the paper spiral down to the embers and then be consumed by the fire. He would never see what words were scribbled on the parchment now.

Leon stammered, his voice elevating in pitch and his face paling. "What are you doing?"

Kinhar spoke with authority, leveling his gaze at the courier. "Tell the Jarl that the Highborn will intercept the stranger on Cyreus to learn why she goads us with lies. I promise you, nothing is to be feared." Kinhar gripped his staff, balancing himself. "The Highborn have always protected the Seven Islands and its inhabitants. We will continue to do so."

Falmagon could not believe how swiftly the courier's countenance changed again, color returning to his cheeks. Leon nodded with a sliver of a smile on his thin lips. "Yes, my lord. We thought the letter to be a ruse. Likely a girl from the mainland without proper parenting or discipline."

"You are wise to think so," Kinhar said.

Falmagon bit down to keep his tongue from wagging. Any man with half a brain could tell Kinhar was misdirecting the courier. Falmagon hoped his mentor did not think him to be equally stupid.

"You heard the Spearhead," Falmagon said in an attempt to hurry Leon out the door. "Ride back to Narthwich. You are dismissed."

"Of course, my lord," Leon said, rising to his feet. He looked at Falmagon and then Kinhar as though he were looking for a proper way to say goodbye. Then, without finding anything more to say, he dipped his head and exited out the door.

Falmagon listened to the footsteps fade before turning toward Kinhar, who made his way back to the desk and sat. The Spearhead did not look at him but gazed out the only window in the room, his head wrinkled with thought.

An awkward silence filled the room for several minutes with Kinhar staring out the window and Falmagon looking to Kinhar. He kept his gaze from the ashes gathering in the fire, the remains of the burnt letter, hoping Kinhar would enlighten him as to what words had alarmed the Northmen.

His mind was riddled with thoughts of the stranger he crossed along the coast when Kinhar finally said, "You were a young boy, barely able to walk, when my path intercepted yours. Just an orphan being raised by your poor grandfather." Falmagon tilted his head at the known story, finding it ill-placed in the sudden moment. Kinhar had recited the story several times over the last fifteen years, but usually upon request.

He twisted his neck to watch Falmagon with an intense, unblinking stare. Instead of continuing the story, telling of his grandfather's farm or his parents' early demise, Kinhar changed course. "The craft of Koldovstvo was imprinted on your soul. I knew it the moment I laid eyes on you that you had magic running through your veins. Many children, born of the Anshedar over the years, proved to be something more, having the capacity to touch the divine power. You, Falmagon, will be the greatest of any. Your parents may have been taken from you early, but the gods blessed you with Koldovstvo. Dahz the White-Clad blesses you."

Falmagon caught his breath at the mention of the god's name. "The Lightbringer?" The Highborn were not to have allegiance to any gods among the wide pantheon. The gods may have created men and even Highborn, gifting them with blessings, but never had the Highborn paid homage to a god or believed one to be more special than another. "Why would you say the Lightbringer?"

Kinhar maintained his heavy gaze, hobbling around his desk. "What I tell you must not be shared with any other Highborn. This is a pact between you and me. Understand?"

Falmagon dipped his chin, mouth drying considerably. He forced his response through his lips, his heart thudding against his chest. Secrets were what young boys kept from adults to duck punishment. On the other hand, to keep the confidence of his superior somehow made him feel important, loftier. "I understand."

"The power of the Highborn is imbued by Dahz, the White-Clad," Kinhar said. "Although the Thunder-Bearer,

Perom, created man, it was Dahz who asked Svarog, the Lord of Lords, to construct those who are worthy."

Falmagon swallowed hard. He was quite familiar with the high gods. Svarog sat at the pinnacle, governing over Thrice Ten Kingdom, masterful over any other god or goddess. Perom had created man, and Dahz protected men. Yet Falmagon had never heard of Dahz giving the Highborn the power of Koldovstvo.

Kinhar echoed Falmagon's thoughts. "While made by Perom's hand, the Lightbringer's voice first brought us into creation, and our power would not exist without Him. And remember, even when Perom found displeasure in men, Dahz persuaded Svarog to let us remain on Aenar." Kinhar folded his hands near his waist, bobbing his head as he spoke, as though the words flowed from the Most-High and not his own mind. "We Kadari are those few Highborn who know this truth. We have pledged our lives to Dahz the Lightbringer, defending Him as much as He defended us. We Kadari take the *Kalamyr Oath* and, as a result, are blessed with divine protection. Dahz's light shines favorably on us!"

His head lightened at the words. A sect existed among the Highborn, and the Spearhead guided its guileful hand. Falmagon ran his fingers through his long brown hair, trying to swallow Kinhar's revelation. "I—I do not understand. Why would you keep the truth hidden? Why would we not bind all those within these walls with the Kadari?"

Kinhar looked to the window, a shadow falling over Melkorka—like a divine sign—as the clouds swept over the sun. His voice dropped so that Falmagon had to struggle to hear him. "Someday all the world will know the blessing of the Lightbringer, and every Highborn will worship him. But in prayer I learned an evil lurks within Melkorka. Koldovstvo is a divine gift, allowing the Highborn to bend the elements of this world, but it can be perverted for terrible deeds in the wrong hands. Until I discover the origin of what darkness skulks, we can say nothing of the Kadari." Kinhar turned his eyes back to Falmagon, eerily flashing blue with the return of the sun's light gleaming through the window.

"Is the stranger I met to blame for this evil? Or the one awaiting in Cyreus?" Falmagon pressed.

"We will see," Kinhar replied faintly. "You will be my sight and prepare to become a leader in the days to come. You must be battle-hardened, physically and spiritually. Dahz demands that you be tested. You must pray to Him. Let Him guide you."

"Pray?"

"Always pray," Kinhar said.

Falmagon swelled his chest, sitting in his chair. He had never prayed before, but he suspected he could learn. Kinhar promised honor and glory, coupled with unwavering duty, long forgotten by most. Falmagon had heard stories of the Highborn fighting against demons and protecting the Anshedar, but in his years at Melkorka, he had only seen them be varlots bowing at the whims of the Jarls and the Anshedar.

The Highborn might return to greatness under the name Kadari, and he would be honored to be at the forefront.

"What must I do?" Falmagon asked. "What does the Lightbringer ask of me?"

Kinhar smiled, his teeth nearly hidden under the thousands of strands of white hair. He stepped forward with an echoing thud, clasping his hand around Falmagon's shoulder. "Take the Kalamyr Oath as I did years ago, swearing your fealty to Dahz."

Falmagon bobbed his head. Kinhar grunted, tugging Falmagon to kneel on the floor in front of him. Once he was down on both knees, head hanging, Kinhar said, "Good, good. Repeat after me."

> *Held fore'er by a simple word,*
> *To defend against the impious,*
> *Ne'er to kneel nor fall nor lured,*
> *Lest blood and death descend.*

The words rolled off Falmagon's tongue, line by line, with ease. He closed his eyes, feeling the warmth of the sun coming from the window; Kinhar's hand on his shoulder was a welcome weight, holding him fast to the wooden floor beneath his knees.

> *Beyond wealth and a princely home,*
> *Trust held fore'er unto the sun,*
> *We war, we worship, we roam,*
> *Lest blood and death descend.*

The sunlight brightened on the opposite side of his eyelids, coloring his vision in spotted colors. Yellows. Oranges. Reds. Sounds from the other Highborn and the Kras outside disappeared. Only Kinhar's voice echoed in the room.

> *Rise above the frail and weak,*
> *Fore'er standing beyond frailty,*

Let all men hear us speak,
Till blood and death descend.

Falmagon sucked cool air into his nostrils, listening attentively for the next words. The melody reverberated in his ears. He had never known the power of the gods before, but the strength of Dahz was undeniable.

He had been chosen.

Feel the warmth of the White-Clad,
Blessing the Highborn in eternal glory,
Let none meander or fall to gad,
Till blood and death descend.

When he finished, Kinhar's voice blended with the soft wind. "Rise as one of the blessed Kadari and receive the Lightbringer."

Falmagon opened his eyes slowly, the brightness fading as the sun disappeared once more behind the clouds. He rose to his feet to meet Kinhar's eyes. The old man's lips were pressed firmly together.

"You are the first Highborn to join the Kadari at Melkorka." Kinhar smiled, his eyes creasing with immeasurable excitement. "I have been waiting a long time for this moment. You were always meant to be the first."

"Now what?" Falmagon asked.

Kinhar widened his eyes. "We prepare you to become a Longwalker. You will go with Nedezhda to meet the stranger on Cyreus, but first let me teach you how to pray."

Chapter II
Falmagon

Falmagon Sej strode onto the rocky shoreline of the island called Cyreus and decided he hated the place. He tried to push all profanities from his mind and instead silently reiterated the beginnings of a prayer to Dahz as Kinhar had taught him.

Honor to the Lightbringer. Protect me. Guide me.

The ongoing forceful wind stalled his thoughts, whipping across Strega's Deep, cold as the world's heart, and stinging him to the bones. If the past years at Melkorka were any indicator, the northern gale would not calm for several months, eventually bringing winter to the Seven Islands with its unwelcomed might.

Honor to the—

The clouded sky caught his eye, blocking the too-distant sun and shading the world in a dim grey. The sight unequivocally added to his sour mood. His brown cloak and cowl did nothing to safeguard him from the biting weather on this miserable island. Despite Kinhar's promise of glory and becoming a Longwalker, he suddenly wanted to return to Melkorka to take shelter.

"Four days on the water and we are still haunted by Strega's breath," Falmagon mumbled faintly, turning his back to the wind and giving up on the prayer. He grabbed at his cloak to keep it from needlessly belting around his frame. The effort was wasted as the fabric flapped against him as wildly as his lengthy strands of hair.

Nedezhda Mager, his declared guide and the Highborn's acclaimed Longwalker, straightened next to him, arms folded under her hooded grey cloak. She ignored her own mantle buffeting behind her lithe body. She stood as a statue, barely reaching Falmagon's chin, squinting at the lofty red alps with her light blue eyes. Her reddish-brown hair whipped over her pale cheeks. Save the stranger with the staff, Falmagon only knew two Highborn who had red hair: Nedezhda and one other Highborn, Faina Zholdan.

He eyed her thoughtfully.

A week had passed since Kinhar secured him into the secret sect among the Highborn, and today, he was still treated like a pawn among his brethren. A moment after pledging his allegiance to Dahz, Kinhar directed Nedezhda to be in charge of their expedition, and then directed Andrik Hjlavok, another apprentice, to go with them.

Falmagon knew Nedezhda the Longwalker must come. She was known to travel the Seven Islands, while he had never left Folkmar. Besides, he'd rather have her lead him than Jhar, who would bellow and complain the whole way. Yet he could not understand why Andrik was with them, and praying to Dahz, like Kinhar suggested, gave him no answers.

He spoke again, louder, nipping the edge of his hooked nose with his knuckles. "Even these too-tall mountains cannot shield the weather. Seven Islands of Forghar and this stranger chooses to come here. By Mulafell, why did she not sail to Melkorka?"

"We have our duty, Falmagon," Andrik said behind him with bated breath. The Highborn jerked the faering onto the rocks by its curved bow.

Falmagon turned to the wooden death-ship. The wind snatched back his cowl with the movement. He did not bother catching the wool hood. Instead, he regarded Andrik, a steadfast man raised with him at Melkorka. Andrik frequently offered reminders of duty, as though Falmagon might forget.

The early onset of adulthood had not been kind to Andrik. His large lips stuck too far past his flat nose. As a result, no matter what words escaped his lips, Andrik's bizarre facial features gave him the façade of arrogance.

All the same, he was not asking for a reminder or to listen to Andrik's smug tone. Unlike the other two, Falmagon was with Kinhar when the rider from Narthwich delivered the message. He had not read the words, but he knew enough to be aware of the impending doom it threatened.

Falmagon folded his arms against his broad chest. "I am familiar with our responsibilities. The safety of the Anshedar and the world is our charge. The only threat to either, including the Highborn, would be demons rising out from the Netherworld, and no demon has bled from the Crags in over ninety years." He took in a breath, continuing to peer over Nedezhda's head at Andrik, who squatted in her slim shadow. "I do not know what game this stranger is playing, but the Highborn are hardly fated for whatever doom the letter suggested. We should have stayed at Melkorka."

"Neither of you have stepped a foot off Folkmar since your early induction and already you know the fates. How very impressive." Nedezhda clicked her tongue.

Falmagon turned from her to scowl at the shoreline; her sarcasm was thick enough to clog his ears. The waves of the sea looked grey, sloshing against one another before roiling onto the coast like ghastly fingers clawing from a watery grave. He would expect her to suggest he and Andrik were inferior for not traveling beyond the scope of Melkorka.

As she went on talking, her tone held as much emotion as the scattered rocks under their feat. "The Highborn are the guardians of the *Seven* Islands, not just one. It benefits us to come and reassure the Anshedar, even if we only speak against a stranger who spits lies. Now stop flexing your muscles and help Andrik flip the faering before the sea takes it."

She took several steps toward the dark red mountains, seemingly uninterested in hearing his reply.

"You wish to reassure them." Falmagon fumbled to say something grand in response to her insult. "Best not tell the Northmen how few of us exist."

Nedezhda twisted her head, making a point of rolling her eyes at his snide remark. "Or how many of us cannot defend against old men with crooked sticks." Falmagon bit his tongue at her comment. "Keep your juvenile thoughts to yourself and help Andrik." She crossed her arms and turned back to the mountains.

Falmagon growled. Nedezhda would no doubt report to Kinhar that he was nothing but a bungling clotpole on his first real excursion from the castle.

He ambled over to Andrik, who attempted to lift the boat on his own. Falmagon grimaced at the other Highborn's strained face, listening to the dramatized grunts slipping from his thick lips. With a sly smile, Falmagon gripped the faering under the edge of the worn wood. He had nearly twice the mass as Andrik. Ignoring his windblown hair brushing over his eyes, he shoved the boat up and over, tearing it from Andrik's hands.

It cracked against the uneven rocks.

"We may not have to worry about waves. The very wind could fracture this *thing* with its shoddy craftsmanship," said Falmagon nonchalantly with a snort. He kicked his foot against the side.

Andrik retracted his hands, rubbing them against his brown cloak. He turned his blue eyes toward Falmagon with a glare, then turned to face the red rocks. "If we hurry, we could be heading back home by sunset."

"Do we not get to enjoy the warmth of a fire or an evening meal? What? No good night's rest?" Falmagon said sourly. "After half a week of eating fish and dried bread, I am hardly eager to return to the wind and sea." Even he could taste the bitterness on the edge of his tongue.

"I thought you said you wanted to return to Melkorka," Andrik scoffed. "Besides, what do you think they will have to offer at Mjovadalsa? They are fishermen and quarry men. They only have *fish* and *rocks*. Are you going to eat the rocks?"

"Aside from dull meals, I thought you would be glad to see your home again," Nedezhda said.

"This was never my home," Andrik replied. "I was four when I left. Anything I know about this island comes from the scrolls."

Falmagon did not want to hear a lackluster story surrounding Andrik's childhood. Any apprentice delivered to Melkorka arrived before the age of five, himself included. Of course, Falmagon was interested in seeing his birthplace, Arkaim, but he did not need to tell stories with his brethren.

Falmagon growled and pushed his hair from his eyes again, thinking back to whether any other village existed on the island besides Mjovadalsa. He could not see any sign of human civilization from the shore. He would kill for dried pork and cheese. "All I am saying is I have no interest in jumping back in the boat."

"Unless you replace your arms with oars, you won't get far around the Seven Islands without a boat," Andrik said evenly. "So you best get used to it."

"You are not much older than me. Why don't you keep your wisdom to yourself?" Falmagon shot back.

"Seeing as neither of you are Longwalkers, you won't have to get used to anything. You shouldn't have left the castle," Nedezhda muttered. She faced the rocks and began trudging across the shore. Her hair whipped around her too-small ears and nose.

Falmagon gritted his teeth and followed, wondering how Kinhar might be testing him. He apparently had not informed Nedezhda of the intent to make Falmagon a Longwalker. If Kinhar said nothing, Falmagon knew his place was to stay silent as well.

He would watch and learn from Nedezhda.

Nedezhda the Longwalker was the only one who answered to the Anshedar's summons. Since Falmagon came to Melkorka, she was the Highborn's voice, their eyes, and their ears. She seldom journeyed outside Melkorka unless bidden by the Jarls for counsel. The king, Merreider Kar, certainly never summoned the Highborn; at least, not in Falmagon's lifetime. In fact, as far as Falmagon knew, no Highborn had been to Arkaim since Kinhar returned with him years ago.

Come to think of it, he was not certain Kinhar had left the castle since. Other Highborn like Dorofej were too old to travel, and Highborn like Jhar and Faina were too defiant. Falmagon bit the inside of his cheek, considering the weakness of those meant to be his brothers and sisters. Their collective onus was to protect the world and its people, and none left Melkorka except Nedezhda. Until now.

He wondered how often the Northmen had to protect themselves. In truth, they were not much different from the Highborn, except for their inability to wield Koldovstvo. To him the difference was everything, but he had never known a world without magic. Kinhar said the Highborn were chosen by the gods. This simple explanation suited Falmagon. He liked the sound of being chosen.

He acquired the ability to touch Koldovstvo at the onset of puberty, like every other Highborn, which meant he only gained the ability in the last five years. In the beginning, he was addicted to feeling the magic pulsate through his veins. Manipulating the physical elements of the world—fire, stone, sky, and sea—made him a god among mortals. But the cost of casting magic was too great to idly amuse himself. With every invocation, he would drain life from his body, drawing him closer to death. Lifting a stone with Koldovstvo may steal an hour, whereas hurling a large rock could cost him a year from his life.

He had no intention of hurrying his life along.

He kept his mind active to steer his thoughts away from the cold. When Nedezhda eventually led them into the mountain pass and away from the beach, Falmagon noticed the frigid current from the north nearly stopped altogether. With the gale reduced to a whisper, Nedezhda opened the dialogue, repeating much of what she had told them while sailing on the faering.

"Remember, the Anshedar believe demons still spill from the Crags of Kazimir, like during the old wars," she said. "We will not give them any reason to think otherwise. That does not give permission to be telling any stories."

"You mistake us for Dorofej," Falmagon said with a smirk. He was never certain who was older, Kinhar or Dorofej, but at least the Spearhead had some sense about him. Dorofej always seemed to be telling outlandish stories.

Nedezhda stiffened the corner of her mouth to hide her amusement. Falmagon was glad to get some reaction from her. An unsmiling woman made a grey world all the darker.

Andrik chortled at the joke.

Falmagon did not need a reminder of why they lied to the Anshedar about the demons. The Highborn's existence hung on the Anshedar's generosity. While they rarely had any need for *shana*, or silver, they were always in need of food and other basic goods. Even the boat they came to Cyreus in had been borrowed from the Jarl at Narthwich.

Falmagon blamed the Highborn's slaves, who rarely produced what was needed for the handful of occupants at Melkorka, especially during winter months. While Kinhar claimed the Kras had purpose, Falmagon did not see any reason to keep them around. Not only were they inhuman, but the little beasts were hardly respectable. The red broods were discovered during the old wars when the Highborn marched into the depths of the mountains.

Falmagon stroked the quills of hair on his upper lip. The underearth was the home to demons and nothing else.

Nevertheless, without a threat looming over Kalamaar or the Seven Islands, the Highborn knew the Anshedar would be less likely to support the lone castle. So they bent the truth a bit. All Highborn knew someday the demons would return, and the Anshedar would need the Highborn to protect the world. Falmagon liked to think that telling the humans they continued to fight demons was not so much a lie as a veiled prediction.

"What of this stranger?" Andrik asked, breaking the sound of their footsteps crunching against the rocks on the path. The wind whistled in attempt to circumvent the mountain. "If she is going around Mjovadalsa saying demons are *coming*, I think that alludes to their recent dormancy."

"Kinhar said the letter said *doom*, not *demons*," Nedezhda said.

"Same thing." The lankier Highborn pursed his lips, narrowing his eyes at her.

Falmagon held his breath. For most of the journey, he listened to Nedezhda and Andrik guess at what was written in the letter. He suspected Kinhar told Nedezhda something before sending them off, but he could not guess what was shared.

"Hardly." Nedezhda drew her mouth tightly, any evidence of a smile lost as she spoke through her perfect teeth. "Rest assured, we will correct whatever unbalance we find. The Anshedar of Mjovadalsa are a proud people. If she lacked the forethought to keep her mouth shut about the truth of the demons, I doubt the humans would change their beliefs at the words of a stranger."

A moment passed and then Andrik spoke his true thoughts, blurting out, "I wonder if she is pretty."

"What if she is?" Falmagon asked. "Will you be more likely to believe her story?"

"I might." Andrik laughed.

"You two must learn to be Highborn." Nedezhda rubbed her small nose, leading them left at the first fork in the mountain pass. "Clear your heads. The Highborn have no room for tenderness and love."

"No place?" Falmagon scrunched his nose. He followed behind Andrik, watching Nedezhda. Her words came across with a harshness that surprised him. "Surely we can love?"

"Love clouds judgment. Best to leave it as a luxury for the Anshedar," Nedezhda answered.

Rubbing his scruff again, Falmagon briefly contemplated her words before catching sight of the mountaintops where snow idly sat. He never considered *love* much, bearing in mind his pickings were sparse at Melkorka, but he had not closed himself off from the idea either. Besides Faina and Nedezhda, he rarely saw a woman, except the few at Narthwich when he helped gather supplies for the castle.

Nedezhda certainly was the prettiest among them, but she acted more like a mother than a wife. He could not see himself holding her hand, let alone sharing her bed.

The next couple of miles were quiet, with Nedezhda leading the way and him shaking the images from his head. She treaded along the path as though she had made this journey a hundred times, taking two more lefts and then a right.

Falmagon heard rushing water moments before the mountain split, leaving a steep and narrow ravine on his left side. The dark red mountain rock almost shimmered in the paled world. He clung to the smoothly cut mountainside with his right hand, cautiously peering down at the fast stream rushing over rapids a hundred feet below them. The water sloshed against the underside of the rock, flowing with incredible speed to the sea somewhere in the far distance. The gulch expanded fifty feet wide with a walkway positioned twenty feet higher on the opposite side. Falmagon scarcely saw movement before a broad-shouldered, bearded Anshedar scooted to the edge, carrying a shortbow at his waist. He did not bother to nock the arrow in his other hand.

"Strega's beard, where'd the lot of you come from?" he called out louder than necessary. "Are you traders from Kalamaar?"

"We are not," Nedezhda replied, keeping her hands folded under her cloak. "We are Highborn from Folkmar. Is Jarl Ashwin occupied?"

The Anshedar shrugged, waggling his beard with a twitch of his nose. "I haven't been to town since the Lightbringer attempted to show his face this morning." He waved his hand at the sky and scoffed at the thick clouds. "Though I suspect the Jarl will never be too busy to grant the Highborn an audience. You know where to find him?"

Nedezhda dipped her head and started back down the tapered path without saying goodbye. Andrik lifted his hand but the man from Mjovadalsa had already turned his back as well.

"A bit tight-lipped, are they not?" Falmagon said.

"They likely have as many visitors here as we do at Melkorka. Pleasantries toward strangers would be foreign to them." Andrik tread behind Nedezhda around the next bend to suddenly enter Mjovadalsa.

Falmagon's eyes caught sight of the round domiciles of the village, sturdily built on both sides of the widening chasm. The two dozen buildings were all carved from rock with round stone roofs, built partially into the mountain and partially on the snaking path. Falmagon guessed they were large enough to comfortably fit several families inside.

Several roped bridges with wooden planks stretched over the gulch, wide enough to carry a cart if necessary, connecting the many homes. Men, women, and children walked across the swaying bridges casually as though the swinging enhanced their ability to walk. Some stopped and pointed at the Highborn as they came around the edge of the mountain. The children smiled widely while the parents pulled them along without looking twice, as though the day-to-day hustle was more important than visitors.

"You should probably stop scowling," Andrik said, twisting to look over his shoulder. "You are going to scare the children."

"Do they not know we are Highborn?" Falmagon asked.

"They, too, probably think we are traders from the mainland, but does it matter?" Andrik asked, then widened his eyes. "What were you expecting? A celebration and their finest wine?" Andrik laughed, jerking his head back so as not to wander off the cliff. "We are Highborn, not royalty."

Falmagon grumbled. He thought the two should go hand in hand, but before he could say anything, Nedezhda hissed at them to hold their tongues. Then, biting her lip, she weaved in and out of the roving commoners—scrawny women, bearded men, and bug-eyed children—while he and Andrik kept to her heels.

She passed the first two bridges, then stopped at the third. Falmagon hesitated, thinking she aimed to pass over the rocking rope bridge. The long drop would give him time to scream at least twice before hitting the bottom. To his relief, Nedezhda turned the other way and made a beeline for the nearest round structure.

The wooden door was constructed from four poorly lined panels, shoddily pieced together. He could nearly see through the slits in the door before Nedezhda clomped up the two stone steps and swung it open without knocking.

He followed her and Andrik inside.

A man with an angled nose, shaved head, and a brown beard down to his mid-chest squinted at them as they entered, shoving a biscuit of some kind in his mouth while balancing a wooden bowl in his hand. Falmagon's stomach growled at the sight of real food. "Lady Nedezhda," the Anshedar mumbled, spraying crumbs into his beard, "I would have thought you to be here a few days earlier."

"Then you must've thought the Highborn walk on water, or better yet, have wings," she said coarsely, examining the ridiculously filthy room. Falmagon trailed her gaze, noticing overturned tables and chairs, a fire barely burning in the hearthfire, and shredded tapestries scattered over the stone flooring. "Nine Lands, Jarl. What happened here?"

"Was there a fight?" Andrik asked, his voice almost a whisper, but the sound carried off the walls.

Jarl Ashwin grinned, the chewed morsels of his bread sticking to his teeth. "Several, actually. We always fight when we celebrate. Come to think of it, someone should write a song about last night."

Falmagon rubbed under his nose, feeling the prickles of his budding facial hair. "What were you celebrating?"

The Jarl held the smile, swiping his scalp from front to back with his hand. In a fluid motion, he slid his fingers around to his left ear and tugged at something stuck through the earlobe. At closer look, Falmagon saw the object was a ring of silver. The Jarl had pierced the hoary hoop through his flesh!

"You know, my memory slips, but it looks as though we had a good time," the Jarl finally said, beaming. He waved his hand as though the action swept the topic from an invisible table. "But you came to talk to the *weird* girl, right? She has been ambling around our village for days waiting on the Highborn. Refuses to be shipped to the mainland until she talks with you."

Falmagon lifted an eyebrow.

Nedezhda may have tightened her little nose, but otherwise, her face was carved from stone. "Where is she?"

The Jarl rubbed his head again before he popped his mouth open as though suddenly remembering. His bright blue eyes fell on Andrik and then Falmagon. "She is naked in the gulch. Wanna see?"

Chapter III
FALMAGON

Naked. Although half sloshed, Jarl Ashwin avowed the female stranger dawdled *naked* near the river. After emptying his supper from its wooden bowl in a monstrous gulp, the Jarl aimed to prove his claim. With a gregarious laugh, he headed them down eight flights of stone steps to the gulch below.

The island of Cyreus was no brighter upon exiting the Jarl's abode. The clouds may have even thickened, giving more shadow to the red mountains surrounding them. Falmagon peered distastefully at the colorless terrain. As they descended the carved stairs, the stench of dead fish stung his nostrils. The rotten flavor circumvented into his mouth and laced his tongue, nearly causing him to gag.

As they bounded from the bottom rock to solid land, they crossed a handful of young men, no older than Falmagon. The lot of them giggled like girls in attempts to return to the stairs. Yet before they could begin their ascension, the Jarl briefly shared in their mirth, slapping their backs as they swarmed by. Falmagon turned his head to watch the men incredulously, quickly pairing their jollity with the potentiality of a nude woman nearby.

He could not imagine anyone willingly standing without clothes in this frigid air.

A moment later, a woman came into view a couple hundred paces away, striding along the bank with the cold wind whipping over the water and striking at her exposed, pallid skin.

The words had to be spoken. "I don't believe it." Fully clothed, the cold stung at Falmagon's flesh like a finely sharpened tooth, and here the stranger was, bare as a babe first wiggling its way into the world.

"Quite a sight, is it not?" the Jarl chortled, pulling the wine cup he had carried with him to his lips. The tall, slender woman ahead of them tugged at her tangled black hair hanging only inches above her shoulders. Her hair against her skin was like ash against snow. Admittedly, Falmagon's eyes swept swiftly over her body, captivated by her perfect form. She definitely was not the stranger he encountered on Folkmar. The Jarl suddenly slapped him on the back with a snort, nearly sending him sprawling to the dirt. "If my wife had a body like that I wouldn't need so much wine."

"She is pretty..." Andrik murmured under his breath.

Falmagon bit his tongue, unsure how to respond. The woman was like a sheet of ice in the grey light. His mind was suddenly mush. "Where are her clothes?" he managed.

"Somewhere along the bank," the Jarl suggested with an innocent shrug. "Unless those boys hid them again."

"We will be topside soon enough to share a bowl of stew," Nedezhda said flatly, aiming to change the subject. She squinted at the strange woman.

The Jarl snorted again, seemingly aware of his place when compared to the mighty Highborn. "I will have it prepared."

Nedezhda lifted her round chin and marched toward the stranger, leaving the Jarl to follow the young Anshedar up the staircase.

Andrik scooped his hand through his brown locks, lifting his eyebrows at Falmagon with excitement before setting off after Nedezhda.

Falmagon swelled his chest and held his breath. Any thought of their mission was fleeting, his eyes glossing over while staring at the naked stranger. He forcibly blew air through his lips, then trailed behind them.

He had to keep his wits.

Nedezhda unmistakably was the least affected, stopping an arm's length from the other woman.

The black-haired stranger twisted around to acknowledge them. The sliver of a smile twisted across her face as she folded her arms casually under her uncovered breasts.

Nedezhda spoke with authority, leaping to the point of their discussion. If the woman wanted attention for her nakedness, Nedezhda would not be the one to offer it. "We have come from Melkorka. I am Nedezhda Mager, daughter of Donn Mager. I hear you wanted to speak with the Highborn about some threat."

Andrik and Falmagon stopped short of reaching Nedezhda's side, falling under the brooding gaze of the strange woman. She preserved the smile, tapping her foot lightly against the hardened earth. She slowly raised a finger to her chin in speculation. Then, with an exasperated sigh, she matched Nedezhda's imposing tone. "You are a bit short to be a Red, but I know the Mager name. It is older than the castle you call Melkorka. How long has your family been in the East?"

Falmagon had no way to place the accusation of being a *Red*. He had never heard a Highborn referred to by such a name, but from Nedezhda's expression, she knew its meaning. He wondered if the woman simply meant Nedezhda had reddish hair. Regardless, Nedezhda's eyebrows disappeared under her reddish-brown bangs in surprise. She held her ground. "Who are you?"

"Erzebeth Navenka," the woman said, tightening her crossed arms so that her breasts swelled. Falmagon's eye twitched in an attempt to maintain eye contact with the woman. She had brown eyes. He had never seen brown eyes before today. The Highborn's eyes were always blue. The quality should be fascinating enough to hold his attention.

Should be.

Nedezhda's eyebrows dropped as quickly as they had risen. "I am not familiar with your name. You are not from these lands."

"I am not. I suppose you aim to keep our histories to ourselves then. Very well," she said with an air of disappointment. Falmagon thought his ears were going to bleed trying to make sense of her words. He knew no place besides Kalamaar and the Seven Islands of Forghar. The stranger continued, "Where is Kinhar Sayan? I expected him to come, not his underlings."

Her choice words caused Nedezhda to scowl. Her cheeks reddened, becoming as taught as dried skin on a skeleton.

Some bizarre mumbled sound reverberated in Andrik's throat next to Falmagon as though he were trying to form a coherent sentence but forgot the structure of words.

"Where do you come from?" Falmagon asked, folding his arms with the same demeanor as the other woman. He did not appreciate being called an underling any more than Nedezhda. While he was not the Spearhead either, he was now a member of the Kadari.

They all had their place.

Her eyes locked on to his so quickly, he nearly stepped back. She flashed her yellow teeth behind her pale lips. "Save your curious questions for Kinhar. If he cannot come to meet me, then I will tell you what I know and be on my way."

"He has grown too old to travel," Andrik struggled to offer an excuse. He combed through his hair with his fingers once more, his large lips twisting to hold back a smile. "Or he might have come."

"Old?" Erzebeth opened her mouth in surprise, turning around to gaze at the river. The water slopped over the rocks, forming a white foam. "How foolish has he been to let himself become old?" she said quietly.

Falmagon frowned. He had never known Kinhar not to be old. If she knew Kinhar, however, he suspected she knew Koldovstvo would age the Highborn quicker than what was natural. But even fifteen years ago, Kinhar was not exactly the ripest of men.

Without her eyes to keep Falmagon's attention, his gaze drooped to her…legs. Odd as the stranger may have been, he admitted the gods had shaped her to perfection.

As with any youthful man, the thought of lying with a woman entered his mind a dozen times a day or more, but Melkorka had slim pickings. Nedezhda was the nearest to his age, and she had a decade or more on him. From the looks of Erzebeth, she may only have been a year or two his elder.

Nedezhda regained control of the conversation, her icy gaze recapturing her inner fire. She nearly shouted the anticipated inquiry. "You sent a warning to the Highborn. We have come to learn of its meaning. What further message did you have?"

Andrik's first string of words overlapped Nedezhda's last. "Please, we have traveled for several days to meet with you. What is this *doom* you mentioned?"

"My message was meant for Kinhar, but if he trusts the fate of Aenar to those he calls Highborn..." Her hands fell to her sides. "So be it."

Falmagon tensed. "Our duty is to protect the world and the Anshedar. If we do not carry the weight of the world, none will."

Erzebeth scoffed, but whatever she may have said to correct his ideology, she kept to herself. Instead, she started her monologue, speaking slowly as though she chose each word carefully. It left Falmagon wondering what she was not saying.

"Years ago, before trekking through the grasslands and forests of Maharia, Kinhar directed me to travel to Anaerfell to witness a...battle. This fight had the propensity to unbalance the world. I was a faithful servant and did as I was instructed. And...what I observed at that holy temple undoubtedly threatens to collapse the world." Erzebeth waggled her head in memory. "None of you need know the details; Kinhar unerringly knows my duty as a Warden. You must tell Kinhar the battle was lost."

"What battle?" Falmagon asked.

"The *battle* he sent me to witness," Erzebeth said plainly, turning back to face them. Her smile was gone, replaced with bared teeth. "I will not upset your scope of the world with what I know. So whatever questions you have, you can ask him when you return to Melkorka. But you will tell him that Moreth and the Kadari move to protect Aenar in the west, and he should do the same here, upon the Seven Islands."

Kadari! Falmagon held his tongue, whispering a silent prayer to the Lightbringer. Kinhar was preparing him for something great, indeed.

"What does that mean?" Andrik pressed.

"Ask him!" she barked, her brown eyes flashing with madness. "The Kadari and their oaths are not my own. I am a Warden. I am not one of you! The bidding is done!" The muscle in her arm flexed, causing Falmagon to take a step back. He was not certain she would strike out at them, but her sudden fury was clear. Her words were biting as she stayed her penetrating gaze on Nedezhda. "The fabric between this world and the next will soon be ripped open again. Demons will bleed from the Netherworld."

Falmagon's mind raced with the new words Erzebeth spit out as though they were common language. Her nudity temporarily slipped to an irrelevant detail. *Maharia. Moreth. Anaerfell.* And she knew about the *Kadari!* Falmagon doubted he would recall half of the names before nightfall, but one word did hang in the air. "Demons," he muttered. "By Mulafell, Andrik said she would threaten with demons."

"Impossible," Andrik said, shaking his head fervently. Apparently he was disenchanted by the threat too. "Almost a century gone without a single beast peeking its head out from the Netherworld."

"How many have you shared this information with?" asked Nedezhda.

"No one," Erzebeth answered. She closed her eyes gently and opened them again, abruptly calm. "I would no more disrupt their fantasy worlds than your own."

"Well," Nedezhda said in her clipped tone, "you clearly have some sense about you."

"You think I am lying?" Erzebeth asked suspiciously.

Nedezhda unhurriedly examined the woman from top to bottom and back again, as though she were just recognizing the woman's nakedness for the first time. "I did not suggest anything of the sort. I very much think you believe what you are saying," she finally said. "But my duty is to convey your warning back to Kinhar, not judge its validity."

"Fair enough," Erzebeth said, averting her eyes. "Then go. Go have your fish soup with the Jarl, and may the gods be with you."

Falmagon's gut roiled at the thought of fish soup. He had secretly hoped the slop held some other meat.

"How did you know we—" Andrik started, looking back to where they had been standing with the Jarl. They had been too far for Erzebeth to hear their conversation.

"I do not understand," Falmagon said, ignoring the other Highborn's curiosity. He focused on Erzebeth's wide brown eyes. "Sending your letter to Melkorka and then waiting for us to arrive took more time than delivering your warning to

Kinhar yourself. Why didn't you just come to Melkorka?"

Erzebeth took a breath. "I hoped to speak to Kinhar without an audience. I did not think he would send you and stay behind."

Andrik stepped forward. "You don't trust us?"

"I do not have faith in the Highborn like him," she replied.

"Is that why you are being so secretive about the details? I thought this message was important," Falmagon said.

Erzebeth bit her lip, considering Nedezhda as though she could read some unseen future. "Your questions require more knowledge than I care to impart."

"Try us," Falmagon said, pulling her attention to him.

"Hmm," she sighed, a puff of cold air forming at the end of her lips as twilight set. "Mortals take action based on their beliefs, their feelings. This strength is also their weakness."

"What weakness? What are you talking about?" Andrik asked.

"Faith," Nedezhda replied sourly. "Faith may breed the dutiful disciple, as seen among the Highborn, but nothing is more dangerous than a throng of fanatics."

Falmagon summarized her argument, hardly believing the veiled accusation. "You think the Highborn are immoral extremists? You think our truth is false?"

The smile found its way back to Erzebeth's lips, mocking Nedezhda's earlier assertion. "I very much think you *believe* what you *believe*."

Chapter IV
Maelili

Frothy seawater splashed against Maelili Kluk's wind-chapped bare knees. She waded through the shallow waters, her gaze fixated ahead on the foreign shores of Kalamaar. Morning broke about an hour earlier, but the sun remained behind a sheet of idle clouds. Maelili doubted they would see the full strength of its light today.

Her feet sank an inch in the mud beneath the water's surface. Luckily, her boots were cushioned with wool for warmth and bound with two thick layers of leather. Before exiting the boat, she had fastened the knots tightly, so no water could seep through to her toes. She was glad for it. The droplets splashing under her low-hanging brown tunic gave her a taste of how miserable she could have been traipsing across this foreign land with frozen feet.

With a few more steps remaining until reaching solid ground, she stopped and turned around to see Brigita Mather and Velkan Amaria, her traveling companions. She looked beyond her long red cloak rippling over the water. The two jerked on the knotted rope attached to their longboat with loud grunts.

"Let the sea take it," she said heartily, her voice almost lost in the wind. She pulled at the thick, knotted string under her chin and cleared her throat. The fabric of her cloak grew heavy, as though it would soak up the sea, pulling at the cord around her neck. "We will find another."

Velkan's long red-gold hair whipped across his face in the northern wind, clinging to his bushy beard and mustache. He looked hesitantly to the boat, and then to Maelili and the barren coast. His face twisted in contemplation. The man's loyalty to her family spanned back to the years of her father's governance over Lairhein. Though looking at him, one would not guess him to be much older than she. He had stayed clear of most wars, protecting his youth. The Stuhians did not age like the skin-switching Vucari or the giant Ispolini from the broken islands of Tundris Mor. They were ageless after adolescence, except when they touched their magic, Koldovstvo.

Of course, every Stuhian could manipulate the four elements—sky, stone, sea, and fire—but their individual bloodlines gifted rare magics to each of them. Velkan came from the Amaria family, one of the few curators of the sacred bloodline, titling him a healer among their people. Brigita, on the other hand, hailed from the Mather bloodline. She could access primal magic, manipulating nature or modifying her body, much like their ancient rivals, the Vucari, also known as skin-switchers. And Maelili was a Kluk, who—like her eternal enemy, the Kaligulas—could touch void magic. Though undeniably, she had not touched the void since her earliest years. Her father had instructed her to limit herself to elemental magic and remain clear of the magic of their foes, fearing it might corrupt her too.

Beyond the three, the only other magical crux was profane magic, which allowed wielding unholy energy; Maelili had never known a Stuhian to have this ancient magic coursing through their veins as it had been declared a curse over a century ago.

Maelili realized neither Brigita nor Velkan had moved, still gawking at her with confusion. "I said to leave the boat," she repeated.

Brigita, the youngest—barely old enough to know the taste of magic—tightened her jaw. Upon hearing Maelili's command again, a questioning look decorated her face, but she released the rope, then clung to her belt beneath the water. "You heard the Arkhon. Let it be." She snapped at Velkan as though she were the elder, and not the other way around.

"Ser Velkan?" Maelili looked to Velkan expectantly, who remained dumbfounded, staring at her as though he were a child. Finally, with a grunt, he grabbed the fore of the boat and shoved it back to deeper waters.

When Maelili regained the royal seat of Lairhein, she restored Velkan to her side among the noble classes. In repayment, he promised her that he would find her brother, Kindel. She would have also settled for her enemy, the traitor Dagmar Kaligula, from whom she usurped the title Arkhon, or either of his two despicable sons, Tyran and Drast. For almost seventy-five years, she had sent scouts to reconnoiter the north with nothing promising to be discovered. Until now, when Velkan led them to the far end of the world, believing he finally had located Kindel's whereabouts.

Without bothering to acknowledge Velkan or Brigita further, Maelili stumbled the rest of the way to the shore, dragging her cloak behind her and collapsing to her knees. The sands were soft. Too soft for the upcoming winter. Yet her mind was on the weakness in her legs. Too many days they sailed for Kalamaar; she had started to think the place did not exist.

Yet the cold sand pricking at her skin rattled her senses, promising her the shore was anything but an illusion.

Brigita and Velkan slipped against the sand behind her, crunching pebbles under the soles of their thick boots.

"We made it." Brigita whistled through her teeth, coupled with heavy breaths. She plopped down next to Maelili, falling to her back, wide eyes to the heavens.

Maelili buried her fingers in the sand. "Who knows what scouts may have seen us come to shore? We need to get out of the open. Find a place for shelter." A gust of wind swept over them, whisking her long white-red hair over her face. Her people once claimed she had the brightest hair of any Stuhian, but she was no longer young. Time and the use of magic stole the color. Luckily, though her hair was quickly turning white, the wrinkles at her eyes and cheeks were slower to show her age. She spat several strands of hair from her mouth, twisting to see Velkan pulling his own hair from his lips, his hair being nearly as long as hers. "Ser Velkan, which way do we go?"

His blue eyes were half closed as he considered the eastern plains stretching for miles, the silhouette of mountains dancing on the foggy horizon. His voice was clear and light with the air of a noble, barely strong enough to pierce the wind. "My apologies, Arkhon. I have told you what I know."

"Not good enough," Brigita said. "You have taken our Arkhon thousands of miles from her husband and child… her kingdom. You—"

"Stop, Brigita," Maelili directed serenely, sinking her hand deeper into the sand to feel its weight. The more she dug, the colder the mud. The weeks at sea had turned to months. She missed the feeling of the earth. "We have all made our sacrifices. You left your family and Ser Velkan left his husband behind. He has gone farther than any other Stuhian was willing and should not be reprimanded for his service." She lifted the wet sand and let it fall back to the earth, weighing the land ahead of her. She could not guess what threats waited for them.

She could have brought those who were more battle-hardened than Velkan or Brigita, but few could match the loyalty of her two companions. "Tell us the story one more time, Ser Velkan."

"As you wish, Arkhon," he replied crustily. He had spent the boat ride reiterating his tale. She knew he was not pleased to repeat the words another time and did not care. He was her subject to be commanded. "The skin-switcher claimed one of their Wardens traveled the scope of Aenar to protect the Ash Tree and knew about this northern speck of land called Kalamaar. The people here—the Anshedar—look like us mostly, save their smaller size and dark hair."

"They cannot touch Koldovstvo, though," Brigita inferred from the many conversations they had on the boat. "If they cross us, we will crush them."

"The Vucari did not say whether they could," Velkan said, frowning, his lips tensed under his thick beard, seemingly disgruntled for being interrupted. "But could they know of our magic anyway when theirs is such a perversion?"

Brigita combed her hair back to braid it with her long fingers. "We have come across the world at the word of a skin-switcher. We cannot even be certain this is Kalamaar. You better hope we see home again, *Ser* Velkan."

"We have heard your concerns, Brigita. For a thousand miles and more. Now silence your tongue." Maelili kept a stony face, swiftly scanning the horizon. They already sat for too long, and Velkan had not finished his story. She needed something she could use to pinpoint a way to travel. "Keep going, Ser Velkan. Every detail."

He cracked his knuckles, returning her gaze. "From what I know, the people here are difficult, bent on their ways and their religion. They are quick to resort to violence, protecting their beliefs, although they are equally apt to change positions on any given topic throughout their short lives."

"A bunch of motley-minded louts," Brigita mumbled.

Velkan gripped the pack holding their rations and supplies in his meaty hand and said, "The Vucari I spoke with knew little about their settlements, but based on what he said, I would expect the Anshedar to build their cities along the coasts." He paused, lifting his shoulders to his ears. "Except in this wind, they may seek the shadow of those mountains ahead."

"What of Kindel?" Maelili insisted. "What did the skin-switcher say of him?"

"Arkhon," his voice trembled, reiterating the warning he had given a hundred times over, "we cannot know if he, or your enemy, or any Stuhia are on Kalamaar. Though standing on its beaches gives me hope we might find something worthwhile."

"Tell me what was said. I need to hear it."

He cleared his throat, lifting his voice as another draft whipped by them—this time springing sand grains up from the extended bank. "The Anshedar have dark colors to them, like the Vucari. Brown hair and black hair. Never red, like our people." His beard waggled with intensity as he talked. He swelled his thick chest. "The scout claimed a handful of young redheaded people have been spotted here—on southern islands and northern forests. Though I cannot say where we might have landed."

Maelili knew how ridiculous his words sounded; they came here because of a rumor of hair color. But if she heard the tall tale often enough, she would make herself believe it.

Every Stuhia had red hair. Dagmar was too old to be considered young by the feeblest of minds, and his sons were too wild with their magic to keep their youth. They were nothing like Velkan, who clung to his youth like a miser clung to his money. She held hope that her brother was the heart of the rumor. She needed to find him, and then she would worry about her revenge.

Her husband, Nevyn, and child, Eisliev, remained in Lairhein—her kingdom—on the other side of the world. They struggled to understand this near century-long quest, but soon, she would be freed from her charge. Her brother would be returned to Lairhein.

Of course, Nevyn had begged for her not to leave them; the feeble man never did understand honor. Maybe that was why he agreed to take her name at their wedding instead of her taking his. Of course, the Kluk name was centuries old, notorious for its honor and power. The same could hardly be said of Nevyn and the other Connocks. In fact, he was lucky to be a Stuhia with his weak-willed heart. The more prominent families of Lairhein had frowned on Maelili choosing such a weak husband, but she preferred not to worry about him rising up against her. She could not say she loved him, but she was safe in his company.

Nevertheless, Maelili would make certain Eisliev would not be plagued by the same diluted thinking as her husband. Her son would keep the surname Kluk, no matter what happened to her on Kalamaar.

"We are here because one Vucari supposedly whispered rumors to another Vucari, and then Velkan beat it out of them. What is to say the skin-switcher wasn't lying?" Brigita questioned. "We should never have come, Arkhon."

"It is hearsay," Velkan said weakly.

Maelili remained gentle, standing up. "You followed me here of your own choice, Brigita, and you knew the story then. I am not holding you prisoner. If you want to return home, the boat can be found that way." She pointed to the sea behind her, knowing full well the boat had already disappeared in the dark waves.

"You know I would give my life for yours, Arkhon," Brigita said, dipping her head. The woman was tough until met with equal toughness, a telltale sign of her youth.

"Then give it with a dull tongue," Maelili replied.

"How can you be so certain?" Brigita asked.

"If your heart is true, the gods will steer you to the path to see your duty done," she answered, repeating the wisdom of her deceased father. She dusted her tunic with her hands, then gestured inland with her chin. "Our road is east. We will find a hollow in those mountains ahead for tonight's shelter. You still have the black walnut husks?" she asked Brigita. The bright-eyed woman nodded, unwilling to split her lips after being reprimanded. Maelili continued, "We will dye the red from our hair so we might blend with the natives. Tomorrow we will set off to find whatever hamlet or city is nearby. If Kindel is here, we will find him."

Without anything more to say, the three of them spent the rest of the day hustling across the landscape. The little light emitting from the sky came and went by the time they reached the edge of the rocky foothills, soon erupting into mountains to the northeast. The grasslands still stretched farther east and south, but Maelili's focus was on the towering red peaks. If the mountains were anything like the Shade Fells back home, finding a way through might take weeks.

Maelili did not want to take weeks, though. She lost count of the many months she had been away from Lairhein. She missed Nevyn and little Eisliev, barely three years old when she left, with his corkscrew red hair.

"Arkhon, you torture yourself with this quest." Brigita found the nerve to start again while they searched for refuge. "How many years has it been without vengeance?"

Maelili sucked the cool air through her nostrils before responding. She did not always welcome the niggling sound of Brigita's tongue, but the younger woman's pragmatism frequently proved to be good counsel. Regardless, she hoped to teach the girl something valuable before returning to Lairhein. "Dagmar has kept himself hidden for seventy-five years, as have his sons."

"A long time to be missing," Brigita said. "Who is to say they are not dead? We cannot live in the past. Our people need—"

"Justice." Maelili finished Brigita's sentence with a pitched rumble in her throat, which may have sounded more natural coming from Velkan than her. "As you know, time means little to our people and even less to the Kaligula bloodline. They are ever patient and planful. You do not know how long they brimmed beneath the surface of our governance, planning their sour schemes. If they are not casting Koldovstvo, they can remain living forever. Therefore, until I see their rotting bodies decomposing before me, they are considered dangerous."

Brigita crumpled her brow, apparently searching for an argument. "I know how magic works. But Dagmar and his sons could have been consumed by Vulkodlak while trying to trek across Maharia. Who knows when the beasts began migrating down from the far north?" she offered. The monstrous wolf-men creatures she mentioned were not only known to plague the skin-switchers on the island north of her city, but they also found evidence of the beasts when traveling across the mainland to Kalamaar. Brigita was spirited—Maelili would admit—and hardly intimidated by the commanding weight of her ruler.

"You were not born during their time. The Kaligulas killed dragons. I doubt they were bested by the Vulkodlak," Maelili said, softening her voice. She would not believe Dagmar or his sons had escaped her retribution through any means, even a natural death. The gods would not rob her of the poetic justice she deserved. The three of them had slaughtered her father, sisters, and brothers, save Kindel. The thought caused her throat to close up.

"The Arkhon is right," Velkan said softly, a distant look in his eye. "I was there when Tyran and Drast led our armies victoriously against the skin-switchers and the *Viy*, Torn'ash." He used the old name for the massive three-headed Father of Dragons. "Neither was powerful enough to defend against their strength. The Kaligula bloodline is more powerful than any Stuhia I have known." He paused to look at Maelili. "I am sorry, Arkhon."

"Do not apologize for speaking the truth. The Kaligulas are stronger than the Kluks," Maelili replied with a cracked voice. "By some strange magic, Drast found my brother, Ghanimer, and me in Lairhein. He came to us as though a beacon of light marked our location. Then, before the night was finished, he pulled a temple down on Ghanimer like it was made of straw." She shook her head at the ghastly memory, holding her tongue from saying she had voluntarily abandoned Ghanimer to save her own life. The shame of not even trying to prevent his death stayed with her daily. The image of Drast Kaligula standing over his unconscious body danced between her temples, even while she scampered away like a hare would from a fox. "From what I know, none of my siblings came close to matching their might."

"Why did Drast let you live, Arkhon?" Brigita asked.

Maelili exhaled. "I cannot say. But his brother, Tyran, had the chance to kill me too and did not." She could feel the tightness in her chest, admitting something she had known for a long time. "Given the chance, I will not make the same mistake. I will not allow the people I love to be hurt."

"Justice has no place for mercy. But we have not come to Kalamaar for the Kaligulas. We seek your brother. The enemy must wait for another adventure," Velkan said. In the same breath, he motioned to the left at the mountain. "We have found a hollow, Arkhon."

The incline leading to the cave was less slanted than expected, and although the ingress into the pitch cavity was narrow, the three of them squeezed through with ease. Each of them quickly got to work setting up their evening camp. Brigita prepared the hair-coloring goop, Maelili retrieved fish and bread from Velkan's pack for their supper, and Velkan kindled the fire. Before long, they were crowded around the flames near the back of the burrowed hole.

Maelili leaned back against the cave wall, peering into the darkness beyond the faint light of the fire, orange sparks popping steadily into the air. The hollow angled deeper into the red rock of the mountain, but the hole tapered off, leaving little space. She likely could crawl through the fleapit if they were ambushed from the front, but the only real outlet would be the way they had come. She hoped for a restful night.

"If the Anshedar knew we were here, they would have come by now," Velkan offered, seemingly reading her mind from across the fire. He had already finished his blackened fish and set to work at sharpening a rock against another rock. The rhythmic scraping sound was more melodic than jarring.

She watched Velkan. The Stuhians were forbidden from crafting weapons to keep them from embedding Koldovstvo into the blades. The law limited the weapon-makers to crafting bows, arrows, and staves. Occasionally, the Stuhians might trade with the giants to the south of their lands for better armaments, but the dealings with the Ispolini were rare. The giants never ventured far from their subterranean cities, and the Stuhians preferred their solitude.

"I hope you are right," Maelili said, taking a bite from her fish. She carefully worked it around in her mouth to check for bones.

"You mean to shave with the stone?" Brigita asked.

Velkan gritted his teeth, eyeing the stone as though he was second-guessing himself. "I did not see a clam shell on the beach and given I did not bring a copper razor…" He groaned with dissatisfaction. "Seems I have but one option. Chazek would not like it, but I should have it grown again before returning home."

Maelili smiled at the mention of Velkan's husband's name. She had forgotten it, though she remembered the man echoed the same tenor of kindness.

Brigita looked at the pulp of black walnut husks mashed against the cave floor. The gritty molding would shade their hair from red to dark brown or light brown, lasting a couple of weeks at most.

"You will not not have enough to color your hair and my beard," Velkan muttered in his light tone, his beard waggling against the center of his chest. Maelili smiled again as she swallowed. Velkan talked as though Brigita's hair and hers were a threat to his manhood when his own head of hair stretched longer than either of their own. He concluded, "Best for my beard to be shortened than your braids."

"Shorten it, but do not scrape at your skin. We do not need you going into town with cuts and a blood-stained face tomorrow." Brigita scrunched her face at the thought. "I think we can spare some for the roots."

Velkan nodded with relief, lifting the makeshift razor to his crinkled hairs.

"Arkhon." Brigita turned away from Velkan as though she could not watch, searching for a topic to pass the time. "I never understood why your brother did not stay and fight against the Kaligulas."

Maelili knitted her brow. "Kindel volunteered to take my father's staff, *Habermani*, to keep it from their hands. Like all my siblings, Kindel watched Dagmar kill my father. You would have fled never to return too." Brigita could not stop from tensing her cheeks with uncertainty.

Maelili embraced patience, knowing the woman was still young. She suspected Brigita thought her brother weak for bolting from Lairhein all those years ago, but Maelili thought him to be rather brave. Venturing off into the world without any direction to protect the heirloom of their family, Habermani—a staff of great power—would have been chilling.

"And what is Habermani?" Brigita scooped a handful of the gook and stepped around the fire to hand Maelili her portion of the concoction. Maelili clawed it from her hand.

"One of the many relics of lost ages," Velkan answered, flinging a handful of red beard hairs into the fire. His face was partially shorn and patchy, leaving a jumbled mess. Without flinching, he grabbed another handful of hairs, his cheek stretching from his face, and then began sawing with the rock. He talked through the side of his mouth. "Many Stuhian families with noble blood kept relics to help them channel

Koldovstvo, like Habermani. More powerful artifacts existed, but they have long been lost. Few remember their existence. Some were stolen by the Vucari, others taken by those who wielded profane magic and were banned from Lairhein. Still others went missing when our people roved through the Shade Fells in hopes of making sense of the world. And a number were stored at *Iriy*, the City of the Gods."

Brigita's eyes lightened up, pausing as she worked the gunk into her red hair. "How many are still in Lairhein?"

"No idea. We do not ask families to reveal their treasures." Maelili massaged the sticky substance down to her scalp. Although the texture was disgusting, it smelled sweet.

"But Arkhon, if these are powerful relics, are they not a threat?" Brigita blinked.

"Of course, but threats arise from their owner's disbelief and distrust, not sudden power from relics," Maelili said with a small smile. Brigita scrunched up her nose as though she did not understand. Maelili's fingers worked at her hair, searching for the right words to help the young Stuhia understand clearly. Her father's words, or some semblance of them, found their way to the edge of her tongue. "Every Stuhian can touch Koldovstvo at a thought, having the ability to snap a neck or worse. But no matter the strength of a Stuhian's blood or brawn or relic, strategy prevails."

"Then the Kaligulas contended for power not because of relics, but because they did not trust in your father?" Brigita asked.

"Dagmar and his sons did not trust in anything but themselves," Velkan clarified, running his hand over his jawbone, looking for longer hairs. "Their family controlled our armies. Some would contest that the Kluks never held power during Maelili's father's time."

Maelili stayed quiet, seeing no purpose in arguing with Velkan. His words, again, were not far from the truth.

"But you feared the Kaligulas and the possibility of them having Habermani," she said.

"I did, and for good reason," Maelili said. "My father always said if you know the enemy and yourself, you will not fear what is to come. Yet the Kaligulas were the greater in both power and strategy."

"You speak as though they were gods," Brigita said.

The flames suddenly sparked in front of her. "I suspect even the gods would fear them," Maelili admitted.

"Then why do you believe Kindel is alive? Would they not have come after him?" Brigita asked.

Maelili did not answer, considering the fire. The thought had haunted her for years.

"No," Velkan said. "Dagmar's ambitions were always far-reaching. He would not have wasted time searching for Habermani in a world full of so many other treasures."

"Like the Ash Tree," Brigita clarified.

Velkan hummed, repeating the words as though they were his own. "Like the Ash Tree."

Maelili gritted her teeth. Velkan gave her hope in thinking Kindel would be found, but she feared she would find little more than his remains. She hated how she anticipated Kindel's untimely death and not that of her enemy.

Chapter V
MAELILI

Velkan meandered ahead of Maelili and Brigita by several feet, plodding between the rising mountains and the expansive grasslands. His new mahogany-colored hair fluttered lightly against his red cloak. Maelili barely recognized him from the rear, though she suspected none of them quite looked like themselves. From the corner of her eye, she could see her own locks bouncing against her cheek. The white-red pigment had been completely swept away, shading her hair nearly as dark as pitch. She pushed the strands behind her ear and out of her mind.

Since dawn, a mist of white hung heavily on the edge of the greensward like morning dew, skirting by their boots as they traipsed along, searching for any sign of civilization. The early morning sun flashed through the scattered mist, striking Maelili's eyes. She blinked repeatedly to see through the rays, finally adjusting her position to stay hidden in Velkan's shadow.

"How far do you think these mountains stretch?" Brigita muttered. The simple question sounded like she was spitting nails. From the corner of her eye, Maelili glimpsed Brigita trying to block the sunlight. The rays seemed to ricochet off the morning haze.

Maelili smiled so she might sound optimistic, though the answer was less than appealing. "The mountains are not growing any smaller on the horizon. And, if I recall, they surrounded us on the shoreline. From where we stand, Kalamaar might be more mountain than anything."

"We should have sailed around the coast until finding a city or at least an inlet," Brigita said, her tinted brown hair bouncing against her back in a braid. "I have not even seen a water source since we left the coast."

Velkan spoke but did not bother to turn his head. "We could have been caught by the Anshedar on the water and given no chance to mask our origin. We were lucky to avoid prying eyes. A few days' march will not hurt us."

"Our supplies are already low, Ser Velkan," Brigita said.

"We will be fine," Maelili said, reaching out and resting her hand on Brigita's shoulder. The woman flinched but quickly relaxed, as if realizing the error of recoiling at the Arkhon's touch. Maelili repeated the words, hoping they would give some sense of comfort. "We will be fine."

The next many hours were consumed in idle chit-chat, admiring the modest terrain of the country. The farther they traveled, the higher the red rocks reached toward the heavens; the prairie, in turn, slowly waned in the shadow of the mountains. In their simple passing, they rustled wild rabbit and red-tailed pheasant from the field, noticed several birds—including sparrows and grosbeaks seen in their lands—but left them alone, continuing their march and hoping to soon finding a village or hamlet.

Velkan kept them along the edge of the mountain for the length of their journey. Twice they stopped to rest their legs and drink what water they boiled the night before. After a while, Maelili noticed their heading was more north than east, but without knowing the land, she figured one direction was as good as any other. Without bothering to look over her shoulder at the sweeping backdrop, her popping ears signified that they were gaining altitude. In addition, the sun swelled above them, promising warmth, but the sudden chill stinging at Maelili's cheeks, nose, and ears bespoke its unintended deception. She secretly hoped Velkan did not plan on leading them over the mountain, but she trusted his instincts.

In short time, with the sound and smell of the sea long forgotten, she struggled to ascend behind Velkan, trying to ignore the burn in the back of her legs. She suspected Brigita also found difficulty when her breath, too, hastened with her attempt to maintain the hearty pace in the thinning atmosphere.

"Arkhon," Velkan said after a long while, stopping ahead of her. He pointed at an ingress in the mountain, sitting between two tan sarsen stones.

"Another cave?" Brigita coughed from behind Maelili. She spat out her argument in a hurried rasp. "We still have plenty of daylight left. No reason to make camp yet."

Velkan rubbed the stubble on his chin, softly shaking his head. He spoke in his usual honeyed tone. "This may be our path. Look at the unnatural position of the stones. I would guess that this leads somewhere important."

Maelili turned from her old friend and studied the cavity in the rock. The height barely reached her chest, and it was narrow enough that they would have to travel single file. They suspected the Anshedar were near to their own size, but this entrance—if it was an entrance—meant the Anshedar were half their size, at most. Scooting closer, she stared helplessly into the blackness. "What do you expect to find down there, Ser Velkan? Do you think the Anshedar build their cities underground?"

She saw him shrug in her peripheral vision. "I would doubt it, Arkhon. But maybe this will lead through the mountains to a city."

"Or," Brigita spoke between her teeth with a piercing tone, "it could be a footpath to the Netherworld filled with demons or worse. We should stay on the surface where we have visibility and the advantage." Maelili pondered the path ahead. Brigita scraped her foot across the ground irritably and added, "Did we really travel so far to be slaughtered by demons in a hole?"

"We cannot be sure any entrances or exits to the Netherworld are on this island," Maelili said softly. "This land is strange to us all."

"We still do not even know if we are on Kalamaar," Brigita argued. "You have your duty to Lairhein as the Arkhon, and you also have a duty to your family. We should remain cautious."

Maelili shook her head, facing Brigita. "My brother is my family. I will leave no stone unturned."

"Arkhon—"

"I will not risk returning home empty-handed and with uncertainty," Maelili spoke over her. "We will either find my brother or know we did all we could to find him."

Brigita widened her light eyes, which appeared all the brighter under her brown bangs. She moved in front of

Maelili with a grim look, facing the underpass into the earth. "Then stay between us and watch your head."

Velkan tilted his head sideways to better examine the path. "Lead the way, Brigita. And give us some light."

Brigita mumbled something unintelligible, likely an insult toward Velkan, considering she did not have to speak to cast her spell. Swift as a sunbeam, two balls of reddish-orange light sparked in front of her, floating a foot in front of her face. She channeled Koldovstvo, adjusting the brightness of the two bulbs, so they would light the path without blinding them, and then sent them ahead into the darkness.

Maelili trailed, blinking several times to adjust to the limited light, which bounced like fireflies in the dark, bobbing through the air ahead of Brigita. Whereas they had been traveling at an incline most of the morning, the depression in the earth was instantly evident, taking them at a harsh angle downward.

"No one has been on this path in a long time," Maelili said, immediately gripping at the rock-strewn walls. Moisture clung to the uneven rock, making it difficult to hold herself steady. She dug her feet into the soft sands. She nearly fell to her bottom, which would be followed, undoubtedly, by slipping into Brigita's bowed legs. She hurriedly pushed the thought from her mind, hoping to keep the idea from spurring into reality.

Velkan whispered, "Appears not. Should we turn back for the surface?"

"No," she replied, shaking her head as though he could see her clearly. "We should see where this goes."

Brigita harrumphed loudly but said nothing.

"Keep it slow." Maelili frowned. The young Stuhian was loyal but awfully impertinent, even when she said nothing.

The ground abruptly changed to loose gravel before changing and hardening into solid form. She followed Brigita's lead, who softly grunted, leaning her shoulder against the eastern wall while clinging to the western wall with her hand. The position gave them considerably more leverage and control during the descent.

Ahead, the two bulbs of light swept back and forth briskly, recoiling from the walls and low-cut ceiling. In short time, the red rock, dull in the pale light, changed into soft brown sediment and greyish clay.

Maelili touched it delicately, peering over her shoulder at Velkan edging along in the shadows. Whatever surface light may have existed behind them was already lost.

Velkan's trusting eyes met hers. His feet fell heavily behind her. "Worry not, Arkhon. We will be victorious. The savants will write about your reign for ages, through the lives of your children and their children."

"You know I do not seek glory, Velkan," Maelili said with a smile. "Glory may be for Kindel to claim, if he wishes it. I only want to bring him home. No song needs to be sung."

"You retook your father's seat as Arkhon and saved us from Dagmar Kaligula's tyranny," Velkan said, his fingernails scraping against the wall in attempt to keep balance. He reiterated what he had told her for the last many years. "Much will be said whether you want it to be or not. You avenged your family and guided us back toward decency."

"The Stuhian people never lost decency, even under Dagmar's thumb," Maelili said. "They only needed the courage to rise against him."

"And you gave them the courage," he replied.

Velkan's wisdom bothered her. She may be their Arkhon because she led the revolt against the Kaligulas, but she had no interest in being forever idolized. She did not want statues or praise. She only wanted to live in peace with her family: her husband, her son, and her brother.

"Arkhon." Brigita turned her chin slightly, speaking over her shoulder without fully turning her head. The orbs drifted farther ahead, augmenting their light to illuminate a widening cavern. "Look at this."

Maelili poked her head over Brigita's shoulder, straining to see in the expanding reddish light. The cavity stretched farther than the light, the brightness powerless against the shadows; though she did see the ground leveled out under their feet, giving a solid path to walk across. Hundreds of jagged stalagmites stretched up from the cave floor, and a hundred more brooding stalactites drooped from the ceiling like icicles. The brownish-red color of clay and underearth painted everything without a sign of stone or gem or anything decorative. If anything of worth ever existed in this place, it had been stripped clean.

"I do not think men came down here, Velkan," she said, scanning the ceiling and floor. The underground haven looked untouched by mortal hands. The crisp smell of fresh water hung on the air. She breathed the scent in deeply as though she might be able to discern its location. "An underground spring must be nearby."

"The fresh water would be a delight," Velkan said in a sing-song tone. "Yet I do not hear any water. Might only be water seeping through from the surface."

A clitter of nails across rock cut Velkan from saying any more. The sound was hurriedly followed by something small flapping past them overhead. Maelili jerked to follow the sound.

"Light, Brigita," Maelili ordered.

With one orb hovering ahead of them, Brigita drifted the other closer with Koldovstvo, the radiance burning through the darkness, shining on the gloomy crevices in the ceiling, where the creature may have fled.

Small claws scuttled against the hanging pillar above them, hidden from the scope of the light.

"Likely a bat," Velkan said.

"No," Brigita said, straining her neck to look closer as the creature poked its miniature horned skull around the rock. Its forelimbs had a small membranous skin attached, serving as wings when outstretched. The demonic-looking thing almost looked like a bat, but as it rustled farther around the stalactite, Maelili could clearly see the scrawny body and spindly legs.

"A skyrz," Maelili said, stepping back and hastily scanning the rest of the cavern. "I have read about them in my father's library. The little demons are rare but also exist in the Shade Fells."

Brigita scoffed. "I would rather have more of those pipsqueaks threatening our outerlands than the Witiko." The undead demons of the Deep that roamed through the underground caves of the Shade were larger than the

Stuhians; she prayed none lurked nearby. Brigita went on, "It does not look like it could do much damage." In response, the skyrz bared its little fangs at Brigita and hissed menacingly.

"Maybe not alone, but a drove of them would tear the skin from your bones like locusts over a crop," Maelili said in a near whisper. "Luckily, I do not see any others."

Velkan cooed from the back, pulling at Maelili's arm. "We should return topside. Clearly the humans are not down here, and this is not a pass. Best not to chance a battle with demons of any size."

She agreed, allowing him to pull her back into the tunnel leading to the surface. "Come on, Brigita. Looks like we will be traveling over the mountain after all."

"Yes, Arkhon." With a twist of her hand, she crushed the skyrz with Koldovstvo, its bones cracking under her power. The little creature squeaked and fell silent, plummeting from the ceiling and smacking against the cave floor.

Chapter VI
FALMAGON

Falmagon never suspected his homesickness would be so intense after less than a week away from Melkorka, but by the time they returned on the faering to Narthwich, he was dreaming of his stone bed. He scratched the back of his head, straining his eyes in the dim light of Kinhar's study, Nedezhda and Andrik standing on either side of him. He wanted nothing more than to fall flat against the solid surface and pull a few soft skins over his head.

He could sleep for days, if not weeks, but first Kinhar wanted a report.

"I am telling you the woman was mad," Falmagon said a second time, directing the conversation away from his real thoughts. He sat rigid to keep his eyes open, feeling the heat from the center fire pit behind him. The flames burned too low for the forthcoming Months of Frost. "She prattled on about a war lost and demons returning from the Netherworld, but she offered nothing of substance to prove her claims. She kept telling us to ask you what she meant."

"He is right. She was the prettiest thing I had ever seen, but she was absolutely mad," Andrik breathed, crossing his arms. He bit at his thick lips, gazing out the curtainless window cut into the northern wall as though he'd been overtaken by a musing. Falmagon followed Andrik's gaze to see what he might have been looking at in the failing light of the sunset, only to see the skirting stone wall surrounding Melkorka. The distant Crags of Kazimir had already vanished on the horizon.

He could hear the other Highborn chattering, calling out to the Kras slaves to hurry along with their evening duties. The raspy responses of the red broods acquiescing to their masters created a constant buzz. Falmagon was glad to be inside and away from the little beasts. He had no interest in looking at their long hooked noses or deathless eyes.

Andrik continued, "She said a man called Moreth led the Kadari to defend Aenar in the West. She spoke as though something more existed across the ocean."

Kinhar shuffled his feet on the floor behind his desk, saying nothing. His knotted hair lay coiled in his lap over his shoulder. Falmagon looked for some change in Kinhar's expression while listening to Andrik's recap. The Spearhead could have been a sculpture, sinking further into his chair and patiently interlacing his fingers as though they were of more interest.

Nedezhda turned her chin upward, glaring at Kinhar. "What does it all mean? Who or what are the Kadari?"

Kinhar lifted his shoulders as though it were a chore, dropping them with a heavy breath. His eyes darted around the room. His voice was eerily calm and deep. "I must ponder her message. I do not know who she is or what she is talking about."

"She seemed to know you well enough," Nedezhda said swiftly, leaving Kinhar with his mouth hanging open on his last word. Nedezhda stepped forward.

The scrolls positioned beneath stacks of books rustled in the breeze that whipped through the window. Kinhar's mouth clamped shut, and he squinted an eye at Nedezhda. Then he dropped his chin to his chest and mumbled, "I think I would remember. All the same, we will continue as we always have, remaining vigilant to any threats we perceive."

"Kinhar—" Nedezhda started with a clipped tone, hands clenched at her sides. "We have plenty of threats in need of response. Not one but two strangers have come to the Seven Islands in the last month, one of whom attacked Falmagon right outside Melkorka's walls, wielding magic the Highborn have never before seen, and we—"

"Nedezhda," Kinhar broke in, saying her name with equal contempt and blinking slowly, "the woman you met is mad. We must think of our well-being and prepare for winter. You will hurry and return to Narthwich and forget about…what did you say her name was?"

"Erzebeth." Nedezhda shot daggers at the old man.

"Yes." Kinhar nodded, his beard bouncing lightly. "Do not worry about her. Go to Narthwich."

"Kinhar!" Nedezhda shouted. "We only returned moments ago. You cannot send—"

"Grain needs to be collected for the winter. Take Jhar with you," Kinhar finished. "He could use the fresh air."

Nedezhda snapped. "Why did you not fetch extra food while we were running your errand? Forestor or Faina could have gone. By the gods, you could have sent Dorofej and a pack horse."

"Do hurry." Kinhar modestly shrugged, disregarding her disrespect. "Andrik, you are also dismissed. Falmagon, stay for a moment more."

Nedezhda gaped before giving Falmagon a pinched expression. Then, turning on her heel, she grabbed Andrik by his brown cloak and pulled him along. From her grip, Falmagon wondered if she would drag him all the way to Narthwich with her. The poor Highborn widened his eyes before being jerked out of the room. The wooden door slammed against the frame as they made their exit.

Falmagon spun around, his question falling off the tip of his tongue. "So you do know Moreth. Is he the stranger I saw with Jhar?"

"By the gods, Falmagon," Kinhar fumed, hitting his desk with an open palm. "Moreth is not your stranger. Erzebeth is not your stranger. Will you forget about the stranger already?"

"I cannot." Falmagon lightly touched the side of his head. The soreness was long gone, but the memory of the redhead was fresh. "He said the Highborn did not deserve Koldovstvo and we should die. Seems worth remembering."

"Do not get smart with me. I said before if we come across the stranger again, we should retrieve the staff, but otherwise do not let him rule your thoughts." Kinhar glared. "Have you been spending time praying to the Lightbringer?"

Falmagon bit on his tongue, trying to regain some moisture in his mouth. He dipped his head. "Some."

"You must pray. Every day." Kinhar sighed, his hand shaking as he rubbed his forehead. He grunted with frustration. "Excuse my poor mood. Erzebeth has let her tongue wag and now everything the Kadari have worked for is threatened."

"I will pray, Kinhar," Falmagon mumbled insincerely. He perked up, almost springing to Kinhar's side. "Then you know Erzebeth too?"

Kinhar leaned back with a dead gaze, answering Falmagon's question without words. The Spearhead eased his tone. "What I know, and what you will learn, is not to be digested by all those who share Melkorka with us. Many of their minds are twisted by being brought up in the lands of the Anshedar."

Falmagon pressed his luck. "You mean to say more lands exist in the West?"

"Have you been listening to me?" Kinhar coughed, his beard shaking with the reverberation in his chest. He took in a deep breath and rubbed his lips with the back of his hand to stifle another cough. "Together, we will show the Highborn another way. We will teach them the way of the Kadari and save the world from the coming darkness under the guidance of the Lightbringer."

"I am trying to understand," Falmagon said.

"Nedezhda will ruin us," he hissed over the table, darkness clouding his eyes.

Falmagon huffed with excitement and moved closer to the desk, the heat of the embers dying down in the small study. "Why did you send her to Cyreus if you did not want her knowing about Erzebeth or the Kadari? If you know Erzebeth, you would have known she'd say something when you did not come."

Kinhar's face softened. "She was upset?"

Falmagon nodded. "She did not even bother trying to hide her frustration at seeing the three of us."

Kinhar dropped his hands to the table and sighed with defeat. His spiraling emotions only heightened Falmagon's intrigue. He watched Kinhar bob his head, the folds of his cheeks quivering. "You are right," he said. Falmagon attempted to make sense of his explanation. "I must have known, even if I did not know I *knew*. The Lightbringer guided my hand and my tongue to help see the truth unravel."

Falmagon dipped his head, indicating he understood the methods of the gods. He was unsure what to say next.

"I told you a darkness resided inside our walls. I have been working tirelessly to discover the source, and when Erzebeth's warning of doom arrived...I...I was terrified," Kinhar said. "You went to Cyreus as a trusted Kadari, and the confusion clouding your fellow Highborn after speaking to Erzebeth proves that you held true to your vows."

"Of course, Kinhar." Falmagon smiled, realizing he passed Kinhar's test. Of course, the Spearhead sent Nedezhda and Andrik with him to assess his loyalty. "I would not falter."

Kinhar nodded. "I know, my son. In the wake of the journey, another among you showed her true allegiance."

"Nedezhda," Falmagon said without hesitation. He noticed that Kinhar calling him *son* sounded more welcoming than when coming from Jhar.

"Nedezhda the Longwalker," Kinhar repeated as though his cheeks were filled with poison. "We saw how she attacked me tonight. Her unwillingness to serve the cause of the Highborn cannot be denied. The gods only know how she has schemed against us while traversing among the Anshedar. Only the gods know what darkness she has welcomed into her heart. No doubt she plots against us."

Falmagon was stunned, wondering how many signs he may have missed that spoke of her treachery. He swallowed, dipping his head in unison with Kinhar.

"We must speak to Erzebeth again to learn more of the impending doom and prepare ourselves for whatever evil Nedezhda will bring upon us."

"What must I do?" Falmagon asked.

"Tomorrow you will travel to Arkaim on the mainland with Andrik. You will seek out your kin, Unnvar Grondahl. He will be about your age now, maybe a few years older," Kinhar said, rubbing his chin through his beard.

Falmagon could not keep the smile from his face. He always found a sense of comfort at Melkorka, but to travel to see his birthplace on Kalamaar was exciting. "I will, Kinhar," he said with ardor.

Kinhar raised his hand to slow Falmagon. "Erzebeth will likely go to the mainland. You will find her and tell her that you have taken the Kalamyr Oath. And then you will see what else she may tell us."

"Kinhar," Falmagon faltered, "she insisted on speaking with you. Why would she tell me anything more?"

"Because she will know you are Kadari," Kinhar said.

"What do you expect her to say that she has not already said?" Falmagon asked.

Kinhar paused, looking around the study with a concerned eye. "We need to know everything she knows."

Falmagon swallowed hard. The answer gave him no direction. "And what about Andrik? What am I to tell him?"

"Tell him you are training to be a Longwalker. Tell him that together you will be safe from this stranger you saw. The one you are so concerned over," Kinhar said off-handedly. "I am certain the redheaded man will come up in conversation regardless. Take the opportunity to explore his relationship to Nedezhda and his allegiance to the Highborn."

Falmagon wrinkled his forehead.

"Go. Eat. Rest. Pray." Kinhar waved his hand. "We have much work to do. This will not be the last of your journeys and the winter is long."

"Yes, Kinhar," he replied.

Falmagon's hands were shaking as he left Kinhar's study. He walked down the staircase and out the keep door into the courtyard. He was excited at the prospect of becoming a Longwalker, but he was not blind that he was being tested again. Clearly by Kinhar, who was sending Andrik with him again, but also by the Lightbringer. He would prove his worth to them both, returning with Kinhar's full respect and the Lightbringer's blessing.

A full blanket of clouds had blocked out the stars, leaving the castle in dim torchlight. He had every intention of returning to his cottage, which he shared with Andrik, so he could rest like Kinhar suggested. Exhaustion had pulled at Falmagon's eyelids long before returning to Melkorka. He would not be surprised if Andrik was already asleep.

The stone house with its thatched roof was positioned against the far wall among four similar domiciles almost fifty feet away. Kinhar once told him stories of when every home held five or six Highborn, but nowadays, only two or three remained in each. If Erzebeth was right and demons were coming again, the Highborn lacked the numbers to defend Melkorka, let alone the Anshedar or the Seven Islands.

Melkorka's triangular twelve-foot walls outlined the keep, the two towers, and a crumbling courtyard. The stables, next to the keep, were barely strong enough to hold their few horses. The guardhouse was empty of anything besides what little grain they had left for winter. And the unstable gate sitting cockeyed at the entrance only added insult to injury.

Furthermore, except for the occasional quarterstaff, the Highborn did not create weapons. Falmagon always believed a bow and arrow, or even a copper dagger may be useful if demons were to return, but truthfully, he would not know how to wield either one.

He only knew Koldovstvo.

"Lord Falmagon," the raspy squeak of one of the red broods reached his ears. He turned to see a Kras slave—half his size, red-skinned, with a hooked nose and pointed ears—swiftly skitter closer. The creatures were not only hideous, but dangerous. They were quick on their feet and could vanish from sight at will. He recognized the slave as Dorofej's favorite pet, Branimir Baran. "Lord Falmagon!"

Falmagon squinted with disgust at the creature. "What do you want, Kras?"

Branimir nervously pulled at his long nose, staring up at him with his two pale-black orbs. "Lord Dorofej asked for you."

"What does the old codger want?" Falmagon asked.

The Kras winced. "I…I did not ask, my lord."

Before Falmagon could scorn the Kras, a rattled, deep voice emerged from one of the homes not far away. "Branimir Baran, I trust you told Falmagon I wished to speak with him, yes?"

Falmagon lifted his eyes about the time the Kras dipped his head. "Yes, Lord Dorofej."

Standing in the doorway with the wooden-planked door swung open stood Dorofej, drowning in his grey robes with his white eyebrows, as white as his mustache and braided beard, arching over his icy eyes. Falmagon had never learned the Highborn's last name; in fact, he was not sure the old man had one. Dorofej smacked his thin lips, looking expectantly at Falmagon across the short expanse.

"Run along, Branimir," Dorofej said, "Lord Falmagon and I have much to discuss."

"Do we?" Falmagon snorted, taking a few steps toward the aged Highborn. "I was about to return to my quarters to sleep. I am meant to leave tomorrow."

"Leave?" Dorofej raised his eyebrows, stepping sideways to allow Falmagon entrance to his own home. "I say, wherever would you go when you have only just returned?"

Falmagon sighed, looking past Dorofej into his home where the hearthfire burnt bright. Without a word, he snubbed the invitation, stubbornly fixing his feet to the earth. He would not get caught up in hours of storytelling with the old codger. "An errand for the Spearhead, Dorofej. I am to become a Longwalker."

"Are you now? Never before have the Highborn had two Longwalkers, yes? Hm," Dorofej said. He did not seem even half surprised, and despite his pitched tone, he did not seem to be asking an actual question.

Falmagon almost repeated himself, thinking the old Highborn had not heard him. Instead, he watched Dorofej shuffle out the door a couple of steps when realizing Falmagon was refusing his hospitality.

"Curious, I am, about what you, Nedezhda, and Andrik discovered at Cyreus. Investigating a message of warning, you were, yes?"

Falmagon rubbed his upper lip.

Dorofej had that perceptive twinkle in his eyes, like a parent asking their child where the pie went after watching them steal it from the windowsill. Not only was the old Highborn always poking where he did not belong, he seemed to enjoy poking at Falmagon the most.

Falmagon glanced over his shoulder to the window leading into Kinhar's study. He was not concerned about Kinhar hearing anything he might tell Dorofej, especially when Falmagon had no intention of telling Dorofej anything worthwhile. However, he wondered what Dorofej might hear from the courtyard below.

He turned his head back to see Dorofej following his gaze, smiling derisively. The expression nearly infuriated Falmagon, but the thought of being accepted into the Kadari—and being chosen—gave him the strength not to return the jeering look. Dorofej did not know everything. Falmagon cleared his throat. "The journey was a waste of time. The threat was hearsay and nothing to worry over. Kinhar said we will continue doing as we always have."

"Hm." Dorofej waggled his beard in thought, squinting his eyes at Falmagon. "A relief to hear, it is. Yet, I say, when before did you leave Folkmar without a guide? Your first journey away from Melkorka, Cyreus was, yes?" A moment passed and Dorofej hastily spoke again to cut off Falmagon's response. "Or misunderstood, I am, thinking you were leaving alone tomorrow. I say, Jhar said nothing about a departure. Then again, rushed from our home to join Nedezhda to Narthwich, he did. Join you, Conn or Faina might, yes?"

"Andrik is coming with me," Falmagon grunted. "I told you I am to become a Longwalker."

"Young, you both are," Dorofej said.

Falmagon ground his teeth. "We are no longer children needing to be watched."

Dorofej crossed his arms, stroking his braided beard with his wrinkled fingers, carefully studying Falmagon. "I see," he finally said.

Falmagon shivered under the old Highborn's gaze and blamed it on the evening chill whipping over the wall. With a subtle shake of his head, he turned toward his home. He needed to follow Kinhar's advice and pray to the Lightbringer. "Good night."

Dorofej mumbled softly enough that Falmagon scarcely heard his response. "One of our last, I fear this night will be."

Chapter VII
FALMAGON

Tying his hair back with a leather cord, Falmagon glanced to the crashing waves. An extra chill fanned off the sea this morning promising the frightful winter to come. He could not say how long they would be gone, traveling to Arkaim and back, but he thought they might return to Melkorka before the first snowfall.

Images of the frost troubled him while he and Andrik traipsed along the beach toward Narthwich. For too long, he worked his numb fingers around his russet-colored hair, loosening and tightening the slack strap in an attempt to weave a knot. Several times he stumbled over his feet, kicking sand up and nearly falling over.

Eventually, he gave up and wrapped the cord around his hand. He then pulled his hood up and tucked his hair into the folds of the cloth.

"Narthwich is over the next hill." Andrik yawned, plodding along to his left. Like himself, Andrik had a thin rope wrapped around each shoulder, attached to a rolled-up blanket full of rations and other gear. He tugged at the makeshift straps. "Good luck finding a boatman to take us across the sea. The waters are choppy, and the overcast will make it too difficult to navigate."

Falmagon huffed, choosing to scowl at the rolling hills instead of his companion. Andrik spoke omen after omen since leaving Melkorka, which was no more welcomed than the invasive wind. "Sounds like you are an expert in sailing now," Falmagon scoffed. "Someone will take us. We are Highborn."

"I guess. Do you not think it is bizarre that Kinhar is sending us to see your kin?" Andrik asked gruffly from his side. His voice held a morning rasp, causing him to sound much harsher than he likely meant. "We only returned to Melkorka yesterday. Did someone die?"

"What?" Falmagon tucked his free hand inside his brown cloak to keep it warm. If his own rations were not wrapped up in the blanket on his back, he might have pulled it loose from the ropes and used it for additional warmth. "No one died. I told you Kinhar wants me to become a Longwalker."

"I know what you said, but the Highborn only have one Longwalker. Why would we need two? And why go to Arkaim? Not even Nedezhda goes to Arkaim without a summons from the king, which I might add has never happened." Andrik ruffled his brow as they started up the hill leading to Narthwich. "Moreover, you have not seen your family in fifteen years. How will they even know you?" They took several more steps and then Andrik added in a softer tone, "Who are you supposed to meet?"

"Unnvar Grondahl," Falmagon said quietly, unsure how to respond to the barrage of questions.

"And who is he to you?"

"My kin. The child of my father's sister."

"But you do not know why you are visiting him?" Andrik cleared his throat, his eyebrows popping up at the same time.

"I already told you why," Falmagon said, trudging up the hill. He did not expect Andrik to challenge the journey so much. He expected the man to be excited to have the opportunity to see the lands they were meant to protect. He was going to have to be careful not to say anything of the Kadari or Erzebeth. He looked for some way to bring the conversation to a close. He did not want to be debating his purpose in Arkaim for the next week. "Kinhar is the Spearhead and his hand guides my purpose. My position is not to question his motive."

Andrik stepped away from Falmagon, dropping his jaw in bewilderment. "What are you hiding? You cannot expect me to believe you are not the slightest bit interested in what is really going on here. Drop the act, Falmagon."

Falmagon gulped a mouth of cold air, turning his gaze to the sea. "I don't know what you are talking about."

Andrik muttered. "You have never been a good liar."

"By Mulafell," Falmagon growled, snapping his head back to look at Andrik. "Leave it be."

Andrik smirked as they reached the top. "Ah, you do know why Kinhar is sending us, but will not tell me? You could have simply said as much."

"I did not say that," Falmagon hissed.

Andrik opened his mouth to respond, but two figures coming up the opposite side of the hill halted him.

"Falmagon! Andrik!" Nedezhda's familiar voice gave Falmagon pause. The redheaded woman led a painted horse by a rope. Jhar Gurov, with his dark beard and burly chest, stood next to her, pulling along his own black mare. Both animals were weighed down with grain sacks where the riders should have been sitting.

Neither of the two Highborn seemed to take notice of the cold. Jhar was not even wearing a cloak.

Falmagon gulped, staring at Nedezhda. His luck would be to cross the one person who Kinhar said meant to betray them. Her muddled expression was evident with her shoulders pulled back and her hand angled over her brow to examine them, despite the lack of sun rays to block.

Jhar's mouth hung open like a noose, as he more firmly gripped the rope to his mare.

Raising a hand slowly in salute, Falmagon started down the hill to meet them with Andrik on his heels. He rattled his mind for an explanation that might send them on their way with little fuss. Whether intentionally or not, Kinhar sent them in the same direction as the other Highborn without providing an excuse for their journey to Arkaim; at least, not one that would be easily accepted. And Nedezhda, no doubt, would be more critical than Andrik.

He needed to watch his tongue.

As he neared, he adjusted his cowl, then tucked both hands inside his cloak for warmth. The material was thick enough to protect his body from the chill, but his nose and cheeks were so cold they burned. He hoped the color would not be mistaken for embarrassment. He sucked in a breath with the hope it made him appear more confident. He was not doing anything wrong; he was following the commands of the Spearhead.

Nedezhda pressed her throat with two fingers as though she were checking her own pulse. Her eyes bulged. "What in the Nine Lands are you two doing out here?"

"You boys running away from home?" Jhar grunted beside her, seemingly bemused by them.

"We are going to Arkaim," Andrik said, his fat lips flapping faster than Falmagon would have liked. His shorter companion folded his hands across his waist sheepishly as though he were hiding the world beneath his tunic.

"To see my kin," Falmagon hurried to add, adjusting his pack, "at Kinhar's command."

"He is sending you to Arkaim? Alone?" Jhar snorted. He turned his head to Nedezhda, angling himself away from Falmagon despite the pinned accusation. "Neither of you know the way."

"I have seen the maps and read the texts. The road is not hard." Falmagon was being honest; he could draw a map in the sand showing every city, nook, and cranny on the Seven Islands and the mainland if asked, and for the last decade, his nose had hung over the writings in Kinhar's study. He was not certain Jhar could even read.

"Not everything on the road can be seen on a map or read on a scroll," Jhar said. "Nothing helped you defend against the stranger on the beach. Have your welts even healed?"

Falmagon bit his tongue from pointing out Jhar's lack of study did not help him, either. He tightened the folds of his cloak. "I appreciate your concern but Andrik and I will be fine. Kinhar thought it would be a good opportunity to train me to become a Longwalker." Falmagon bit his tongue a moment too late, hearing his words as he spoke them.

He winced under Nedezhda's cold stare.

"Nedezhda is our Longwalker, boy," Jhar raised his voice, his muscles tensing under his grey tunic. He stepped closer, putting his shoulder in front of Nedezhda like he could protect her from Falmagon's words. "She is the envoy for the Highborn across the Seven Islands and Kalamaar. The Jarls and the Anshedar know her, and her alone. In the history of the Highborn, we have never had two Longwalkers. So if you are going to lie to my face, you best be a bit craftier."

Falmagon inched closer to the older Highborn. If he were to be a Longwalker, he would be of equal standing with the other Highborn. He would no longer be an apprentice. He would not be treated like a child. "I am not lying."

"No, you are not." Nedezhda tapped her index finger against her lip. "You would be quite gutsy to make up a story of that magnitude."

"Nedezhda, you cannot believe him?" Jhar kept his gaze on Falmagon.

"He is telling the truth," Andrik piped up weakly.

His assurance was unheard under Falmagon's louder tone. He loosened his hold on his brown cloak, raising a finger in Jhar's face. "Return to Kinhar and ask him yourself if you do not believe me."

"Why don't you come back with me?" Jhar growled.

"My orders come from the Spearhead. Not you."

"Falmagon," Nedezhda eased, pulling the Highborn next to her back to his mare with a tug on the shoulder. Jhar made a fist and then tugged at his dark beard, following her subtle direction. She hummed, pushing a rogue strand of red hair behind her small ears. Her face had become a mask of serenity, despite the condescending tone of her voice. "You two should run along and do as your Spearhead commands."

Falmagon swore he could see a vein pulsating on the side of Jhar's neck.

Andrik huffed, squishing his thick eyebrows together in surprise. "That's it?"

"Find Rowland near the docks. Tell him I sent you and he will take you across to Kalamaar," Nedezhda offered. "Jhar and I wish you a safe journey."

"Thank you," Falmagon said with uncertainty. He rubbed the fuzz on his upper lip.

She smiled. Then, with a jerk of her wrist, she pulled at her horse to step around him and Andrik.

"You are going to get yourselves killed," Jhar declared, squeezing the reins until his knuckles were white. "We cannot let them wander off, Nedezhda. We have our duty. Fifteen years of training should not be pushed aside so easily. Too few of us remain at Melkorka as it is."

She ignored Jhar, giving Falmagon and Andrik unspoken permission to shuffle around the larger Highborn.

Falmagon watched Nedezhda from the corner of his eye. He was not sure what to expect from her, but she did not so much as turn in his direction. She remained focused on the coastline leading south to Melkorka.

Jhar, on the other hand, watched his every step, scowling so fiercely he could have drained the color out of the sea. He maintained the glare until Falmagon and Andrik reached the bottom of the hill and were entering the outskirts of Narthwich.

Falmagon gave the crotchety Highborn a final look before turning his back for good.

The village was small, fitted for the fishermen who lived among the scattered buildings. He meant to lead Andrik straight to the docks, bypassing the great hall and the few homes. He could see some people, women and children mostly, meandering between the gaps of the buildings. None of them so much as looked in their direction while they walked.

Even though Falmagon did not know the Anshedar personally, he was familiar with Narthwich. Over the years, he traveled to the village to collect supplies or, most recently, to gather the long boat to travel to Cyreus. The faerings would be found tied off to the wooden docks.

"I thought Jhar was going to fling us over his shoulder and carry us back to Melkorka," Andrik said, picking up his pace to stay next to Falmagon. "I am surprised Nedezhda let us continue."

"What choice did she have? She could not stand at odds with Kinhar," Falmagon said. "She probably thinks we are going to die out here anyway."

Andrik stifled a nervous laugh. "Surely not. She has always thought well of us." Falmagon snorted, then swiftly tried to maintain his composure. He was glad he was ahead of Andrik, where he could not see his face. Andrik went on, "Do you think Kinhar means to have you replace her as the Longwalker?"

Falmagon wrinkled his nose. He had not given the idea much thought. While Kinhar was suspicious of Nedezhda, he did not give any indication of removing her from her station among the Highborn. At least, not anytime soon.

"I am not sure," Falmagon finally said. "Someone needs to learn the task of a Longwalker. She will not live forever."

"I suppose not," Andrik said, his awkward laughter catching in the back of his throat. "Come to think of it, I wonder who the Longwalker was before her."

Falmagon averted his eyes. The Highborn typically relied on the enslaved Kras to keep their history, and the slaves did not share what they knew unless asked. He supposed any one of the little red broods would be able to tell him who had come and gone from Melkorka over the years, which would likely be paired with long tales about the troubles of the Highborn over the past thousand years. Falmagon supposed he should be curious like Andrik and ask the Kras what knowledge they tucked away in their tiny heads, but in truth, he did not care. He did not know when Melkorka was founded or by whom. He only knew Kinhar was the Spearhead for the past several generations, and anyone who lived in the castle came after him.

Kinhar very well could have been the first Highborn.

While Andrik may like to poke around in history, Falmagon preferred to focus on what was in front of him. His concern was on the future. Between the threat of Nedezhda and Erzebeth's warning, he could not risk getting caught up with old tales. He would do whatever he could to avoid a history lesson. Besides, the past could not be changed; he only had power over the future.

"The docks are this way," Falmagon said.

Falmagon spotted Rowland leaning against the rear post of the docks, overlooking the choppy waters of Strega's Deep. Falmagon remembered him from when they acquired a faering a few weeks ago before traveling to Cyreus. He was approaching Rowland from the back, but the knotted grey hair over the tattered brown cloak gave away his identity. The torn piece of fabric appeared to be more of a blanket than a cloak, having more holes than a fisherman's net. If that were not enough, the thin line of smoke coiling over the man's head suggested the long pipe he saw last time had not steered far from the man's thin lips.

"Rowland," Falmagon said as he approached. The boatman turned with a gruff snort, pushing grey smoke from his nose. He lifted his chin to gaze at Falmagon from under his wide-brimmed hat. "We are heading to Kalamaar. Nedezhda said you might give us passage."

"Did she now?" Rowland peered through heavy eyelids, holding his pipe in his teeth. He scratched the scruff at the side of his cheek. "I know you well enough, do I not? Another Highborn. Well, I suppose we should head off."

Falmagon dipped his head as Rowland turned back to look out at the sea. "She did, and yes," Falmagon reassured him, unsure if he should begin walking down the docks. Rowland certainly made no movement toward the boats.

"So…are we ready?" Andrik asked, shuddering at Falmagon's left.

Rowland grumbled.

"What are you looking at?" The dock creaked beneath Andrik's weight as he stepped onto the first wooden plank. His shoulder nearly brushed against Rowland's. "Is the water too rough to sail?"

"No, we can make it to Kalamaar all right. The Jarl sent a couple men out with a boat, and they have not come back is all," Rowland said, pulling his pipe from his lips and gesturing with it in his right hand. "Four days have now passed. The rusalki begin swarming about this time of the year. I am guessing the lot of them are dead."

Falmagon wrinkled his nose. He heard stories of rusalki from Nedezhda, referring to the so-called half-fish, half-women who lived in the sea. He never knew whether they were real or not, but he did not doubt their existence. In a world of demons and magic, he suspected most anything could be true.

"You are worried about the men, then?" Falmagon assumed.

Rowland snorted. "Hardly. Men come and go. I am worried about my boat."

Andrik stifled a laugh like he usually did, his face scrunching up horrendously. He must have caught Falmagon's odd expression, because he swallowed hard and asked, "How close to shore do they come?"

"I have never seen one near Folkmar, if that is what you are needing to know," Rowland said. He lifted his eyebrows at Andrik, blowing smoke from his nostrils. "I imagine we have too many Highborn for their liking."

"They fear the Highborn?" Falmagon asked.

Rowland's eye twitched. "The magic upsets the creatures, Highborn. They are as old as this world, and they feel it. Like dragons, I imagine. Do you not know anything? What do they teach you in that castle?"

Andrik mouthed the word, turning to wink at Falmagon with sudden amusement. "Dragons, he says."

Rowland grumbled but did not act as though he heard Andrik's comment.

Falmagon did not respond. Any halfwit in the Seven Islands heard tales of three-headed dragons flying overhead in the early years, long before Melkorka or any other place had been given a name. If the monsters ever existed, Falmagon suspected the Highborn killed them long ago.

Rowland sucked on the end of his pipe, then cleared his throat. He spoke through a cloud of billowing smoke. "My apologies, Highborn. You two surely spend too much time fighting demons to wonder about the nature of every creature roaming Aenar. Worry not. I will teach what I can. Come along."

Falmagon cleared his throat and then clumsily muttered his thanks. He shadowed Rowland to the nearest faering. It looked like he would get a history lesson after all.

Chapter VIII
FALMAGON

"She was mad, mind you, but her beauty was something to be marveled at. Was it not, Falmagon?" Andrik drummed his fingers on the side the boat and forced a wink. The wide grin that followed was terrifying enough to send any woman running. Luckily, the boat lurched over the dark waves, lifting Andrik from the central wooden plank stretching across the middle of the faering, stealing the smile from his face.

Falmagon averted his gaze. He did not disagree with Andrik. His own mind reforged Erzebeth's nakedness against his will several times a day, painting a picture of her standing before him, which did nothing more than leave him squirming and uncomfortable. While he would not refuse the chance to see her without clothes again, he feared how he might be weakened in her presence. He unquestionably fantasized over the few women at Melkorka during his youth, but fighting the urge to daydream about them was not this difficult. The memory of Erzebeth seemed to fester with every passing day. He hoped against hope his tongue would remember its purpose—to learn more of her warning— when he found her in Arkaim.

Andrik hit the outside of the boat a bit harder with his fingers while speaking to Rowland at the stern. "You should have seen her. Her hair was dark like a moonless night, and she had the palest skin I've ever seen. She stepped straight out of a fireside tale, I tell you."

"Really? Pray tell what type of tales you tell around a fire?" Rowland straightened the hat on his head.

"You know what I mean," Andrik snorted, waving off the boatman. "She was beyond words."

"You are certain she was not a rusalki?" Rowland squinted an eye warily, pulling his pipe free from his teeth and blowing smoke from the corner of his mouth. "You said you saw her near the riverbend, right? Rusalki can always be found near water. Does not have to be seawater. And they never wear clothes."

"She had legs," Falmagon said.

Andrik laughed. "She had a lot more than legs."

"A rusalki can twist its tail into legs when they need to reach the shore," Rowland said, returning his pipe to the gap between his teeth. He continued to talk around the thin piece of wood. "How do you think the devilish things feed outside fishing season? Men cannot always be found on boats."

"Do they really eat men?" Andrik stopped laughing and paled. "I cannot think I would be foolish enough to follow one into the water, no matter how pretty she sings."

"That's the thing. You are enchanted by the song, young Highborn. You would not have a choice but to plunge face first into the saltwater." Rowland lifted his finger. "You would drown yourself."

Andrik scrunched his face in disgust, looking across the open water as though a rusalki may surface and start belting out a song at any given moment.

Falmagon sighed, returning to the point of the conversation. "The stranger—Erzebeth—was not a rusalki and she did not eat anyone." He used his thumb and forefinger to smooth out the hairs on his upper lip, as small as they were, and searched for words that might soothe Rowland. He needed the Anshedar to return to Folkmar and assure the people they were safe, not talk about women prancing around naked on Cyreus. "Forget her beauty. She was mad. Those on Folkmar have nothing to fear, and even if something were to be feared, the Highborn would protect the Seven Islands."

"It does my heart well to hear that, Highborn," Rowland said. The boat rocked over the waters, bobbing over another wave, and he caught his pipe between his lips with a grunt. As he resettled himself on a wooden plank, he added, "Though I would like some explanation for her beauty and her nakedness. I have been all over Kalamaar and the Seven Islands. According to you, she is as pretty as Lada. No woman is that pretty, and none of them go prancing about without any clothes, especially in weather this cold."

Falmagon smiled at the reference to the Lady of Flowers, the Goddess of Love. He looked for a reason to satisfy the old man. The challenge was not difficult. "I cannot say why she was naked, but—if we are being honest—the stranger was the first woman Andrik and I ever saw naked, being at Melkorka and all."

"Ah, I see!" Rowland gaped, laughing hard enough for his gut to jiggle. He took a moment to regain his composure.

"Say no more. I imagine that to you, anything with tits would have appeared to be fashioned from a goddess. Even the old fat hag I have waiting for me back home."

"No. Gods, no." Andrik covered his mouth in disgust, having no reference but Rowland's ungodly description. He spoke between his fingers. "Erzebeth really was as pretty as we say."

Falmagon smiled. The boat sprang over another wave in a fit.

"Sure, sure," Rowland said, gesturing ahead with an incline of his chin. "Kalamaar awaits."

Falmagon twisted around from the aft. Land appeared on the skyline.

The last couple miles to the shore were relatively quiet until Rowland jumped from the faering into shallow water to pull the boat ashore. Falmagon and Andrik followed his example, grabbing the sides of the boat and heaving the hunk of wood to the rocky shoreline. Tall grasses stretched in every direction to the foot of the red mountains rising toward the heavens a short distance away.

"No matter where we go on the islands, we cannot escape the Crags of Kazimir," Andrik commented, looking to the mountains.

"I heard if you travel far enough north, you will see them no more," Rowland said. "Beyond the mountains are far-reaching forests and marshlands. Even the men of Kalamaar avoid the far north."

"Why?" Falmagon asked, pulling his pack out of the base of the boat. The blanket had accumulated several wet spots from the splashing water. He hoped the food stayed dry.

Andrik followed his lead, snagging his own rolled-up pack from the faering.

"Not sure, to be honest. Maybe they fear falling off the edge of the world," Rowland said, leaning against the boat and crossing one leg over the other. "You are not heading that way, are you?"

Falmagon shook his head. "Our road takes us to Arkaim."

"Ah. Good." Rowland reached in his pocket to fetch more stuffing for his pipe. "Must be important business to go to the city of the king." Falmagon held his tongue and was thankful when Andrik did the same. "You will be heading northwest, then. Make camp tonight and you might reach Valishul tomorrow."

"We know the way," Falmagon assured him.

Rowland hummed to himself, pulling a small bag from his pocket. "Well, the last one of you that I brought over seemed to be a bit confused, so I thought I should be certain. I suppose we can only know what we know." Rowland cleared his throat. "I pointed him in the direction of Arkaim, but he ventured off in the opposite direction like a lout. He did not even respond when I called after him. I feared he was abandoning his charge at Melkorka." Rowland averted his eyes, stumbling over his words. "But I would not question the Highborn. You have your way."

"The last one of us?" Andrik stuck his fat lips out and squinted an eye. "Who are you talking about? What was his name?"

"I have never been much good with names, but his hair was flaming red like fire. Much like Nedezhda, or the other woman from Melkorka who visits Narthwich from time to time."

"Faina?" Andrik offered.

Rowland shrugged. "Said I was never good with names."

"Red hair?" Falmagon gaped. The similarities were too great to be a casual coincidence. The man Rowland spoke about must be the stranger who attacked him and Jhar on the beach. "Did he carry a crooked staff?"

"He did," Rowland said.

"When you were with this man, what did he speak about?" Falmagon asked. His chest tightened with excitement. While Kinhar said he should not worry about the stranger, he had admitted the Highborn would do well to gain possession of the staff. "Anything."

"He did not say more than a few words." Rowland paused, clutching the small pouch in his hand. He wrinkled his forehead. "You mean to say you did not know him? By the gods, what is happening with all these strangers walking across the Seven Islands. The world is not big enough for strangers."

Falmagon tensed his shoulders, knowing the world might be bigger than any of them realized.

"You thought he was one of us?" Andrik piped up.

Rowland gave Andrik a flat look, surprised by the question.

Falmagon could not forget the odd magic the stranger displayed on the beach. Not only did he seem to vanish without a trace, but he could move quicker than the eye. He suspected Rowland saw the magic and assumed the power came from Koldovstvo, but he pressed the question anyway. "Why would you think he was a Highborn?"

"The fire hair, of course," Rowland said. "While not all of you have the mark, anyone would think he was a Highborn," Rowland said. "We Anshedar are not like you; we are not touched by the gods."

Falmagon raised an eyebrow with interest. His and Andrik's hair was as dark as any Northmen. While he knew Nedezhda and Faina had red hair, he never thought them to be *touched by the gods*. Again, he recalled Erzebeth's use of the title *Red* to greet Nedezhda on Cyreus; he did not think she was claiming her to be a Highborn.

He rubbed his nose with the back of his knuckles. He probably looked foolish asking the boatman to explain something he should have known firsthand. He felt stupid.

Andrik began to speak, but Falmagon hurried to interrupt him. "What way did you see this man go? How long ago?"

"Like I said," Rowland replied, gesturing to the northeast with his finger, "he went away from Arkaim into the mountains. I would say no more than a couple weeks have since passed."

Falmagon gazed in the direction Rowland pointed. Every bone in his body wanted to give chase, but two weeks was a long time, and from the maps he studied, nothing existed to the west except the wilderness.

Andrik cleared his throat, drawing Falmagon's attention away from the unexplored terrain. "We will report this stranger to Lord Kinhar when we return to Melkorka. For now, we head to Arkaim. We better make what progress we can before we cannot see beyond our noses."

Falmagon grumbled in agreement. "Will you be camping with us tonight, Rowland?"

"Me?" Rowland laughed. "No. I'm going to pack this pipe and go home."

"Are you not afraid of getting lost on the water? The light will disappear before you make it more than a league off shore, and you have no stars to guide you," Andrik said.

"I've been sailing these waters since before you were born," Rowland said, stretching his legs. "I could cross them blind if needed."

"Let's hope it never comes to that," Andrik said.

"Yeah." Falmagon squinted, uncertain how to properly tell the Anshedar goodbye. He smoothed his tunic. "Well, thank you."

He waited for Rowland to reply with a grunt. When the boatman turned his back, Falmagon did the same and began walking west to where the town of Valishul would be waiting. He knew they would not make it before losing the light, but he would go as far as they were able.

Behind him, he heard Andrik usher a final farewell to Rowland and then skitter across the rocks to catch up with him, slowing as he neared. Moments later, the two were walking stride for stride, shoulder to shoulder, along the southern coast of Kalamaar.

Falmagon enjoyed the silence while it lasted, exploring his surroundings away from the castle. The smell of the seasalt tickled at his nose, no different than walking along the beaches near Melkorka. The sound of water slapping against itself was also familiar, echoing only feet from them to the south. In the distance, he could see the outline of trees, bespeaking of a small wood that should contain Valishul.

For miles, he watched the red crags to the north rise and fall against the skyline, no more than a few hundred paces from them. Tall grasses, higher than Falmagon's waist, stood between them and the mountains. He was glad. He had no desire to near the Crags of Kazimir, once home to the Kras and then demons, or so he once was told. Every towering peak was said to have tunnels running through, some which might lead to the depths of the Netherworld itself.

The treeline disappeared in the evening shadows when Andrik finally spoke. "This will be as good a place as any to make camp. I will gather some brush and sticks to start a fire."

Falmagon rumbled in agreement and they set to work.

In little time, he and Andrik lounged around their small fire with their blankets strewn on either side of the dug hollow. Falmagon had retrieved a pear from his pack and bit into it half-heartedly. He then broke away a chunk of dried bread and stuffed it between his lips to blend the flavors. He was not necessarily hungry, but he knew if he did not eat something now, he would wake up before daybreak feeling the toll on his stomach.

"What is the plan once we reach Valishul in the morning?" Andrik asked, already finishing his meal and putting the remains back in his sack.

Falmagon chewed slowly, waiting to swallow before answering. "We will find another boatman to take us to Arkaim."

"You wish to travel by boat?"

"Why not? The route will be faster than traveling over the mountains or going along the coast," Falmagon said. "The quicker we reach Arkaim, the quicker we return home."

Andrik lifted his nose. "Twice, you and I have left Melkorka, and each time, you only speak of returning. For someone wanting to become a Longwalker, I would think you would have a greater love for seeing the world."

"This is not about love; it's about duty," Falmagon said, using Andrik's general rhetoric against him. Andrik scrunched up his face. Satisfied that he successfully redirected the other Highborn, Falmagon went on, "Our path home will be more difficult. The waters will freeze so taking a boat south will be nearly impossible. I suspect if the cold sets in too quickly, we may not make it back to Melkorka before spring."

Andrik smacked his thick lips in thought. Leftover crumbs stuck to his lips as he talked. "Kinhar would have been wise to wait until spring to send us."

"He is the Spearhead of the Highborn, Andrik. He knows what he is doing," Falmagon said.

"He is old," Andrik said.

Falmagon frowned. "We are Highborn. Hardship will do us well; we will learn."

"I am still uncertain why I must be out here learning with you. I am not a Longwalker, nor do I have any desire to be one." Andrik lifted his eyebrows. "Tell me the truth. You wanted to go east, didn't you? You wanted to search for the redheaded stranger Rowland saw. I could see it. Tell me, is that why Kinhar sent us here? Is that why we are really on Kalamaar?"

Falmagon looked hard at Andrik, clenching his jaw in deep thought. The fire danced between them, thrashing at the darkness. His desire to find the stranger burned with the same intensity. And, in this moment, Andrik gave him the chance to track down the man and his staff. He would return to Melkorka with it. They could discover its purpose and what magical properties it possessed. More importantly, he could determine what threat the *stranger* really held for the Highborn.

He only had to lie, but then he would be unable to seek out Erzebeth. Kinhar would never approve.

"No," Falmagon said. "I told you why we came to Kalamaar. Arkaim is our destination. We are here to visit my family."

"But you would prove yourself as a Longwalker if you found the stranger." Andrik rubbed his hands together.

"The thought crossed my mind," he said, wondering at Andrik's intent. Falmagon knew Kinhar was challenging him on this adventure. *Could Kinhar have sent Andrik to test him and not the other way around?* He leaned closer to the other Highborn. "Are you eager to seek him out yourself? Your words are misleading."

"I am curious," Andrik admitted, leaning back on his elbows comfortably as though he had not a care in the world. "Your story of the stranger's magic is fascinating to us all. While Jhar said very little of the encounter, he attested the magic was different than what we know of Koldovstvo."

"What do you mean *what we know?*"

Andrik shrugged. "What other magic exists beyond our own? I think the stranger may know something of Koldovstvo that we do not."

"Kinhar would know. He is the best among the Highborn." Falmagon rubbed his chin. Andrik tilted his head to look off into the darkness, avoiding his pointed gaze. It was his turn to test Andrik's loyalty. "You think Kinhar is lying to us about what he knows of Koldovstvo?"

Andrik cleared his throat. "I did not say that, but I do think some Highborn know what others do not."

Falmagon placed his food down on the blanket. "What do you mean?"

"Dorofej, for instance," Andrik said. "I heard stories how he once healed the injuries of others with Koldovstvo. Before he got too old, they say the Anshedar would bring their ill to Melkorka for Dorofej to heal them. I do not know any other Highborn who has ever done such a thing."

"We all have heard stories of the old codger healing wounds. Kinhar has admitted few Highborn ever have the skill to mend—"

"He used to be strong enough to bring men back from the dead, Falmagon," Andrik interjected.

"What?" Falmagon laughed. "Those are stories you heard from Dorofej, no doubt. No one has seen him so much as cast a single spell in fifteen years."

"Of course not. He can't. He does not have much power left in him. I think he would outright kill himself if he tried to touch Koldovstvo," Andrik replied. "He does not have many years left the way it is."

Falmagon grimaced. "He is not as old as Kinhar."

"Maybe not," Andrik agreed. "But that is not all. I have seen Nedezhda do things too. She has cast spells that I...I am almost afraid to speak about."

Falmagon caught his breath, seeing the fear in Andrik's eyes. The other Highborn turned back to the fire. "By Mulafell," Falmagon cursed. He may find the evidence he needed against Nedezhda through Andrik and be able to test Andrik at the same time. Nine Lands, Kinhar may have known Andrik would be able to help them find the underlying evil at Melkorka. Perhaps that was the real reason he sent him with Falmagon. He coaxed him to continue. "What have you seen her do?"

Andrik visibly swallowed, lifting his hands to warm them by the flames. He took his time in responding, his voice somewhat shaky. "Remember several years ago when we had that sickness sweep over Melkorka? We Highborn survived it—barely—but it killed many of the Kras: Fardin, Mir, Gulab, Rana, Anosha…"

Falmagon slowly nodded. He remembered thinking the Kras would all die off during the winter, which would not have been entirely terrible. He was surprised Andrik knew the names of those who died, while Falmagon still struggled to remember the Kras who were alive. He thought to say something cruel but decided to let Andrik continue his story.

"I was directed by Kinhar to bury the bodies outside the castle walls with Nedezhda. We carefully wrapped them in linen and went out during the midday, hoping that the red dirt could be softer. It wasn't." He briefly smiled to himself. "We dug five separate graves. Deep. Nedezhda helped with the chore every step of the way, even though she was the Longwalker and I was but a simple apprentice. We hoped the sickness would stay buried beneath the earth."

"I thought you were meant to burn the bodies. We always burn the dead."

"Not the Kras. They bury their dead, returning them to the ground and all that. I think Kinhar was trying to show them respect. They lost so many caring for the sick Highborn."

Falmagon bit his tongue, uncertain why Kinhar would care enough to bury them. "What did you see?"

Andrik met Falmagon's gaze over the fire. "I am getting to it. She and I had just finished putting the bodies in the ground when she instructed me to fetch us water while she began filling the holes. I scarcely walked twenty feet and heard her mumbling words over their bodies."

Falmagon reared back. "She was praying for the red broods? To what god?"

"I do not know. We Highborn do not pay homage to any god, and we certainly do not say words over our dead." Andrik scratched the back of his head. "I did not think much of it. I was parched and the whole ordeal was bizarre anyway. So I hurried to get our water skins. When I returned I…"

"What, Andrik? Spit it out," Falmagon ordered.

"Nedezhda was chanting and tendrils of energy, like smoke reeling off a burning candle, flowed from each of the bodies into her."

"Into her?"

"I could see her skin glowing under the power of her magic and her hair reddening. Sitting here thinking about it, I think she was stealing whatever life force they once had and was adding it to her own. She was making herself younger."

"By the gods! What kind of dark magic could she have been wielding?" Falmagon whispered. "Why did you not tell anyone? Why did you not tell Kinhar? She could have been the very reason the sickness struck Melkorka."

Andrik gulped, rubbing his mouth with the back of his hand. "Oh, I do not think she would bring harm to us. The Kras were already dead, Falmagon."

"Were they? Or did she kill them?"

"They were dead, Falmagon." Andrik scratched at his dark hair. "I do not understand how Nedezhda used Koldovstvo, but I do know she is one of us. She is a Highborn, an ally, and a friend."

"You really believe so?"

"I do," Andrik replied.

"I hope you are right." Falmagon frowned. "For the sake of us all."

Chapter IX
MAELILI

The clay hearth in the center of the near-empty alehouse, Kal'bane, heated the room along with the evening stew. Maelili heard nothing beyond the four walls, even though the busy streets of the capital city of Arkaim had been bustling hours earlier. The smell of mixed vegetables and beef filled the one-room tavern, causing her stomach to rumble. She could not remember the last time she, Brigita, and Velkan had eaten a decent meal.

She sipped at the alcohol in her copper cup, watching the young innkeeper, Unnvar Grondahl, speak to his two younger children, while his wife readied their food. Unnvar was a large man with a belly stretching over his britches and more muscle than most, and although he seemed kind enough, he was not pleasant to look at. Even now, he scratched at his rearside while speaking, his yellow teeth visible over his thick, messy beard.

Maelili looked into her cup, keeping her gaze from the rest of the room. The few patrons who sat around the scattered tables seemed to be from the city, likely speaking in hushed voices while staring at them. Maelili was glad they were able to sell the red cloaks they wore for a decent amount of silver. The color was vivid compared to the greens and greys most of the Anshedar wore and had drawn more attention than any of them wanted.

Beyond the few tables were several bedsteads made of straw and covered with sheepskin. Unnvar assured her he had room for the three of them to take up residence for the night, even though his family shared the beds strewn across the room too. If more travelers came, she suspected they would end up sharing a bed or resting on the floor. Yet after spending weeks sleeping in a boat and upon the ground, either option was inviting.

Relaxing her shoulders, she tipped back the copper cup and gulped. The liquid was cool until touching her throat, and then surprisingly burned. The ale was certainly stronger than anything brewed in Lairhein. She stifled a cough. Then, putting the cup on the table, she spoke to Brigita and Velkan across from her. "Tomorrow we will head farther east and explore these inland towns. They cannot be too far."

"We will only hear more of the same, Arkhon," Brigita commented, folding her arms over the table and leaning forward. "These people know nothing about a redheaded man. The only red-haired people any commoner has *heard* of comes from the south at Melkorka…these so-called Highborn; and they alone are talked about as though they are mythical creatures. May I add, they have only spoken of *women* with fire hair and not men."

"She does not need your reminders," Velkan said in his honeyed tone, peering through the loose strands of his mahogany-colored hair, setting down his own cup. "We have not come so far to leave stones unturned."

"No, we have not, Ser Velkan," Maelili agreed. She ran her hand through the lengths of her hair, pulling it around to see the dark pigment. Two days ago, they had to reapply the paste to their hair to keep the shades of red hidden. "We have taken measures to blend in with the Anshedar. We have no reason to think Kindel would not have done the same."

"We should go to the place called Melkorka." Brigita stubbornly tightened her jaw. "Every man, woman, and child has pointed in its direction."

Maelili took a deep breath. "You are right. But if we travel a hundred and fifty leagues to the south and find nothing, we will be traveling a hundred and fifty leagues back to finish exploring Kalamaar. We must search the villages nearby before venturing south."

"I understand, but if we find what we are looking for…" She sighed and hung her head in defeat. "We have just been away from home for so long, Arkhon."

Velkan cleared his throat to interrupt the younger Stuhia from continuing. "Your Arkhon gave you permission to leave if you wished. The offer stands if you miss your family so much, or you can stay and fulfill your duty."

"I intend to serve my Arkhon." Brigita snapped at him, turning her nose up. "You mistake me for being selfish. I do not think only of my family, but also of our Arkhon's family. A husband, a child—a nation—await her return."

"We all have family back home," Velkan whispered kindly, his face softening.

Maelili breathed slowly, noticing a few heads turning their way with Brigita's elevated voice. Even the innkeeper had left his children to gather their bowls of steaming stew from his wife so that he could glance at them between balancing the bowls on his hand and forearm.

Maelili did not want to think of her husband, Nevyn, or her son, Eisliev. Thoughts of them made her stomach flutter, but no matter how often Brigita mentioned them, she would not allow herself to be weakened by the affection she felt. She did not find Velkan's gentle nature in herself. She hissed across the table at Brigita, reiterating the young Stuhia's words. "A husband, a child, and a nation *who*—through my example—will understand how duty demands sacrifice."

"And what if you die out here? What lesson will be learned?" Brigita challenged, unaware of Unnvar swiftly closing the distance behind her.

Maelili spoke through gritted teeth, hoping only Brigita would hear her. The chair legs scraping against the wooden floor around her indicated several patrons had grown interested in their exchange. "They will know their Arkhon held herself to the same measure as her people. They will know that when duty demanded death, Maelili Kluk did not balk!"

Velkan cleared his throat again, when Unnvar suddenly reached around Brigita and slid the bowls in front of them one by one, along with a handful of rolls wrapped in linen. He must have heard part of their dialogue, because he said, "Every year winter comes and our tongues twist, speaking of death until spring arrives." He chuckled nervously. "Let us hope no dies tonight at the Kal'bane. I have never been one to fear death, but dead bodies are bad for business."

Maelili looked down to her stew, forcing a smile to touch her cheeks. "If it comes to it, I will help throw some salt on them until they can be buried."

Unnvar paled for a moment, eyeing her before smiling. "I prefer to save my salt for the stew."

Maelili nodded. She pushed Brigita's intolerance from her mind, hearing her stomach rumble once more, embarrassingly so.

Velkan grabbed at his bowl, pulling it to his lips, and slurped up a mouthful. He spoke while he chewed, hurrying to change the topic. "This is delicious, Master Unnvar. Compliments to your wife."

Unnvar flashed his yellow teeth wider. "Dahz has blessed us with a healthy supply of meat this year. With any luck, the winter will not be as harsh as yesteryear."

Brigita cleared her throat, raising her eyes at the innkeeper who hovered over her. Already, her face was twisted with discontent, but her nose wrinkled further at the mention of Dahz the Lightbringer. The Stuhia knew the god to carry the sun across the sky on his stag wielding his hammer, Mulafell, but none paid the White-Clad homage.

Unnvar looked down casually to meet Brigita's bright eyes. His smile froze in place, mouth opening in wonderment. "Your eyes…I have never met anyone with green eyes before. How remarkable!" He looked around the table, his grin fading and jaw further dropping. "By the gods, you all have green eyes. How did I miss that? Where did you say you were from?"

The color faded from Brigita's cheeks, looking hastily to Maelili. She adjusted the pin holding her dark green cloak, and then reached for her bowl of food.

Maelili's instinct was to look away too, to hide her eyes for as long as she might from Unnvar, but she put on her best smile and looked at him. At closer inspection, she saw the brute of a man had blue eyes, and while blue eyes were rare among Stuhia, they were not altogether uncommon. She had not thought their own eyes would set them apart from the Anshedar.

When she could not think of a word to say, she turned to Velkan for help. She did not know the land well enough to name a place.

"The north," Velkan finally offered, snagging a biscuit and avoiding the exchange of blank stares. He took a bite, the crumbs falling to the bowl beneath his chin. Maelili could see his red scruff already dotting his face, hidden mostly by the long strands of colored hair. If Unnvar came closer, he would see the red hair sprouting from Velkan's chin and upper lip.

"What?" Unnvar managed to reply.

Velkan bobbed his head like he was riding on a cart, appearing all the more confident. "We are from the far north, a farm outside the city."

"The far north." Unnvar repeated with a bewildered shake of his head. Again, Maelili noted movement from the other men and women in the small alehouse, leaning closer or moving their chairs. Whoever was not listening before certainly paid attention now. Unnvar's beard waggled as he stepped away. He awkwardly put his hands on his hips. "Outside Jh'tutat, I assume? I cannot say I know any Northmen who have ventured beyond the town. The gods only know what beasts roam in those dark forests and marshlands. Are you not afraid of falling off the edge of the world?"

Velkan hooted, nearly spitting food from his lips, while Brigita hurried to cover her mouth with her hand, finding equal mirth in the words. Maelili kept her eyes down, fighting back a smile instigated by Velkan's burst of laughter more than anything. She hurried to reach for the bread, shaking her head in response to Unnvar.

Unnvar angled his eyebrows in what looked like confusion. While the Anshedar may look similar and even know the same gods as the Stuhia, they were bizarre people.

The door to Kal'bane swung open, drawing Unnvar's attention. He immediately sounded a hearty welcome—before anyone walked through the entryway—and, to Maelili's relief, stepped away from their table.

The first man to enter the alehouse was no older than Brigita, with a head full of black hair and lips that were too large for his face. His grey cloak fluttered behind him as he stepped out of the chilled wind. He rubbed his hands together, scanning the room.

His companion looked barely old enough to be called a man. His long russet hair was tied back with a simple cord and hung against his brown cloak. He stroked the fuzz on his upper lip, standing with his shoulders pulled back and his chest puffed. His blue eyes sparkled, penetrating the dim light of the hearth fire, as though nothing could be hidden from his sight.

Maelili took a bit of food, watching them in silence.

Unnvar approached, motioning for them to close the door behind them. "Welcome, welcome. Are you looking for a bed or simply a bite to eat? Supper is ready with plenty of malt to wash it down."

The second man stepped in front of the first, surprisingly taking the lead. "My name is Falmagon Sej, and I'm looking for my kin, Unnvar."

Maelili watched with fascination. The burly innkeeper stepped forward, cocking his head with interest. "Falmagon? Falmagon Sej?" He widened his eyes, looking over his shoulder at his wife. She stood up from a chair in the back, shushing the small children at her heel. "We thought you to be dead."

"You mean to say that you are Unnvar?" Falmagon smiled. He reached for the large innkeeper, clasping him on the arm. "I am anything but dead. I went to Melkorka to become a Highborn."

Maelili stifled a gasp at the revelation.

"Certainly. The whole family knew you went to Melkorka," Unnvar said, rubbing his hands on the side of his pants. "After all these years, we suspected you were taken by demons, or worse."

Whatever reply Falmagon provided Unnvar was lost as Velkan pulled Maelili's arm. "Arkhon, it may be wise if we take our leave. The innkeeper seems a bit too interested in our origins. Staying any longer may give away our identities."

"What about them?" Maelili asked, nodding at the two strangers.

Brigita scraped at the table with her fingers, clearly oblivious to the conversation behind her. "They will likely need a bed too, and I do not want to share the lodge with unknown travelers. I say we take to the road and sleep beneath the open sky."

Maelili narrowed her gaze at the young woman. "The stranger said he is from Melkorka. If we stay, we have the opportunity to learn what we need to know without going south. Besides, the weather is turning colder; the hearthfire would be more welcome."

Brigita whipped her head around to study the man named Falmagon. "He said that? How can we know whether he is telling the truth or if he knows anything worthwhile?"

Velkan pushed away his empty bowl. "We have already drawn quite a bit of attention. Might be best to at least find another place to stay for the night, and then watch for him in the morning."

Maelili watched Unnvar take Falmagon and the second man to meet his family. The wife grinned widely, then hurried to fetch them a bowl of the same steaming stew, her dark flimsy braids bouncing. She acted as though she had known Falmagon and his companion forever.

"We will not risk losing sight of these men," Maelili said.

"As you wish, Arkhon," Velkan hummed, lifting his cup for a refill.

The next several hours lagged for Maelili while she sat at the table near their beds. Velkan, Brigita, and she maintained casual talk around the table for the sake of appearances, watching customers come and go. After a while, the few patrons remaining in Kal'bane barely gave them a second look.

Maelili watched and waited for an opportunity to speak to Falmagon or his companion, who she learned was referred to as Andrik. But Unnvar kept the two men in the back corner with his family, seemingly giving a history lesson on their family lineage. She could not hear much, and what she did hear was useless.

Eventually, none were left in the alehouse except the two Highborn, Unnvar and his family, and the three Stuhia.

"If anything, we can agree these two Highborn certainly do not have red hair," Brigita said, rubbing the end of her nose while peering over her shoulder. She lifted her eyes back to Maelili. "Do you have any idea what you might say?"

"Not entirely," she replied.

"We have the ability to overpower every Anshedar in this alehouse and question the Highborn as we see fit," Brigita said. "You must only give Ser Velkan and me the command. If either of these men know where Kindel is, they will tell us, I can assure you."

Maelili frowned, her vision clouding from the strong alcohol. "We did not come here to destroy their civilization or to place a beacon on our own. We are not like the skin-switchers." She knew the words would cut deep for Velkan and Brigita, who knew the Vucari historically invaded their lands every summer from the north. Until recently, that is, when the skin-switchers' nation began to break apart. They had not engaged in war with their enemy for years.

"We understand," Velkan said.

Maelili nodded. She was not worried about Velkan, a man who had proven his loyalty to her family since her father's reign over Lairhein. Brigita was the one who needed instruction.

Taking a breath, she watched Falmagon venture away from the corner alone. His empty cup swung in his left hand as he made a beeline to the pitcher of ale sitting on a table near the hearthfire. He took little notice of anything more in the room, seemingly caught up in his own thoughts. She was not surprised. He scarcely looked away from Unnvar or Andrik all night.

She hastily reached for her own copper cup and downed the ale. The burning caused her to snort through her nose. "Listen to me. I want us here and gone without the Anshedar knowing we walked among them. Now, the two of you stay put, and let me discover what I can."

"Arkhon?" Velkan challenged.

"I am ordering it," she said. "Drink your ale and shush."

She scooted her chair back from the table. Her legs were wobbly, bespeaking the amount of alcohol she drank over the past several hours at Kal'bane. Her vision blurred all the more as she stood, the pit of her stomach churning with ale.

She was downright drunk.

Steadying herself with a single hand, she pushed off the table to intercept Falmagon.

She reached the young Highborn at the hearthfire while he was already pouring his drink. She stumbled over her feet inelegantly, feeling the full effect of the Anshedar's drink. In fear of falling, she reached out and grabbed his upper arm to steady herself. He flexed in surprise beneath her sudden touch.

"If I could persuade you, my lord," she smiled, tracing her hand down to his elbow and holding tight, "would you mind filling my cup, too?"

His bright eyes examined her beneath his bangs. The surprise did not disappear from his face, eyebrows disappearing under his shaggy hair. A smile formed, the corners of his mouth touching his cheeks. Unexpected dimples appeared on his face, causing her to naturally smile in delight. They fit him.

Despite his positive response, he did not say a single word. Instead, he continued to pour liquid from the pitcher into his cup until it overflowed. The ale rolled over the edges, soaking his hand and splashing to the floor.

"Falmagon," Unnvar laughed from the corner. "You are going to stain the wood."

He gasped, faltering back and lifting the pitcher. She followed his lead, hanging onto him like he was an extension of her own body. "Oh, look what I have done," Falmagon laughed. "I am sorry, Unnvar." His speech was garbled, but clear enough for her to understand.

"I was hoping you would put it in the cup!" She joined in his laughter. She heard a chuckle from the table behind her and ignored it. Admittedly, the young Highborn was more attractive up close than she initially thought, but she did not intend to do any more than intrigue the man enough to speak with her in private.

Velkan and Brigita could withhold their judgment until morning.

"I am happy to be of service." Falmagon held his grin. "What is your name?"

"Maelili," she answered.

He lifted the overfilled cup to gulp from the edge ravenously. He then guided her to the nearest table to sit the cup down. She followed his lead, freely offering her cup when he reached for it. He seemed to fight to keep his attention on the cup and not her. He spoke while he poured. "You have an unusual accent. I feel as though I have heard it once before. Where are you from?"

"The north," she answered quickly. "And you?"

"Melkorka, from the Seven Islands." Falmagon grinned. She could not help but see the swell in his burly chest. "I am a Highborn and soon will be a Highborn Longwalker."

She cooed, feigning delight, without having any idea exactly what the words meant. She reached for her drink.

"Falmagon!" the other Highborn called from across the alehouse. "Are you coming back to speak with your kin or am I meant to entertain on your behalf?"

"Mind yourself, Andrik!" Falmagon called over his shoulder.

"I have more than one story I am sure you would be displeased for me to tell," Andrik shouted back.

"Ah, leave him," Unnvar chuckled. "Someone is going to have to share a bed anyhow."

Falmagon waved off Andrik and Unnvar with less fervor. He looked on Maelili again, asking, "What do you know about the Highborn?"

She bit her lip playfully, reaching for his hand. "So very little. Please tell me everything."

Chapter X
Maelili

Maelili stepped outside from the empty alehouse, covering her eyes with the full of her arm to block the intense light of the afternoon sun. The wind was crisp and refreshing after being enclosed in the dark building. She should have woken up hours ago, yet the morning hours had somehow slipped away without notice. She groaned, running a hand through her tangled hair. Her head ached with enough intensity to take her to her knees.

"I am pleased to see you found your clothes this morning, Arkhon," Brigita said loudly from her right. Maelili emptied her lungs, turning to see the young Stuhia standing on one foot, leaning against the alehouse with the other foot kicked up under her. Her arms were crossed, and the glare painted on her face was unmistakable. "A long day we would have had if this morning we were yet again subjected to what *everyone* saw last night. And not just Velkan or Unnvar, but the children too." She scoffed, shaking her head. "Here and gone without being noticed? Is that not what you said? I promise, Arkhon, no one is going to forget last night. Not Falmagon Sej, and certainly not I."

Maelili's throat tightened as segments of the night flashed across her vision. One moment she was drinking with the Highborn, and the next he was stripping her naked and taking her to bed. Worse yet, she recalled welcoming the invitation with gleeful giggles. Even now, she could nearly feel his weight on top of her, his lips pressed against her own. The few furs had scarcely covered their nakedness while she had shouted his name.

Falmagon.

Brigita pushed off the wall, her hands turning to fists at her sides. "Please explain to me how humping the Highborn helps us find your brother?"

Maelili's mouth dried, bile creeping up her throat. The taste of the Anshedar ale was still thick on her tongue and teeth. While she had the authority to silence Brigita, she lacked the desire, especially when the young woman ridiculed her with the truth.

She searched for a reply.

Falmagon, although a great deal younger than her, was certainly handsome. He presented himself as everything her husband lacked: strong, confident, and determined. He would, no doubt, be powerful in future days. But now, in the light of a new day, none of those reasons would persuade her to lie with him.

"I had too much to drink," she said. The excuse was pitiable, but it was all she had. Perhaps she could have said she longed for the touch of another, or she thought the action would force him to tell whatever secrets he held. Though in truth, no explanation was worthy.

She was married, she was the Arkhon, and she slept with a stranger with a pretty smile.

Brigita tensed her jaw in response.

"Did we learn anything from him?" Maelili asked.

"What? Did we—" Brigita growled, pushing her dark hair from her eyes. "You were the one with his ballocks banging against you! I am never going to unhear it!"

Maelili turned away from her, forcing a cough from her throat. The more Brigita spoke of the incident, the more she recalled Falmagon hovering over her with his long hair canopying their pressed lips. If the pounding in her head was not so strong, she might have been more concerned about the fluttering of her heart. She needed something to take away the intense throbbing. She asked, "Where is he?"

"The Highborn?" Brigita asked, flaring her nostrils. "I do not know. He and his friend were out the door before breakfast, and I thought it might be a bit forward to ask Unnvar about your lover's whereabouts."

Maelili withheld her disappointment. She could not blame anyone for losing track of Falmagon and Andrik except herself. "And what about Ser Velkan?"

"He did not comment on your nighttime undertaking, if that is what you are asking," Brigita said.

"I mean, where is he?" Maelili scowled.

"Looking for the Highborn, I assume," Brigita said, stepping away and calming her tone. "The pretentious fop fixed his hair and then stormed from the alehouse right after sunrise, telling me to stay and watch over you. Unnvar and his family left shortly after to gather meat from the market. They said no one comes by until the late afternoon, and you were free to sleep as long as you wanted."

"Keep an eye out for Ser Velkan while I get ready."

Maelili did not wait for Brigita's response. She went back inside Kal'bane, letting the door slam shut behind her. At re-entrance, she could not help but take note of the overwhelming smell of sex in the air. The hearthfire burned low, giving little light to the room and less warmth. She moved through the shadows toward her bed. The tussled sheets caused her stomach to tighten with disgust.

While frowned upon, no law prevented her from sleeping with other men. In fact, as long as she only lay with men or women beneath her station, she was protected from the ruling of magistrates sitting on the newly formed Ninth Council back home. And being the most powerful woman in Lairhein meant she could hump anyone she chose. Yet she was not some saucy, common-kissing flaxen wench who lifted her skirts for random men in alehouses. In all actuality, since being wed to Nevyn, she had never been intimate with another man.

Her eyes watered unforgivingly. The remaining bedsteads were not far from her own, giving a clear indication of how close the others were while she and Falmagon shared each other's company. Maelili covered her mouth as though the action would halt the tears from sliding down her cheeks. She wished that she could return to a sober state. Her mushed mind caused her thoughts to scatter.

She could not understand what she was feeling. Sadness tugged at her heart, guilt filled her gut, and fury swelled in her chest like a feral fire. Yet she was not mad at the Highborn who shared a night's embrace beneath skins. Nor was she angry with Velkan or Brigita, who traveled a world away to help her find her lost brother. If anything, she may only have held ire for herself.

Maelili wiped the tears from her face and began pulling at her snarled hair. No matter whether she lost the respect of her companions or exited the Kal'bane while continuing to feel like ale was flowing through her veins, she could not forget her duty. Kindel must be somewhere on Kalamaar or the Seven Islands, and she needed to bring him home. The opportunity last night may be lost, but the Highborn was not beyond reach. She would find Falmagon and discover if he knew anything of her brother.

He owed her as much.

The door creaking open behind her grabbed her attention. She dried her eyes again and turned around.

"My Arkhon," Velkan said in a gentle voice, his large frame nearly hiding the door behind him. "Have you rested well?"

"As well as I am going to," she managed to say. Her voice was weak, cracking with each word as though she might burst into tears again. She did not bother trying to correct her broken speech.

Velkan offered a weak smile. Even in the dim light, she could see he had freshly shaven with new cut marks on his cheeks and chin. He pulled his hair back over his shoulders with either hand. "Arkhon or not, you cannot blame yourself for being mortal."

"I am held to higher standards, Ser Velkan," Maelili said. "In order to see my charge done, my heart should lead me, and here I have betrayed myself."

"No great man or woman in history has pledged themselves to a moral code and kept their foothold. While I respect you for pushing to become better, only the ignorant believe their leaders to be inhuman. I do not follow you because I think you to be perfect. I would be blind and stupid to believe so." He took two large steps, folding his hands in front of him. "I follow you because, like your father, you are capable of recognizing when you make mistakes, and you act to rectify them. At times, every one of us bends the knee to indulgence, yet not all of us learn from our faults."

Maelili thought of her father, Jonafel Kluk, a legendary leader of the Stuhians before he was killed by Dagmar Kaligula. He guided their people fairly with kindness and logic better than any other before him. "I am not my father."

"You knew your father in one way," Velkan said, "and I in another. He battled against himself as much as any other, I assure you."

"How so?"

Velkan chuckled. "If I tarnish his memory, he might return from the Netherworld to haunt me. His misdeeds should stay with him in the grave, safe from waggling tongues and history books."

"I would never tell. I promise." Maelili smiled.

"I believe you," Velkan replied, coming close enough to offer a hand, "but I have made promises. Much like those I keep to my husband back home about his own mistakes. And the same of which I extend to you. What happened last night between you and the young Highborn is irrelevant to our quest, and therefore I will never tell the tale. Carry it with you or share if you must, but while we are on Kalamaar, we have a greater responsibility. If we can find Kindel Kluk and your father's staff, Habermani, the fine details of our adventure will be forgotten."

"And what of Brigita?" Maelili asked, taking his hand. "She is less than pleased with her precious Arkhon, swearing to never forget."

Velkan enclosed her hand in his own. She could feel his warmth. "We have a long journey ahead and she is young. I am certain she will grow to understand."

Chapter XI
FALMAGON

No matter how hard he tried to keep his feet planted, Falmagon could not keep the spring from his step. The extra bounce came as naturally as the unchanging smile planted on his face. The capital city of the Anshedar, Arkaim, promised to be more exciting than he imagined. After one day, he had reunited with his kin and secured his manhood, romping the prettiest thing in all Kalamaar and the Seven Islands.

His heart melted at the thought. He was the luckiest man alive.

"I am blind out here," Falmagon said, walking adjacent to the docks. He angled his head away from the sunlight ricocheting off the icy blue water. The cool wind stung his nose and ears, roiling off Strega's Deep nearby. He was beginning to think every city built by man was stationed by the sea.

He convinced Andrik to explore the city an hour before the sun lifted, venturing to the market and the many different shops. By now the two of them had walked almost every inch of Arkaim two or three times. Falmagon told Andrik that exploring the city was part of doing his duty as the next Highborn Longwalker. He was meeting the people and becoming familiar with the capital, while in truth, he was secretly searching for Erzebeth Navenka.

As much as he tried to stay focused on the city streets, the events from the night before replayed in his mind, often causing the people and buildings to blur around him. He experienced each breath and gentle touch in his head again and again. He lost count of how many times he had to shake his head to free himself from the agreeable memories.

Despite a perfect night, his task of finding Erzebeth Navenka was more important. Kinhar said she would have come to Arkaim. Yet the few intertwining roads were mostly empty of wandering bodies, and those he crossed held no resemblance to Erzebeth.

"I cannot see anything." Falmagon complained again, letting loose a breath. "The Lightbringer rides his chariot too close to Aenar."

"I do not know what you think you are missing. We have been down this street half a dozen times." Andrik rubbed his half-open eyes, his feet scraping against the solid road.

"Are you not enjoying yourself, Andrik?" Falmagon cooed. "This is the capital of the Anshedar. King Merreider Kar, Twelfth King of Kalamaar, Bearer of the *Svehla*, resides here. Not even Nedezhda has seen the likes of the city."

"That you know of," Andrik sighed, "and we saw the king's courtyard and keep twice already. The building is less impressive than Melkorka. Besides, he is not even in Arkaim. The people said he went to Farmas."

"Still…" Falmagon shrugged.

Andrik spoke through gritted teeth. "And if you are blinded by the Lightbringer, I suspect it's due to your head being stuck in the clouds. You have not stopped smiling since you woke up."

"Would you be any different?" Falmagon hurried his question when Andrik took a breath. The Highborn's sour look deepened. Andrik maintained his wicked mood most of the morning, yet only now he hinted at Falmagon's humping last night. "Come on. I know you have never experienced the touch of a woman. Be happy for me. By Mulafell, I became a man last night, which is more than most *men* at Melkorka can claim." He pushed Andrik playfully. "Are you jealous?"

Andrik grabbed Falmagon's shoulder to stop him in the street and scowled. They lingered between the scattered homes and shops. What few citizens could be seen passed with little interest. The shorter Highborn spoke under his breath. "I doubt Kinhar sent us here so I could hear you grunting and sloshing about in the midnight hour with a woman twice your age. You said you were training to become the Highborn Longwalker."

"I am." Falmagon knocked Andrik's hand free and leaned inward. No doubt his friend was envious. "Who is to say the affection of women does not come with the title?"

"She was too old."

"Maelili looked young enough to me. Besides, name a woman we know who is not twice our age or more?"

Andrik grumbled in response.

"You are myopic. Age does not matter," Falmagon pressed, rubbing his knuckles against his nose. "I am glad to have slept with an Anshedar. Better to have Maelili than a woman back home."

Andrik looked at his feet, his thick eyebrows angling in contemplation. Falmagon scoffed, turning to admire the wooden homes and thatched roofs surrounding them. The hum of the passing men and women chatting to one another filled the silence. Finally, Andrik stuck out his lips and raised his eyes to stare at Falmagon with determination. "It matters. Do you feel nothing for her?"

He patted the side of Andrik's shoulder with a soft chuckle. "Of course I do. Maelili was perfect. Better than anything I could have imagined. I hope to see her again tonight."

"What? Why would you see her again?" Andrik blubbered as Falmagon began walking down the street once more. "We have completed your task. We met Unnvar. I thought we would be on our way back to Melkorka today. We have our duty, Falmagon!"

"We can spare another day." Falmagon combed his hair back from his eyes, hearing Andrik's footsteps hurry along to keep up with him. "I am not going to hump a woman and disappear. She was charming, beautiful...flawless."

"You do not know anything about her, Falmagon."

"What is there to know? She liked me, and I find no reason not to like her back. I might even make her my wife."

Andrik grabbed the side of his own face. "Your wife? Do you even hear yourself? You cannot bring her back to Melkorka."

Falmagon smiled, pushing his hair back over his shoulders again. "Why not?"

"You are a Highborn. Do you not remember what Nedezhda told us while we were on Cyreus? She wisely advised us against love. We do not have the luxury of being in love," Andrik insisted.

Heat flushed from Falmagon's neck to his cheeks at the mention of the other Longwalker. "Does Nedezhda also tell you how to piss? Do you squat behind the castle walls like a dainty girl?" Falmagon picked up his pace. "I bet she has never loved anyone in her life."

"What has gotten into you?" Andrik struggled to keep up with Falmagon's long legs. "You do not have the authority to speak to me like that. You should not speak about Nedezhda like that either. We came—"

"Kinhar would disagree." Falmagon spat to the ground and whipped around. "You have the audacity to quote a woman who, by your own admission, plays with death magic."

"I did not say it was *death* magic." Andrik wrinkled his nose.

"She sucked the life out of the dead!"

"I should not have said anything to you," Andrik sneered, looking cagily from the corner of his eye.

"Bah! Go back to Kal'bane and leave me be. Get some rest while you can," Falmagon barked over his shoulder, harshly twisting away and stomping off once more. "Another long night likely awaits and tomorrow we begin our journey back home."

He did not wait to see whether Andrik complied with his instruction. Instead, he stormed off down the street without looking back, keeping his eyes on the people and buildings ahead. After several blocks, when he did not hear the pitter-patter of Andrik's feet fighting to keep up, he finally slowed his pace.

For all Falmagon cared, Andrik could keep his arrogant opinions about Maelili, Nedezhda, and the-gods-knew-what-else to himself. The Lightbringer did not choose Andrik to be among the Kadari, nor was he meant to be a Longwalker. Falmagon considered Andrik as Kinhar would—and the gods would—an inferior, half-brained Highborn.

Pulling his hood up over his long hair, Falmagon skimmed the scattered clusters of Anshedar on the sides of the street. Men, women, and children, each with dark-colored hair and blue eyes, jibber-jabbered as though no work was left to be done, despite midday barely passing. He guessed the Anshedar had less work this time of the year with the ground being too hard to be worked and expecting snow in the next quarter year.

He meandered his way away from the docks and back toward the eastern entrance to the city. Along the way, he searched the faces of the many families and friends walking in huddles, talking loudly about the gods, the weather, and the king. Some of the citizens gave an extended glance back, scrunching their faces or turning away uneasily, but most paid him little mind.

He stopped dead center in the street, wondering if he should abandon the quest when the light pierced his eyes again from above. Realizing how much time had passed since he prayed, he whispered, "Lightbringer, you have steered my feet to Arkaim. If I am fated to find Erzebeth and the truth of this doom, now is the time to reveal her to me."

The cool wind stung his left cheek, guiding him to the right. He twisted his neck as though he were guided by Dahz's very hand, knowing the slender woman with the tangled black hair and pale skin would be revealed to him. Yet his heart still stalled in his chest when Erzebeth Navenka appeared through the city gates, no more than thirty paces away.

He almost did not recognize her wearing clothes. In fact, he nearly expected her to be naked, her snowy skin and dark nipples bared. However, the woman clad herself appropriately to blend with the Anshedar around her. The brown boots, black pants, grey tunic, and sandy cloak looked worn as though she might have pulled them off the back of a dead man. With the thought fresh in his mind, Falmagon noted that she did not carry a weapon.

Her brown eyes magically flashed to a bluish tint in the sun, immediately locking on him as she advanced. She flashed her yellow teeth, showing more kindness than he saw on Cyreus, lifting her chin in recognition.

"You came a long way to talk with me, young Highborn," Erzebeth said, approaching him until she stood within arm's reach. "Come with me. We will speak privately."

"I did," he managed to say, wondering how she knew so much without having any way of truly knowing. She slipped by him without another word, without touching him, and headed to the back end of the city. He swiftly followed, trekking beyond the Kal'bane, where he could hear the heavy laughter of Unnvar within, and to the same docks he withdrew from less than an hour ago.

Once they reached the edge of the water, Erzebeth stopped, folding her arms into her cloak. She smiled with her mouth closed, looking across Strega's Deep. Falmagon stepped to her side, towering over her by nearly a head and a half. She was a good foot shorter than Maelili, and while she looked to be about the same age, she was no less beautiful. He briefly reforged the image of her nakedness again, seeing her standing along the gorge at Cyreus, before his mind twisted the image into Maelili's thin figure beneath him.

He shook the thought from his head, hoping he was not blushing. He recalled what Kinhar told him before leaving Melkorka and hurried to say the practiced words. "Erzebeth, I have taken the Kalamyr Oath. I am one of the Kadari now."

"Of course you did," Erzebeth replied, focusing on the endless ocean ahead of her. She inhaled, swelling her chest to its limit, and then slowly exhaled through her pursed lips. "Kinhar would not have sent you unless you took his precious oaths. Understand your vows to the Lightbringer are sacred. You cannot break them, young Highborn."

"My name is Falmagon."

"Okay, Falmagon," she said. "Do not break your vows."

"I will stay loyal to the Lightbringer until my death," he said. "I assure you."

"Good. The gods will remember."

Falmagon bit his inner cheek, wondering how else to begin. "Are you part of the Kadari too? Do you worship Dahz?"

"I am not, and I do not," she answered. She looked up at him. "Tell me, is that why you sought me out? To ask me about my allegiences to the gods? Should I tell you tales about how I came across the ocean? Must you hear about those who run with wolves, or better yet, those who become the beasts they hunt?"

"What? I do not think so unless that has something to do with what you came to tell Kinhar." He ruffled his brow, feeling a knot in his throat. Erzebeth was more of a mystery now than when he met her at Cyreus. He clarified his purpose. "Kinhar sent me to learn more about your warning of doom."

She blinked several times, staring at him as though he were mad. The silence was deafening.

"That is why I came," he said.

"I told you what was meant to be said, Falmagon. I did not hold anything back when I met with you and the other Highborn," Erzebeth said. "Why would Kinhar think I know something more?"

"He has had a vision…in prayer," Falmagon said.

"I see. I have never known his visions not to be prophetic," she replied. She stared into his eyes, her own shifting between a dark brown and a dull blue. "What did he see?"

"The Lightbringer told him that an evil lurks at Melkorka, and he believes the evil is tied to your forewarning," Falmagon said. Erzebeth crossed her arms, staring at him as though he should continue. He searched his mind for something more to say to her, anything to help her reveal what she might not have said when he was with Andrik and—"Nedezhda Mager," he blurted. "Kinhar believes the evil may reside in her."

"You are speaking about the Red who came with you to Cyreus?" she asked.

Falmagon dipped his head, still unsure of what the title meant, but Nedezhda did have reddish hair. "I am. Why do you call her that?"

Erzebeth rumbled in her throat, almost like a wild beast. "She is not like the rest of you. She has access to a wicked magic that undoubtedly threatens each one of the Highborn."

He could not shake Andrik's story about Nedezhda using death magic to siphon the life from the Kras corpses. He wondered if the stranger with the staff was a Red. His use of Koldovstvo was also unlike anything Falmagon knew. "How did you know that she could…"

Erzebeth met his gaze again, lifting her hand to touch his chest. "You must tell me the truth. Is she the only one among you with hair the color of blood? Are there more who have the ability to touch your magics?"

Falmagon was quick to shake his head. "No, she is not. One more resides at Melkorka, and then there is a…a stranger. I crossed him outside Melkorka weeks before we met you on Cyreus. He was following me. I do not know his name, but…" Falmagon paused, feeling the weight of her hand pressing against his chest. He was speaking so swiftly, she may not have understood half of his words. Her touch was soothing. He slowed his pace. "He said the Highborn did not deserve to live."

"You must think on what you know and what you think you know, young Highborn." Erzebeth paused to correct herself, "Falmagon. I think you know the answer already. I will tell you that Kinhar cannot avoid the coming of demons any more than he can escape his inevitable death. Yet the evil the Lightbringer warns him of must be a Red. Most only know destruction. If you wish to have an advantage in the wars to come, you must kill the correct one."

Chapter XII
FALMAGON

"About time you returned! I feared you got lost in the city," Unnvar boomed as Falmagon walked through the sturdy door of Kal'bane. Unnvar's two children straightaway bolted from his wife's skirts at the site of Falmagon, springing to his side and hugging his legs. Falmagon grabbed at the door frame to keep his balance. Unnvar did not bother calling them off, continuing as though the children belonged swinging on the ends of his trousers. "I thought you came to visit me, yet you spend all day parading around town. Ha! You act like you have never seen a Northman before."

"Rarely, Unnvar," Falmagon forced a grin, closing the door behind him while keeping himself upright. He stumbled forward with the children pulling his drawers partway down. He gripped at his waistband, unsure how to respond. Children were rare at Melkorka.

Unnvar's children had wild dark hair hiding most of their features; Falmagon did not lean close enough to look at them any further. Last night taught him that if you gave them too much attention, they would not let you alone. One evening with the buggers was plenty to tell him he never wanted children of his own.

He wondered if he should have welcomed the distraction of the children, however. The walk back to the alehouse did not give time to shake Erzebeth's words from his thoughts, especially the part about needing to kill someone. Not only had Falmagon never killed, but the Highborn were sworn to protect lives, not take them.

"...the city," Andrik finished from behind Unnvar's hulking body. Falmagon grimaced. He had not noticed the other Highborn hiding at the back table. He had not heard most of what Andrik said.

He spoke in a hurry, hoping no one asked him about his whereabouts. "After being trapped on an island for fifteen years, what can I say? The Anshedar are interesting, but the city is what impresses me."

"Are you mocking your friend? Your friend here just said the same." Unnvar howled with amusement, smacking Andrik on the back. Andrik lurched forward, almost dropping the tankard of ale he held in his hand.

"Whoa there, Unnvar!" Andrik shouted, glaring at Falmagon with a furrowed brow.

"Ah! What do you care?" Unnvar simpered, looking pleased with himself. "Not like you are paying for my ale."

"Children, come away from him," Unnvar's wife finally called, releasing Falmagon from the grip of their little fingers.

He nodded his appreciation and blundered forward to find a chair next to Andrik, glancing over the rest of the alehouse to discover the place was empty. Maelili and her friends were gone. "Where is everyone?"

"Slow night is all." Unnvar nudged his shoulder. "Do not look so down, Falmagon. Your northern squeeze will be back with her friends before closing time. You might get another go at her before you return home." Falmagon did not miss the cold glare Unnvar's wife gave him, resulting in Unnvar leaning down to whisper, "Though best try to keep it down tonight, or the lady is going to have you sleeping with the hogs at your next visit."

"I will do that." Falmagon choked, reaching for a cup and the pitcher of ale. He longed to see Maelili again, but after speaking with Erzebeth, he could not say he was in the mood for another tussle.

Unnvar rumbled in his throat, raising an eyebrow at Andrik. "I was telling Andrik here that he should make a go at the other gal. She is called Brigita. She is a bit feisty—from what I can tell—and might even have less experience than your gal. But I cannot say I've ever seen a field that didn't need a plowing."

"Unnvar Grondahl!" His wife reached out to cover their youngest child's ears.

He waved his hand to dismiss his wife and snorted. "Let her ears alone. I already said it." He leaned in, scratching the underside of his stomach. "I was glad to see you know your way around a woman, Falmagon. I am not sure what all they teach you in that forsaken castle, but you make me glad to call you kin."

"Thanks, Unnvar," Falmagon said uneasily, squinting at him. He lifted the cup to his lips and gulped. The liquid burned deliciously. "I think you should wait until I have had a bit more to drink before we talk about romping women."

"I will drink to that," Unnvar said, reaching for his own copper cup.

"Any chance we could find a more suitable topic?" Andrik appealed. He raised his thick eyebrows at Unnvar and Falmagon hopefully. "We came all this way. Perhaps we could talk about Falmagon's family. You knew his parents?"

"Oh." Unnvar's eyes widened. "That is a story. I suppose you would not know it, would you?"

Falmagon cocked his head at Andrik. "Why would you want to discuss my family when you had no interest in your own when we visited Cyreus?"

Andrik wrapped his hands around his cup and lifted his shoulders. He relaxed his face, joking, "I will talk about anything to keep the focus off your ballocks."

Falmagon smirked. Andrik looked more relaxed in his chair than he had been in the streets earlier. Perhaps the malt helped calm his nerves or, even better, caused him to temporarily forget their discourse over Maelili. Falmagon hoped the effect was permanent. They would be stuck with one another on the long road back to Melkorka, and he would rather the trip be absent of arguments.

"Come, now. Fill your cups," Unnvar said. "I will tell you of Falmagon's beginnings before he was swept away to Melkorka." Unnvar reached out with the pitcher to fill Falmagon's cup and then to top off Andrik's. He adjusted himself in his chair, scraping it against the floorboards so he might look at the burning hearthfire while he spoke. "Well, I will tell you what I can remember from what was passed to me by my mother, Sonia, and our grandfather, Ratimir. Do you remember Ratimir?"

Falmagon looked to Andrik and then Unnvar, shaking his head slightly. Kinhar had told him his grandfather's name was Ratimir, but he knew little else about the man. He said, "When I was younger, I would lie in bed and pretend I could feel the whiskers on his cheek. But I let fairy tales be fairy tales a long time ago."

"Hm." Unnvar grunted. "You were not far off. He always did have a face full of fur." On the opposite side of the fire, Falmagon noticed Unnvar's wife getting the children ready for bed. He had not realized evening had come.

"You were raised by your grandfather?" Andrik asked.

Falmagon dipped his chin, making a note that Maelili had not returned yet. He answered half-heartedly. "Yes."

Andrik frowned. "Where were your father and mother?"

"Wait a moment." Unnvar raised his hand. "Are you going to ask questions or am I going to tell the story?"

"Go on, then," Andrik encouraged, lifting his cup to take another drink.

"Ratimir's wife died birthing Falmagon's father, who was called Falmir, and so our grandfather was left alone to raise his two children in Arkaim," Unnvar started.

"That is hardly the place to start," Unnvar's wife snipped from the children's cots.

"Shush, woman, and let me tell it how I want," Unnvar growled, waving her off. He shook his head, turning back to Falmagon and Andrik. "Ratimir built Kal'bane and intended your father to continue running it after he passed, but Falmir had an adventurous heart." Unnvar chuckled. "My mother said every time they turned around, he was out exploring beyond the city walls and she would have to go fetch him. By and by, when my mother was old enough, our grandfather married her off to my father. They moved to a pig farm in the country and Ratimir was left to raise Falmir alone."

"What happened?" Falmagon asked, reaching for the pitcher to refill his cup. He passed it to Andrik's outstretched hand when he finished.

"He disappeared is what happened," Unnvar said. "No more than a month passed and Falmir was gone. No one knows whether he went to the Crags of Kazimir, the Seven Islands, or to the far north into the wild marshes. Ratimir considered him dead and brought my parents back to Arkaim to learn how to manage Kal'bane. For two years, my father and mother ran the alehouse while our grandfather withered away."

Unnvar paused to refill his own cup, emptying the pitcher.

Falmagon grimaced. His father sounded less and less like a man meant to inspire others, deserting his family and his duty. He chewed on his inner lip, wondering if he should stop the tale before Unnvar spoke of his mother. The last thing he wanted was to leave Kal'bane knowing his mother and father were inept.

How could he be chosen by the Lightbringer to be among the Kadari if his parents were but inferior Northmen?

"After two years had come and gone, Falmir returned to the alehouse," Unnvar lifted his finger, a twinkle in his blue eyes, "with a woman who had *fire hair* and was as close to springing a babe from her belly as a summer sow. Falmagon was born weeks later, right here in this very room."

"Ha!" Andrik suddenly burst into laughter. "Who would have thought you would have lost your virginity in the same room you were birthed? That is rich!"

He bent over to hold his stomach, smashing his forehead into his knees.

"Shut up!" Falmagon threw the few droplets in his cup at the other Highborn, causing even Unnvar to chortle until his belly shook. Falmagon tried to keep the grin from spreading across his face to keep from encouraging the two men laughing without restraint. "Do you mean my mother had red hair?"

"That is what my mother told me." Unnvar slowed his laugh. "Rumor among us Northmen is that some of the Highborn have fire hair, right? Maybe your mother lives with you!"

"Maybe it's Nedezhda!" Andrik laughed harder, springing back upright with tears in his eyes.

Falmagon swallowed hard at the possibility. Andrik may have been drunk, but the potential truth left a ball in Falmagon's stomach. If Nedezhda used her death magic to remain young and was the Longwalker among the Highborn, she could very well be his mother.

His mouth dried, hearing Erzebeth's warning ring in his ears.

Was he meant to kill his own mother?

Falmagon gripped the side of his pants to keep his hand from shaking. "What happened to my parents? Why did Ratimir raise me for so many years before Kinhar took me away to Melkorka?"

"I spent several years trying to get the full story out of Ratimir. I was curious, you know? He probably would have never said anything, but as our grandfather grew older, I swear he spilled every secret he ever kept. Some of the things that came out of his mouth, I am telling you, I would have been better off not knowing." Unnvar looked to Falmagon, grinning at his joke. Falmagon did not return the smile, eager to hear the rest of the story. Unnvar's expression disappeared as swiftly as frost from flame. "Right. I cannot be certain what Ratimir told me was true, but he said your mother disappeared the same night you were born. She abandoned both you and your father."

Falmagon fell back against his chair.

"Was he so ugly as a child?" Andrik sniped between his fat lips.

"No, no," Unnvar said, completely sincere. His blue eyes locked on Falmagon with concern. Falmagon looked to the hearthfire, but he heard Unnvar continue, "In fact, Ratimir said she was overwhelmed by the sight of her child, completely awestruck."

"Why did she leave, then?" Falmagon asked.

"I don't know," Unnvar said. "No one does. Sadly, your father did not stay around much longer, either. He waited maybe a week or so, thinking your mother would come back to the alehouse. When she didn't, he went off searching for her. He never returned." Unnvar cleared his throat. "I am sorry, Falmagon."

"Not your fault that I was unwanted by my parents, Unnvar," Falmagon said, sitting his cup down. His hand would not stop shaking. If Nedezhda Mager was his mother, she would have needed to return to Melkorka to fulfill her duty. But what happened to his father?

Did she kill him?

"Hm." Unnvar scratched at his beard, thinking over his comment. "Might be a stretch to say they did not want you,

Falmagon. Only the gods know your mother's reasons for leaving and what happened to them after they left. I hate to give you false hope, but we thought you were dead all these years. Your parents may be alive yet."

"Let us hope not," Falmagon murmured.

"What?" Unnvar leaned forward to hear him better.

Before Falmagon could come up with a suitable response, the door to the Kal'bane swung open, followed by a shuffle of feet.

Falmagon sighed at the sight of Maelili entering the alehouse with her two friends. Her green eyes hung on him, ignoring everyone and everything else in the room. "Come walk with me, Falmagon. I wish to speak with you."

Chapter XIII
Maelili

Her tongue twisted into knots being close to Falmagon once more. She attempted to speak a couple of times, but she could not seem to form words as they walked out the door of Kal'bane and through the quieting city. After spending the better part of the day with a spirited Velkan and a disgruntled Brigita, she honestly felt at ease in the silence. Falmagon was patient with her. He said nothing, his stride matching hers, seeming relaxed and nonjudgmental. She knew he would not hold her to the standards of an Arkhon. He allowed her simply to be herself.

Maelili smiled to herself. In this moment, walking through the too-cold streets of Arkaim under the white moonlight, she was free. In all her years, she never cogitated about her commitment to duty and family and how each limited her exploration of life. Certainly, her concern for each kept her bound on a singular path. Like her father, she imagined that her life's onus had become a lifelong burden.

Even now, Maelili wanted nothing more than to relish Falmagon's company as she had last night. She could not deny feeling something for this young man, who emanated strength and confidence as readily as warmth from a hearthfire. Yet the advice of Velkan and Brigita, who pestered her all afternoon on how she might siphon the information she needed from Falmagon, echoed in her head. Her obligations prevented her from truly enjoying the moment.

Falmagon's left hand brushed against hers, stealing away her breath and her thoughts of duty. She did not realize how close he had come. The warmth emitting from his skin caused her palms to sweat with excitement, which likely made her ears redden beneath her hair. The nights had been cold traveling across the world to find her brother, so last night with Falmagon had been a welcome change. She longed to hold on to him again and feel the heat of his body.

Once they were beyond the view of the alehouse, she slipped her fingers in between his and held tight. He loudly exhaled, squeezing back, a sign of his pent-up desire to touch her too. She reluctantly gave her stipulation. "What happened last night cannot happen again."

Falmagon slackened his grip with uncertainty but did not let go. "Did I do something wrong?"

"No, not at all," she whispered, strengthening her grip where he faltered. Her jaw shuddered with her words, thinking of Nevyn and Eisliev. She adored her husband as wives were meant to adore husbands, but whatever tremor reverberated from her belly to her throat was unlike anything she knew with Nevyn. Touching Falmagon was like channeling magic. She was liberated. She was whole.

"What, then?" he asked. His gentle eyes glanced down at her while they walked.

She did not have the heart to meet his gaze. "I do not know you, Falmagon Sej. I can only wonder what you must think about me, seeing how I freely offered myself to you, a stranger."

"Only the purest thoughts," he assured her. The strength in his grip returned, his fingers pressing into the back of her hand. She wanted to believe him, but even trusting the Highborn did not allow her to ignore either her position among the Stuhians or her marriage. Her behavior last night—even now—was inexcusable.

She gave a small smile. "You are kind, but you do not know me either, Falmagon. You do not understand."

"Help me, then," he tenderly appealed. She was surprised that she did not hear desperation in his voice as she might expect from another man, specifically her husband. Falmagon stopped her in the street, darkness widespread around them despite the soft moonlight. Only a handful of homes held windows with lanterns or candles burning; the streets seemed entirely empty, save the two of them. "What must you know to love me?"

She almost choked on the word. "Love?" Her fingers grazed the side of her cheek. The smoothness of her skin dissolved years ago, a reminder of the battles she waged when protecting Lairhein against the Kaligulas almost seventy years ago. Being a Stuhian, she was timeless unless wielding Koldovstvo, having the ability to live forever if she left her magics untouched. Though with the white strands colored from her hair, Falmagon would have no way to guess her true age.

Talking of love reminded Maelili of Falmagon's youth and her lack thereof.

Yet her heart quickened.

Did she love him?

He searched her face, speaking in a rush as though he were hoping to speak the right words before she could object. "We will start over. My name is Falmagon Sej. I am a Highborn from Melkorka."

She slid her hand from her cheek to hang her fingers from her chin, accentuating her smile. "And what is meant by being a Highborn? Are you a noble?"

Falmagon scrunched his face in confusion. "What?" He snorted, dimples appearing on his cheeks. "No, I am not a noble. Do you really not know what a Highborn is?"

She shook her head innocently, lowering her hand.

Falmagon turned his head, his long brown locks touching the side of his cheek. "I thought all those on Kalamaar and the Seven Islands knew the Highborn. Have we really been so secluded from those whom we are meant to serve?"

"The far north is a way from Melkorka, yes? We keep to ourselves," she lied, hoping the words would stick without question.

Falmagon looked north as though the blackness on the horizon would confirm her words, repeating them in his ear with bated breath. He lowered his chin to keep her in his sight. "The Highborn are like you—like the Northmen—except we have been gifted by the gods to manipulate the elements."

Maelili did not bother to correct him from grouping her among the Anshedar. She was glad he believed her to be a Northman. "What do you mean?"

"We have a magic within us called Koldovstvo," he clarified, saying the final word slowly with emphasis. Maelili bulged her eyes in surprise, immediately pulling back from his grip. She fought to keep her feet planted on the ground. He responded by touching her forearm, misreading her trepidation. "I know. I know. The concept is foreign to most Anshedar, and if you have never heard of the Highborn…well, you may think I am mad speaking of magic, but what I say is true."

Maelili froze, her mouth drying. The elated feelings sank into the pit of her stomach. For the past weeks, she heard of the Highborn from Melkorka and their duty to protect the Anshedar, but no Northmen spoke of them wielding the Stuhian magic, Koldovstvo. A thousand questions raced through her mind, from how the Highborn came by the magic to the extent of their power.

She was taught that Koldovstvo was exclusive to the Stuhians. The Ninth Council, back home, taught that Wolos, the God of the Dead, gifted the Stuhians with Koldovstvo when he crafted them in the same likeness as dragons, earning them the name, dragon-men. While most Stuhians, including Maelili, believed the wisdom of the Ninth Council, others swore the teachings to be an outright lie.

"Have I frightened you?" Falmagon stooped to look her squarely in the face. "Did I say something wrong? Those on the Seven Islands know what I say to be true. I am sorry the Highborn do not come to Kalamaar more often to teach the Northmen of our ways. We are rarely needed here on the mainland."

Maelili could not answer his questions with so many of her own on the tip of her tongue. Foremost, she wondered what he would say if he knew she could touch Koldovstvo too. "What do you do with this magic?"

"We protect the Seven Islands, Kalamaar, and the Anshedar against whatever demons come from the Crags of Kazimir. We are also sworn to respond to the king or the jarls to maintain peace," Falmagon replied. Somehow, his dimples remained visible, as though he forced the expression to ease her concerns. He went on, "But mostly, we do nothing. We sit at Melkorka and survive like any other Anshedar."

Fighting against the urge to withdraw further, Maelili moved her quivering hands to hold Falmagon. She placed her head against his wide chest, feeling his muscular arms wrap around her, confused by his words. "You do not often fight the demons?"

He looked away from her, stumbling over his words. His composure disappeared. "I…um…" He flared his nostrils with a huff, and then shook his head. "No, we have not fought demons in many, many years. The Highborn would not want me to tell you. They would like the Northmen to think monsters are bleeding from the Crags daily. In truth, I have never seen one in my lifetime."

Maelili remembered the winged skyrz she, Velkan, and Brigita found in the cavern within the mountain the afternoon after coming to Kalamaar. The Highborn were unaware of what stirred beneath their very noses. "You do not go looking for them, then?"

"Absolutely not. We have not enough Highborn to be taking excursions into the mountains." Falmagon rubbed her arm, again misreading her intent. "If you are worried about my safety, I assure you I am not in danger."

"How many are you?"

"Not many," Falmagon said, speaking slower. He blinked a couple of times, possibly realizing he was being asked too many questions about the Highborn. She bit her inner cheek and waited for him to finish. "Though I am not certain there have ever been many of us," he said. "Once in a great while, the Anshedar have a child born with the ability to touch Koldovstvo, and they are called on to bring the child to the Seven Islands." He tightened his hold on her, his fingers running through her long hair. "I was the last of said children brought to Melkorka, and that was over fifteen years ago."

"Separated from your family?" she asked, emphasizing her concern for him.

"Yes." Falmagon placed his hands on her shoulders and leaned back to look her in the eyes. "I hope we will not spend all evening talking about myself and Melkorka. What about you? Why did you leave your farm and come to Arkaim?"

Maelili wrapped the back of his brown cloak around her trembling hands. The fabric was warm against her freezing fingers. She was not certain how much she could say without risking the truth. "I am looking for my brother, Kindel. He has been missing for some time."

Falmagon's face twisted. "You think he is in Arkaim? Did he run away from home?"

She did not know how to explain the full story so simply to Falmagon. Explaining her blood feud with the Kaligulas and the importance of her father's staff, would not serve anything more than revealing her true identity.

Maelili made a humming sound, giving no indication of whether Falmagon's assumption was correct or not. She said, "Kindel could be anywhere on Kalamaar or the Seven Islands. I have asked so many about his whereabouts, hoping someone has seen him. Unless he changed his appearance, he would not be difficult to identify. His hair is as red as the setting sun and he carries a crooked staff."

Maelili inhaled sharply as Falmagon pushed away from her, almost violently, tearing her hands from his cloak. He scowled at her, all gentleness vanishing from his blue eyes.

"Kindel is his name?" He curled his lip. "Your *brother* attacked me on Folkmar."

"What? You have seen him?" Maelili clamped a hand over her mouth. The accusation was overlooked upon realizing the gods brought her to Falmagon to find Kindel. She released her hand, reaching for Falmagon, who withdrew from her touch. "When?" she begged.

"A month or two ago," he said. "He has since returned to Kalamaar. A boatman carried him across to the mainland and supposedly saw him heading east."

"East…"

"Did you not hear what I said?" Falmagon replied tersely, clenching his fist. "He attacked me, Maelili! He threatened me, and for no reason. Why would he do that?"

"I…I don't know." She rubbed her forehead looking toward the east. "I must go now."

"W-what?" he stammered.

She reached for him, grabbed the back of his neck, and pulled him close. She forced her lips against his, the bristles of his budding mustache rubbing against her face. The warmth of his skin warmed the chill on the end of her nose. He rumbled in his throat with confusion—or excitement— it did not matter.

She gripped him tighter, Falmagon's long hair brushing against her fingertips. She could feel his heart thumping in his chest. She swore hers matched the rhythm.

Maelili lingered, treasuring the moment.

She pulled away slowly, breathing heavily; Falmagon must have been holding her tightly while they kissed. His face was riddled with uncertainty.

"I must go, Falmagon," she whispered again. She was glad for the cold of the evening, withholding tears in the corners of her eyes. "Thank you, Falmagon. Thank you for everything."

She ran down the road, leaving him standing in the center of Arkaim. When he called after her, Maelili quickened her pace—more than anything, to keep herself from turning back.

Chapter XIV
Maelili

"We need rest, Arkhon," Brigita huffed, pulling her cloak around her arms and shivering. Her weak tone could as easily have been the subtle wind sweeping in from the north. "Not only have we been walking all night, but we have no idea where we are going. The sun will be rising any moment."

"We are going east," Maelili retold her in a cutting tone. The young Stuhia had been extremely vocal since leaving Arkaim, clearly finding it difficult to keep herself silent despite repeated reminders of their duty. Maelili filled her lungs with a breath of cold air, satisfied that Brigita restrained herself from having the last word.

Noting the first signs of daybreak on the skyline ahead, Maelili blew into her chilled hands. Her breath might as well have been nonexistent, having no impact on her icy skin. Hours ago, clouds moved in from the north blocking out the twinkling stars and indicating rain or snow. Luckily, nothing more than dew and drizzle touched their shoulders. She hoped the clouds would disappear by the time the sun peeked over the horizon to provide a bit of warmth, but no such luck existed. The array, now colored pink and blue, decorated the horizon ahead, the outline of northern forests and southern mountains silhouetted in the dawning light.

"We must go east," she reiterated to herself. "East."

"Arkhon," Velkan attempted, bidding to gain her attention from behind Brigita. His level of exhaustion was audible, his footsteps heavily pounding against the earth in an attempt to keep his balance.

She ignored him, stepping faster down the road until she threatened to topple head over heels. She could hear Velkan and Brigita struggling to keep up behind her. Her own legs burned with every footfall, a telltale sign that she needed to rest as badly as her companions. Somehow, she ignored the fatigue coursing through her slender body and allowed her mind to wander.

She could not be certain whether she ran for her brother or from Falmagon. For many miles, she fought against the pained feeling in her chest, knowing she left Falmagon heartbroken and confused in the middle of Arkaim. While she had no intention of hurting him, she knew any explanation she might have given would have led to questions she was unwilling to answer. If she was being honest with herself, she almost hoped he would hunt her down and demand to know the truth. Images of him sweeping her off her feet and passionately kissing her lips dotted her imagination, but he had not followed her to Kal'bane where she collected Velkan and Brigita, nor did he follow her down the road she now trekked.

He respectfully let her leave.

She was not sure if she should hate him or admire him for allowing her to go and decided to chalk it up to his young age and likely mystification at her running off.

Maelili's head and heart were at odds about their last moment together—how she deserted Falmagon and how she wished he would have reacted—though the ceaseless aching in her chest told her which part of her anatomy was winning the battle. She was brimming with regret.

She did all she could to shove thoughts of the young Highborn from her senses, focusing on the gift he unknowingly gave her. For the first time in seventy years or more, her faith in finding her brother was renewed. Kindel was on Kalamaar.

After a league or more, Velkan ultimately reached her side on the worn path between the capital and the town ahead. His feet thudded inches behind her own. "Brigita is right, Arkhon. No matter our optimism, we cannot keep this pace," he advised. "Jh'terin will not be going anywhere."

"It cannot be much farther." Maelili sighed, shivering in the early morning cold. She stopped on the road, holding her side with aggravation. She knew her body could not take much more. Her eyelids longed to close, increasingly heavy from her lack of sleep, and her feet were as sore as her knees. In fact, every muscle in her body begged for an inn with a warm fire and a warmer bath. She crossed her arms, caving to reason, her chin quivering with every word. "Very well, Ser Velkan. We will take a moment to gather ourselves, and then press forward."

She scarcely stopped speaking before Velkan's hand landed on her shoulder. With a gentle tug, he ushered her to the side of the road. A few remaining brown strands of grass caught her eye in the billowing light, suggesting how close they were to the first snows of the season. Even if they found Kindel in the next few days, they would not be able to leave Kalamaar until spring.

She stumbled along next to him before collapsing to the frozen ground beneath her. The dirt was as cold as her boots.

Brigita sat down next to her. Maelili could sense her green eyes examining her, conceivably searching for some sign of weakness in her. She knew she lost favor with Brigita after Falmagon and would possibly never regain her respect. It did not seem so long ago that Maelili considered how she might teach Brigita to become a better Stuhian, to understand the importance of duty and justice—to understand how her heart and her purpose should be one and the same. However, after recent events, Maelili could not say which of them more resembled a child or who intended to aid the other more.

"What did the Highborn say, exactly?" Brigita asked without hesitation. "We have marched for nearly the full of night, hoping to find further signs of your brother in the dead of night. Though I do not know what we are looking for or when we should start looking."

"You forget your place, Brigita. Arkhon Maelili leads, and we follow." Velkan grunted.

Brigita huffed, flicking her hair over her shoulder, disinterested in his words of wisdom. She did not bother addressing him, pointing her small nose at Maelili. "What did he say?" she repeated.

Velkan opened his mouth again, but Maelili silenced him by raising her hand. She caught sight of the back of her knuckles. Little color was visible in her pale skin.

"It is okay, Ser Velkan." She crossed her legs and leaned forward to draw a makeshift map on the ground. She loosely fashioned the western and southern shores of Kalamaar. "We landed here on the western coast and, in the past month, traveled east to Farmas, north to Jh'terin, and then west to Arkaim. From what we have learned," she continued to dig her finger into the hard ground, "Melkorka is directly south of Farmas, over this mountain range and across a channel of water. The Highborn we met," she swallowed hard, refusing to say his name, "said Kindel was last seen on this southern shore. He was heading east. The plan is to travel back to Farmas in the same way we came, and then follow after him."

"Falmagon was certain this man was Kindel?" Brigita asked, filling in the blank name with a clipped tone.

Maelili slowly nodded. "He said the red-haired man had a crooked staff resembling Habermani. No other has fit the description of my brother or my father's staff so closely."

Brigita exhaled. "And how long ago did he see him?"

"A month or more." Maelili gritted her teeth, knowing how ridiculous the notion sounded; then again, she reminded herself that the three of them traveled across a continent based on information that was years old at best. "If he has been on Kalamaar all this time, he would not disappear in the past months. We will find him."

Velkan hummed with approval, despite Brigita's looming frown. He kneeled next to Maelili. "We have not had a better sign in decades. We will find Kindel, Arkhon."

Maelili clamped his left arm with her right hand, barely feeling the brawn of the man in her numb grip. "We will, and then we will return to our families."

Brigita snubbed Maelili's attempt at giving a few words of inspiration. "You mentioned last night that Falmagon was attacked by the man he saw," Brigita said, falling back on her haunches. She tucked her hands inside the folds of her cloak as a whistling wind whipped across the area. "Should we be worried your brother has gone mad? Or should we think the Highborn are not to be trusted?"

The last question rolled off her tongue like poison from a viper's fang.

Velkan answered before Maelili could, sharing his insight in a gentler tone than Brigita deserved. "Wild speculation will only lead us to suspicion and vile thoughts. Both will impede our ability to see our duty done." He patted Maelili's hand on his arm. "We know Kindel exists somewhere in this land. The better question is whether he truly went east, or he wished to mislead those who watched him wander off."

"What do you mean? Why would he do that?" Brigita lifted an eyebrow.

"The claim is he attacked a Highborn, who certainly are respected in this part of the world. I never met an ignorant Kluk. If he thought he might be pursued, he could have doubled back and gone another way without being seen." Velkan snorted, scratching at the beginnings of a beard resurfacing on his cheek and chin. "I mean, what exists to the east besides the wilderness? I have not heard a single Northman mention there being a civilization beyond Farmas."

Brigita nodded. "You are right. Only forests and mountains exist beyond the forked river. That is what we have heard."

"What are you saying?" Maelili's heart hurt at the implied meaning. She could not risk facing Falmagon again. "We cannot go back to Arkaim."

"No, Arkhon," Velkon assured her. "We should continue to Farmas and even farther if we must. But I would suggest we stay alert every step of the way. Your brother may be closer than we think."

Chapter XV
FALMAGON

Andrik nudged Falmagon's shoulder with the edge of his shoe, speaking in a croaked whisper. "Come on. It is time we got moving."

Falmagon cleared his throat. He thought he heard Andrik moving around some time ago but had been too tired to open his eyes. "What time is it?" he mumbled, feeling a slight burn in the back of his throat.

"Early," Andrik faintly said.

Falmagon squinted his eyes and slowly sat up, pushing the blanket from his chest. Even with the wool covering removed, the heaviness over his heart stayed. The last couple of days were nearly more than he could bear. He rubbed the sleep from his eyes, forgetting whatever dream he had been dreaming, seeing the shape of Andrik turning away from him. The blue hue of the sky, absent of the sun's light, told him the break of dawn was nearing. Regardless of sleep, exhaustion stripped the strength from his muscles and bones.

With a quick glance, he noticed Andrik had already doused their fire and packed his own belongings. "You have been busy." Falmagon figured his companion must have been awake for more than an hour to get so much done.

"Let's go."

Falmagon grimaced. Since parting from Arkaim two days ago, Andrik had become increasingly short with him. No doubt a result of Falmagon humping Maelili, meaning Andrik was holding to either some righteous sense of disappointment or incessant jealousy. Either way, he'd said nothing more since leaving Kal'bane. All in all, Falmagon was grateful Andrik kept his opinion to himself; he had no interest in entertaining his insolence.

Falmagon could not be sure he could keep up with Andrik right now anyway. He was haunted with lingering thoughts of Maelili, and talking about her would only make his emotions more real. She was already the first thought each morning and the last each night. Even now, her smile danced through his mind. Speaking her name would, without a doubt, prolong his agony.

In addition, he could not shake the fact that her brother had been the one who attacked him on Melkorka. Since leaving Arkaim, he had dubbed the brother with the epithet, Kindel the Red.

The name seemed fitting.

"The way back to Melkorka will be challenging enough without your attitude," Falmagon dared to say, watching Andrik shuffle farther away. The shorter man deliberately refused to look Falmagon in the eye. He could not believe such childish behavior.

"I don't know what you are talking about," Andrik replied, reaching down for his pack. He heaved the sack onto his back. "Grab your stuff. You can eat some jerky while we walk."

"I am not hungry," Falmagon snipped back in equal measure. He swung his feet out from under his blanket and grabbed his boots. He and Andrik had no choice but to walk the length of the coastline back to Valishul—or at least south of the village—where they would, with any luck, find a boatman to take them across the channel to Folkmar. As he had expected, no boatman in Arkaim had been willing to sail so far in the freezing waters, leaving the two of them to travel south on foot. With little food in their packs and no guaranteed shelter, Falmagon remained hopeful they could return to Melkorka before the first real snowfall. Though with the scent of winter hanging on the morning air, he doubted their chances were good. "We will do better to save what provisions Unnvar gave us."

Andrik grunted and turned to face the south.

Falmagon took as much time as he dared, rolling his bedroll and examining the rolling waves of Strega's Deep to the west and then the mountains to the east, which had barely been visible when setting up camp last night.

Nothing but the countryside existed for miles.

Andrik stood several feet away with his nose turned up and his arms crossed, remaining speechless while Falmagon worked in silence. He waited until he saw Andrik's ears redden—he hoped from frustration and not the cold—and then rose to begin their trek.

League after league, they walked in silence with Falmagon leading and Andrik stamping behind him like a stubborn mule. The other Highborn's constant blustering and random low growls, which seemed to be more for show than anything more, were easier and easier to ignore with each passing step. After a while, Falmagon did not hear Andrik any more than he did his own breath.

Before long, the edge of the mountain range they slept near disappeared behind them, opening the landscape to rolling hills and grasslands stretching east. Falmagon peered across the land from time to time, noticing nothing more stirred in any direction. Soon, a second set of mountains appeared farther south. He kept their heading along the coast, secretly hoping the Lightbringer would decide to show his face before night returned.

Falmagon chose to eat a few tidbits when he and Andrik rested around midday, and then without a word, they set off again. By and by, Falmagon found he rather liked the quiet, surrounded by the sound of the wind whipping against the outside of his hooded cloak and the crash of the surf in the distance. His heart ached for Maelili, but outside of losing her, he was content in knowing he had completed the task given to him by Kinhar.

It took many hours, but when Falmagon eventually found the willpower to stop thinking of Maelili, he reflected on what he learned at Arkaim and imagined what he might tell Kinhar upon returning to Melkorka.

He rubbed his growing mustache in deep thought. Erzebeth Navenka confirmed Kinhar's concerns about the perils simmering at Melkorka and even went as far as suggesting an enemy would spur the Highborn's doom. While Erzebeth claimed they could not escape the forthcoming demons, she did say they would have the advantage if Falmagon was willing to slaughter the right Red.

The suggestion caused his throat to tighten considerably to the point that his feet faltered while he walked over the flat terrain. Based on her description, he only knew three people with red hair. First, he knew the Highborn, Faina Zholdan, a middle-aged woman who scarcely said more than what was needed to be said. From his upbringing at Melkorka, he knew her to be a gentle woman with a sweet smile and a sweeter heart.

Kindel, the brother of Maelili, was the second. Falmagon absolutely believed the man was a danger. From the moment Kindel attacked him on Folkmar, including the threats he whispered in Falmagon's ear, Maelili's brother seemed to have every intention of ruining the Highborn. Yet he was the brother of the woman Falmagon loved, and despite his hostile words, the stranger had not been seen in months. He seemed far removed from the Highborn and Melkorka.

And lastly, Falmagon knew Nedezhda Mager, the Longwalker, a woman who was meant to be a mentor to the Highborn apprentices and an envoy to the Northmen. Kinhar did not trust Nedezhda, believing her to be audacious and outspoken, always challenging his commands, even though he was their Spearhead. While Falmagon heard the testimony of Andrik and Erzebeth marking Nedezhda as being different from the other Highborn—practicing her *death* magic to warp Koldovstvo to keep herself young and vigorous—he also knew Unnvar's story of his own birth, which identified Nedezhda as possibly being his mother.

How could he kill his own mother?

The prospect of Nedezhda giving birth to him disturbed Falmagon, and not just because he often considered her to be prettier than the other women at Melkorka. The web of lies is what really caused his blood to boil. Of course, he was not so rash as to start screaming at the heavens—no matter how much his emotions urged him to let loose—but if she were his mother, he wanted to know why she never said anything.

He gritted his teeth. To have a child in secret, Nedezhda would have needed to be gone from Melkorka for an extended period of time. He suspected if the other Highborn knew she was pregnant with an Anshedar's child, she could have been challenged to step down as their chosen Longwalker; or perhaps telling the truth about Falmagon would have risked revealing her dark magic, considering she presently looked to be only a few years older.

Yet the most disturbing thought for Falmagon was that, if it were true, perhaps Nedezhda did not even know he was her son.

Without warning, Andrik rushed to Falmagon's side and grabbed his arm, gesturing ahead with an excited shout. "What in the Nine Lands is that?"

Falmagon jumped back, jerking away from Andrik in a frenzy. His eyes zipped to and fro to gain perspective. He and Andrik had nearly reached the second set of mountains and the sun was dipping in the west. The land and grasses were turning bronze in the failing light.

He had completely lost track of time.

"By Mulafell, Andrik! Why are you yelling? You scared me half to death."

"Look." Andrik pointed.

He followed his finger to the mutilated corpse of an Anshedar lying sprawled out on the dirt almost thirty feet away. Falmagon swallowed to keep the acidic bile in this throat from spewing from his lips.

Splattered blood stained the withered grass alongside a gruesome path of smeared blood trailing off toward the mountainside as though something had been dragged away. At first glance, he could not tell if the figure was male or female, but once he inched closer, he noticed the strong cheekbones and flat chest of a young boy, not much younger than himself.

To the left and right of the mangled body were distinct claw prints. The markings appeared large, almost twice the size of Falmagon's foot, and were surprisingly deep in the hardened earth, giving some indication of the size of whatever beast created them.

"What do you make of it?"

"A bear attack, maybe? Killed the boy and took the larger prize. Perhaps the boy's father..." Falmagon rasped, his voice trailing off.

A blood-curdling cry, high-pitched and menacing, echoed from the mountain ahead, causing Falmagon to hold his breath. He snapped his head toward the sound in time to see a shadowed, lanky creature skitter across the landscape and over a hill out of sight, pulling a hefty body with only one hand. At a distance, the thing looked like a distorted Anshedar with long arms and longer legs.

Andrik stumbled back. "That was not a bear. That was unlike any animal I have ever seen."

"Yeah," Falmagon managed. He clenched his fist, pulled his shoulders back, and waited for the creature to appear again. After only a few breaths, the same gurgling bellow reached his ears, followed by the cry of someone in pain, but the beast stayed out of sight.

Andrik scratched at the tuft of hair on his head. "What should we do?"

Falmagon was quick to reply. "We pursue it and protect the Northman if we can."

They were Highborn, after all.

Without an argument, Falmagon led the way, stooped over and hurrying ahead on his toes in an attempt to keep the sound of his movements quiet. He hastened across the terrain with his hands hovering inches above the ground, ready for the beast to spring from the grasses ahead without warning. He soon discovered moving quietly was futile. The dry grass rustling against his boots sounded like falling rain, and the dirt crunching under his toes might as well have been thunder.

The crags rose at a steady incline as they neared with the distant landscape dimming in the fading light. About the time they reached the top of the hill where the creature had dipped from sight, Falmagon could scarcely see twenty feet in front of them.

"It could not have gone far," Falmagon said.

Andrik's eyes were sharp. "There is a cave up ahead," he whispered, gesturing to the rising mountain. Falmagon inched forward, making out a bleak ingress against the flat of the rock. Andrik tugged at Falmagon's arm. "Should I give us some light?"

Falmagon rubbed his hands against his pant legs, feeling the sweat surfacing on his palms. Every bit of Koldovstvo they cast was life wasted. He gulped. "No, I will do it. Stay alert."

Reaching beyond the physical world, Falmagon embraced Koldovstvo, feeling the warmth of the magic run through his veins. With a simple thought, a yellow orb, burning as bright as firelight, materialized in front of him. The light illuminated the area, almost twenty feet in all directions, including the entrance to the cave.

Nothing moved.

Andrik sighed with relief. "I will lead the way," he said, nearing the mouth to the cave, "but I am burning the first thing I see move."

"Do not hurt the Anshedar," Falmagon said, easing in behind him.

Andrik did not respond, craning his neck to see into the cave. The ground sloped down and to the right, giving no indication of what could be ahead. In the magical light, Falmagon could see the muddy mess of blood and soft dirt mixed together under their feet.

Andrik flared his nostrils. "We may find what took the man, if it was a man, but I doubt we will find him alive."

Falmagon nudged him in the back. "Get moving, then. We are wasting time."

Andrik skittered down the slope while Falmagon kept the orb hovering in front of him by several paces. At times the light dimmed, but for the most part, he did well in maintaining his concentration on the magic. With his mind, he was able to whip the orb back and forth in front of Andrik, keeping the narrow path well lit.

After only a few steps, Falmagon gathered the hovel was not nearly as deep as he first guessed. The curved path swiftly opened into a wide cavity almost twice the size of his cottage back home in both height and width. The smell of damp rocks, decay, and fresh feces made him nauseous, but the sloshing sounds of flesh and meat being mashed between teeth is what ultimately caused him to gag.

He grabbed at his stomach in disgust.

Andrik became rigid. "We are too late."

Falmagon braced himself, whispering a prayer to the Lightbringer, and then sluggishly glanced over Andrik's shoulder. Besides the light of the orb, the hollow was pitch black. He guided the light forward with Koldovstvo, eliminating the shadows from the area.

Hunched in the center of the room, an ash-grey monster crouched with its bony elbows resting on its knees, tearing at the corpse at its feet with savage claws. The beast's dark bulbous eyes flashed around the room, widening in the yellow hue of the orb.

The monster shifted away from the light.

Falmagon clenched his jaw, seeing the rotting skin clinging to the bone and sinew of the hairless, unclothed monster. "A demon!" he hissed.

"Erzebeth's warning was true," Andrik gasped.

The demon's death howl echoed off the rock, drowning their words. Whipping its head like a startled serpent, the demon gurgled and tossed the corpse to the side with ease. The demon then rose to its full height, standing almost a head and a half taller than Falmagon.

"Gods!" Andrik cried.

The enormous demon charged, lifting its gangly arms from either side of its long legs, reaching for them. Falmagon reared back as the monster bared its sharpened fangs within its rotting mouth.

"Burn it!" Falmagon screamed in horror, losing control of the orb and extinguishing the light.

Fire erupted from Andrik's fingertips as Falmagon leaped sideways. The flames crackled the air, the orangey blaze replacing what light had been lost.

Falmagon twisted to face the lumbering, shrieking demon as the fire ripped at its decaying skin. The heat burned his cheeks and stung at his eyes. With a battle cry, Falmagon let fire take shape from his own hands, allowing the power of Koldovstvo to fill him as easily as breath did his lungs. The flames stole the chill from his bones, but since he was the one who crafted the magic, he was safe from the blistering heat.

The demon fought against the fire for several steps before turning to run, wildly swinging its clawed hands at Falmagon and Andrik. The hungry howl of the beast turned into a fierce cry and then a whimper as it struggled against the grime on the floor, attempting to flee.

"Kill it!" Falmagon screamed. "Do not let it escape!"

Andrik shouted all the louder, courageously approaching the beast and intensifying his magic. The colors of his flame changed from orange to red, and then to purple and blue. Falmagon lowered his hands watching Andrik. The Highborn bawled with ferocity—with madness—not stopping until the demon fell to the ground and stopped twitching.

Falmagon watched Andrik with concern in the darkness. The smoldering flames dimmed over the demon's body. "Are you okay?"

Andrik grunted.

Falmagon matched the tone, then neared the charred carcass. He recast the orb of light. "Where did this demon come from?"

Andrik continued to say nothing for several moments, covering his mouth. He glanced to where the dead body of the Anshedar had been flung, touching his own cheek with hesitation. "How many years did we lose?"

Low snarls and growls resonated from the back of the cave, drawing his attention to another footpath leading deeper into the mountain.

Something more stirred below.

"Never mind that, Andrik," Falmagon said, speaking as boldly as he could. "Youth is fleeting and duty calls."

Chapter XVI

FALMAGON

Falmagon's hope dwelt with the Lightbringer, keeping the faith that his fate was not to die beneath this mountain.

The trail twisted like knotted snakes, winding one way and then another without any rhyme or reason. He pursued the low echoing rumbles of the demons as well as he could, doubting whether he would ever see the sun again. Attempting to determine where the hum of the beasts originated by navigating the forked paths was hopeless. In short time, he counted half a dozen split trails since entering the first tunnel, but after doubling back twice, he'd already lost the way back to the surface. His rough plan for exiting the damp hole was to seek out the inclined paths, no matter how slight, but first he must find the monsters below.

He would succeed. He was Highborn; he was Kadari. He was chosen.

"We are lost," Andrik said under his breath.

Falmagon snorted with condemnation, keeping his eye on the ball of light he had crafted. With fear of losing more years, Andrik had retreated behind him the moment they entered the deeper passageways, all the while refusing to take a turn in casting the light.

"We are where we are meant to be," Falmagon muttered, furtively glancing over his shoulder.

"I do not think anyone is meant to be down here," Andrik frowned. "We should turn back, Falmagon. We know Erzebeth's warning to be true. Demons exist and they are reaching the surface. Let us leave this place and return to Melkorka. We must inform Kinhar."

Falmagon scowled and shook his head. He planned to tell the Spearhead everything, including Andrik's cowardice, which completely overrode his courageous act in Falmagon's mind. "We need to know what we are up against. One demon does not constitute a threat."

"Nine Lands, it doesn't!" Andrik bellowed a bit too loudly. "We can hear them well enough. Why must we put eyes on them?" As if responding to his claim, Falmagon heard the grating sounds of teeth grinding and nails scraping against rock ahead. He could not guess how far away the beasts roamed, but the sound sent a chill up his spine. Andrik went on, oblivious to the increased ruckus. "If we die down here no one will know the truth. What if we find an Anshedar half dead, and we cannot return with him?"

"What of it?"

"Will you kill him to ease his suffering? You may be able to kill a demon, but can you take the life of the living?" Andrik snapped. "What if I fall? You are not a healer! Will you kill me or leave me to be eaten by demons?"

"I will do whatever I must," Falmagon said.

"What does that mean?" Andrik cried out.

"It means that I will not collapse under the weight of my duty. Turn back if you want," Falmagon retorted, picking up the pace as though he would leave Andrik behind. "I will not stop until I know the numbers of our enemy."

"You are going to get us killed," Andrik argued. He grabbed Falmagon's cloak and forcibly jerked him around. The might of the Highborn was impressive, almost as though he used Koldovstvo to strengthen his effort. "Who are you trying to impress, Falmagon? Your one-night harlot is gone. She left you!"

"What? How dare you!" Falmagon roared, shoving Andrik off him too forcefully. The light wavered over him as he struggled to keep the magic alive. Andrik could not maintain his balance, and the force knocked him off his feet. He buckled, kneeling to the dirt with a grunt. Falmagon hovered over him, bringing the orb of light to his shoulder and seeing fear dancing in Andrik's eyes. "You are taken by weakness and have the nerve to question me. I am performing my duty as a Longwalker!"

Andrik lifted his nose in defiance, his fat lips shaking with every word. "You are unfit to be a Longwalker; you will never hold the title. You're careless and…and conceited. Why would Kinhar allow you to speak for the Highborn?" His pupils constricted in the weak light. "Nedezhda is our Longwalker!"

Falmagon loomed over him, dropping his voice considerably. "You know nothing!"

"I know chasing after demons is reckless!" Andrik cried, hardly hearing Falmagon. "I will tell Kinhar how stupidly you have behaved."

Falmagon gritted his teeth, fighting the urge to ball his fingers into a fist. He was not concerned about Kinhar questioning him, let alone punishing him. He was fulfilling his duty to the Highborn. Kinhar would see that. Andrik was a fool. "Then run away," Falmagon whispered nastily. "Run back to Melkorka and tell Kinhar your little tales. We will see who he believes when I return."

"I will," Andrik spoke in an exasperated breath, eyeing Falmagon uneasily. He repeated himself as he scrambled to his feet. "I will tell him everything. You would be wise to come with me unless you want to die at the hands of a demon."

Falmagon growled. "Do not pretend that you care about me. Leave me!"

Andrik tensed in the feeble light. He kept his gaze firmly on Falmagon for only a moment and then hung his head. The growls of the demons beneath them reverberated through the tunnel.

Without another word, Falmagon left Andrik standing in the dark and descended toward the gnashing demons below.

He smirked to himself as he crunched down the path, holding himself steady against the uneven walls. He found some satisfaction in knowing Andrik would have to use magic to find his way out. Casting the orb of light would not wilt his body much, unlike the fire he wielded against the demon, which likely snuffed several weeks or even a couple of months from his life. But if he wanted to find the surface again, he would be forced to embrace Koldovstvo. No man, Highborn or otherwise, had any hope of traversing these tunnels without a guiding light.

He would not be surprised if he found Andrik curled up and weeping in the dark on his way back out.

Falmagon despised Andrik for daring to think he was being brave for Maelili. The man was completely caught up in his own delusional musings. Maelili had nothing to do with Falmagon's sense of valor. He was not a weakling. He was a Highborn. He was bound to keep the Seven Islands and the Anshedar safe; and if the underearth was swarming with demonic spawn, he would stand at the forefront of the battle, ready and willing to defend those loyal to the White-Clad.

Kinhar said the Lightbringer imbued the Highborn with Koldovstvo and picked Falmagon to be among the chosen, the Kadari. The knowledge encouraged Falmagon to his place and his purpose. He would not turn his back on a god who gifted him with such power. If Dahz the Lightbringer really was the Protector of Man, Falmagon would be his shield.

"See me through," he prayed.

The sound of the demons amplified with each step, but Falmagon refused to feel fear. Clenching his fists, he kept the light steady next to him and grounded himself, focusing on the cold seeping from the walls to his fingers. The demons would not be able to compete against the might of Koldovstvo.

Falmagon would defeat them.

Small demons zipped toward him, flying at his orb. The swift beasts startled him at first, with their bat-like wings fluttering on either side of their gaunt bodies, complete with arms and legs. They peeped and squeaked, turning their diminutive, horned skulls back and forth as though they were communicating with one another.

Acting on impulse, he used sky magic and created a burst of air to fling the lot of them into the wall. The bones in their bodies splintered and their heads cracked on impact, replacing their screeches with shrill cries and then silence. The quiet of the cavern was replaced with the gnashing and scraping of bigger demons below.

Falmagon stepped by the still bodies of the little monsters without taking a second glance. He wished all demons were as easy to dispose of.

Step by step, he listened to his feet scrape and crunch against the cave floor. The cacophony of death echoed below, intensifying, calling for him. Challenging him to come forward and see its face. His thumping heart rattled his rib cage. His head throbbed along with the blood pulsating in his temples.

He did not journey far beyond the array of small demons before the shadow of a lumbering beast blocked the path ahead.

Falmagon slowed, gripping at the wall for support. Even in the darkness, he could tell the monster was the same as the one he and Andrik crossed near the mouth of the cave at the surface.

Whether the orb floating above him marked his position or not, Falmagon knew he would not have been capable of hiding from the demon. The undead monster caught his scent, slanting its bestial face toward him and sniffing. An eerie rumble reverberated from its throat as it rotated its hulking body to face Falmagon. The extended claws scraping against the floor chilled his skin; the raucous noise itched the inside of his ear.

The demon lumbered at him.

He fought the desire to flee, fire forming at the end of his fingers.

The beast's bloodthirsty howl rang out, while the firestorm filled the tunnel—yet the monster was not slowed by the destructive flames. Even as its flesh ignited, blackening and bubbling, it lunged for the Highborn. In a breath, the ghastly, foul demon emerged through the orange and red blaze. Blackened eyes and bared fangs came within inches of Falmagon, spitting saliva with an untamed roar. Falmagon faltered, rearing back as pointed claws raked through the air, splitting the flames in twain and striking him across the chest.

The fabric of his cloak and tunic frayed from shoulder to sternum, and the skin of his chest ripped open. His magical inferno dwindled to nothingness and the orb of light winked from existence. He felt wetness touch the edge of his eyes in shock. His throat closed, pain searing through him. The demon rose to its full height in front of him in the failing light, its head scraping the ceiling.

The cave went dark.

He could not die down here. He was chosen by the Lightbringer. Kinhar promised.

The monster clearly was not hindered by the dark; it struck him again, pitching him sideways into the solid wall. Falmagon threw his left arm up in desperation to temper the impact, protecting his head from smashing against the rock. He cried out, the small bones in his wrist immediately cracking, shooting pain to his elbow.

He slumped over, somehow managing to keep his feet under him. Warm blood seeped down the front of his chest and stomach, sticking his clothes to his skin. A crunch behind him gave little warning before the demon clenched him by his clothes above his shoulder blades and slammed him into the wall. His left arm fell to his side, while his right hand prevented his nose and face from being crushed under the weight of the larger creature. Soil and dust rained down over him as the demon leaned against him.

"By Mulafell," he cursed, choking, managing to get a foot planted against the base of the wall for leverage. The soreness lessened in his body with the threat of death.

The demon hissed, an unnatural clacking rising from the pit of its throat. The stench of decay suffocated Falmagon as the creature bent closer. In desperation, he wriggled against the strength of the beast.

Fangs suddenly impaled his left shoulder, digging into the muscle and spouting blood.

Falmagon screamed, forgetting what other demons may be lying in wait farther down the path. Koldovstvo poured through him. He created a whirlwind of air to push off the wall, hurling him and the giant demon back into the opposite side of the tunnel. He grunted, slamming into the frame of the beast. The ceiling quaked, drizzling them with more dirt. The thing snarled vehemently, ripping its mouth free from Falmagon and releasing its clawed grip.

Dropping to the earth, Falmagon groaned, gripping his injured chest. He rolled away using his right hand as best he could to crawl away and shift into a crouching position. His head spun from the pain, but he knew the demon would not forget him so easily. The din of more monsters rasping and growling arose from the depths, drumming off the enclosed walls.

He kept Koldovstvo empowered in his mind, not caring how many years he would lose. He produced an orb of light above him, its glow allowing him to see through the speckled dust continuing to fall from above. The enraged demon snapped at the air where he'd stood a moment before, and then charged.

The demon only took a single step before Falmagon used magic to elevate it off its feet. The beast hung in the air for a moment, flailing and clawing at him, and then was thrown down the tunnel from whence it had come. Falmagon fought against the darkness clouding the corners of his eyes. He remained crouched in the darkened burrow, making the light follow the demon's descent. He knew his hold could not falter while the demon was still so close. The monster shrieked an unearthly cry, helplessly scrabbling at the underearth in an attempt to slow its forced retreat.

When the demon disappeared from sight, Falmagon lost control of the magic. He tried to fight back another cough, his chest burning. Holding himself upright with his right hand, he scooted across the ground, listening to faint growling. His left arm ached to the point that he thought he might faint.

The snarling increased in volume, suggesting the demon was skittering back to finish him. Even with Koldovstvo, Falmagon knew he would not last another round with the beast. Blood dribbled from the corner of his mouth. He wiped it away, peering down the tunnel. In the dim light of his distant orb, Falmagon saw several shadows racing up from the pathway ahead.

"Gods," he croaked, coughing without restraint. An army of dead resided in this nasty hole.

They would tear him to pieces.

With a pained grunt, he again allowed the magic to pull at his senses. His chest tightened under the stress of Koldovstvo; every breath wheezing through him threatened to be his last. He used his magic to pull at the rock, dirt, and filth circling the burrow ahead. The ceiling and walls shifted. Powdered earth misted the path ahead, dampening his view considerably. The first demon appeared in the hazed light as a large hunk of earth crumbled from the ceiling. The demon growled, stepping backward. The falling section sparked several more chunks to crumble, pulling rock and stone, stealing all light.

The din of screeching demons faded from Falmagon's senses and he slipped into unconsciousness.

The sound of nails clicking and picking at rocks awoke him. His eyes fluttered open to be met with the same blackness found beneath his eyelids. He could not say how long he'd lain on the hardened ground with a rock wedged against his spine and a thick layer of dust covering him. He simply listened to the demons scraping at the rubble, rasping with hunger for his bloodied body. He felt hopeless to stop them.

He waited.

The sound of movement seemed to echo from all around him. He hoped the whole tunnel did not fold in on him.

Falmagon's chest and left shoulder stung as though daggers pierced his flesh, causing him to convulse wildly. He was certain blood pooled beneath him, making a mud in the grime. He could not hold back the guttural moans that escaped his lips with nearly every breath, and he squeezed his eyes shut as though the pressure might redirect his attention from the agony.

Some comfort came in knowing he was alive, although clearly dying. His mind wandered to thoughts of the Lightbringer, where he suspected he should have placed focus to begin with, and he prayed.

"Dahz…Protector of Men," Falmagon sputtered, his good hand gripping a handful of soil at his side. He painted pictures in his mind of the Lightbringer riding in his chariot, wielding the Hammer of Righteousness. "Come on *Mioengi* wielding Mulafell and save me from this darkness. If I should die, take me to the Netherworld so I may walk among the gods at Thrice Ten Kingdom."

He coughed again, his words failing him. He raised his hand and covered his mouth. The small hairs on his face scratched at his palm, and he almost wept. He wondered how much of his life he whittled away. With the pain coursing through his muscles and joints, he could have been any age, even as old as Dorofej or Kinhar.

"Oh, Lightbringer. Protect me," he struggled to say. He could taste salt and copper in his throat. "If my charge is not complete, see me back to Melkorka. See me home."

The earth shifted down the tunnel again, sending rocks clattering from the pile of rubble that kept him safe from the bloodthirsty monsters. The growling demons were abruptly louder.

The sound of quick footsteps near the back of his head caused him to freeze. He held his breath; his heart stilled in terror. One of the demons may have broken through, yet nothing attacked him.

He waited for a moment, and then whispered as loud as he dared. "Andrik?"

Silence.

With the rising racket of the demons, he had no choice but to cast light again. For all he knew, the cavern was shifting from the weight of the earth above him, and he was alone in the darkness.

He cleared his mind, forming the orangey glow of the orb above him.

Falmagon wheezed, his head growing light. The face of the stranger—Maelili's brother, Kindel the Red—hovered only inches above him. His red hair glimmered, angling the crooked staff on his shoulder.

The magic faded.

Kindel pressed the butt of his staff against Falmagon's chin and forced his head sideways. His strange accent echoed off the walls. "Good. You are not dead yet."

Month of Slaughter
Third of Frost
118 CE

Chapter XVII

FALMAGON

The sound of creaking wheels jostled Falmagon from fevered dreams. He sputtered awake with his mouth drier than ashes, eyes fluttering against the weakened sun rays. His body felt numb from head to toe. He grunted, recoiling from the glimmering rays of the Lightbringer. The sunlight was surprisingly warm in comparison to the frigid cold that stung at his cheeks.

He moaned faintly, lying on his back with his arms extended over his head. He tried to pull his arms down, only to discover he simply tugged against rope restraints binding his wrists. His hands throbbed and tingled.

Grunting, he tucked his chin to his chest to see the far-reaching horizon on the opposite side of his feet. While the sky remained clear, powdered snow blanketed every blade of grass across the low-rolling hills. He fell back against the wooden cart, straining against the ties again, realizing the full of his condition. His legs were set, woven against the baseboard with a thick rope. The knotted binding threaded through the boards, up and over his legs several times from his thighs to his ankles. As he inspected the handiwork, an ache crept over his body, bespeaking his injuries still raw and fresh. His lesions did not appear to be bleeding, but he was far from better. The simple effort of examining the cart caused him to grow lightheaded. He fought against the urge to return to sleep.

With resolve, he craned his neck, stifling the cough that built up in the base of his throat. Obstructing his view from the driver's seat were several dead rabbits and foxes swaying on a piece of twine stretch over him. The carcasses were already cleaned, dried with blood, hanging inches from his face. He wrinkled his nose, thankful the cold stole away the smell.

Darkness touched the corners of his eyes, and he was forced to lay his head down before dreams took him.

He focused on the clopping of the horses' hooves and the hum of the driver. The two sounds were quiet compared to the squeaking wheels. He could hear nothing more, further hinting at his isolation from civilization. He was alone out here with whoever had tied him.

The end of the crooked staff bouncing over his head drew his attention. The stick was slanted only slightly over the seat, just far enough to dance in Falmagon's vision. Fear pricked at his chest, suddenly recalling how Kindel had materialized next to him in the cave moments before the demons burrowed through the fallen rock. He needed the staff to escape. He needed the staff for the Highborn.

Before Falmagon could consider if he was dreaming or how Kindel the Red could have dragged him from the hole in the ground, a harsh cough tore through his throat, rocking his head back and hitting the planks with a crack.

Worse yet, the effort sent a sharp sting railing down his neck and shoulders. He cringed, holding his breath, wondering if the cuts in his chest and the wounds in his shoulder had reopened.

"Whoa," Kindel's accented tone resounded as he pulled the cart to a stop. A single horse whinnied and snorted.

Falmagon fought against the scratch in his throat, trying to keep himself from deteriorating into a complete coughing fit. He could feel the burn in his nostrils. He tried to focus on Kindel while chewing on his tongue in an attempt to make saliva in his mouth. He swallowed what little spit he could muster, offering a momentary reprieve.

He listened to Kindel dismount from the seat and land with a thud on the ground. Footsteps crunched against the frost as he walked around the cart. Falmagon saw the red strands of Kindel's hair through the side boards, bright against the colorless backdrop.

Before he could decide whether he should pretend to fall back unconscious or face his captor, Kindel jumped up on the cart, standing over his bound legs. His dark cloak whipped behind him as he stared Falmagon in the eye.

The shadow of the man blocked the light of the White-Clad, making him a blotch against the blue-white sky. After several long moments, Kindel shifted his stance, and Falmagon easily recognized the blue eyes and flaming hair of Maelili's brother.

He grinned, holding the staff outright in his hand as though it were an extension of his body. "I am Kindel Kluk, son of Jonafel Kluk. What is your name?"

"Falmagon," he croaked. "Falmagon Sej."

"You are the boy I met on the island south of here near that crumbling castle, are you not?" he asked. He tilted his chin up. "Tell me the truth. Were you following me?"

"No," Falmagon said hoarsely, spitting his long brown hair from the corner of his mouth. His blood boiled at the sight of Kindel. "I am not your enemy. Untie me."

"Oh, but you are my enemy," Kindel said, clicking his tongue on the roof of his mouth. "While I admit you can hardly be blamed for your position, you are anything but an ally. You wield magic never meant for you. I will see that magic is eradicated from all your kind. One thing Aenar does not need is more arrogant mages."

Falmagon coughed again, his throat drying all the more with every word. "You do not understand…" His muscles tensed, his throat itching uncontrollably. "The gods gifted us with magic to…protect…the Northmen. To protect you…"

"Hardly!" Kindel laughed at him. "Hold on. You are going to startle the horse." He pulled a water skin from his belt and knelt, popping the top from the container. Falmagon gulped ravenously at the clear liquid as Kindel dumped it over his lips. The water was colder than the wind, stinging at his chapped skin. He suspected the missed drops would freeze in the hours to come. Kindel pulled the water skin back, then pushed away the red strands of hair that fell over his eyes. Falmagon could see grey patches among the crimson. Kindel grunted. "Let us hope you do not die in the days ahead. We will be at my homestead in a few days, if you can last. Then I can better tend to your wounds."

Falmagon sighed, laying his head back. His chest and shoulder stung, but he could tell he was not bleeding any longer. "If I am your enemy, why would you care for me?"

"I can learn more from you if you are alive," Kindel said.

Falmagon did his best to sneer at Kindel, knowing his face was probably bloodied and swollen from the fight against the demons. "You want to know about the Highborn? We are the Protectors of the Seven Islands and Kalamaar."

"Are you? I cannot say you have done a very good job of saving these people, *Half-blood*."

"The Highborn have protected them for hundreds of years." Falmagon scowled, unfamiliar with the epithet Kindel gave him. Kindel looked at Falmagon blankly as though his assertion meant very little. Falmagon clenched his jaw. "How long have I been out?"

"Days? Almost a week?" he answered. "I cannot rightly say. You have gathered yourself a few times to drink something before dozing off again."

"Where are we?"

"A long way from where I found you, and even farther from your castle. Though knowing our whereabouts hardly matters," Kindel said. "You will not be returning to your friends. I can assure you."

Falmagon gulped.

He could not be certain if Kindel meant he would forever be a prisoner or if he intended to eventually kill him. "What did you do to Andrik?"

"Your short friend?" He smiled, creases forming at the corners of his eyes. "I watched him run south. I suspect he went home, leaving you to die at the hand of the Witiko."

"The demon?"

"Yes, the demon," Kindel scoffed. He leaned on his staff, studying Falmagon, and then shook his head in clear disappointment. "Some friends you have, fleeing from the first sign of monsters. About as heroic as a field mouse."

"He always was a spineless bastard," Falmagon grimaced.

Kindel chuckled. "At least we can agree on that, which is why I snagged you instead."

Falmagon gave him a questioning look.

"You will see what I mean soon enough." He waved his hand at Falmagon soothingly. "You may be eased in knowing Andrik, as you called him, did not know I was there any more than you did. I was waiting in the hills, tracking the Witiko long before you stumbled across my path. Interesting how fate brought us together once more."

Falmagon coughed lightly. His head ached, making it difficult to understand exactly what Kindel was admitting and what he was keeping secret. "You were tracking the demon?"

"Yes," Kindel replied, looking over his shoulder at the skyline. "I brought a Northman all the way from Farmas to help lure the beast. Though it took almost two days to get the demon to come out from its hole. I thought the poor man would die from his injuries long beforehand, but he lasted."

"What?" Falmagon shot his eyes to Kindel. "You used a man as bait?"

"Men are the best bait for demons." Kindel returned his gaze to Falmagon. "I needed to locate the tunnel so I could stop the monsters from bleeding out. I have been closing tunnels all over this island for years, but the devils keep coming back to the surface. Why do you think I was on the Seven Islands a couple months back?" Kindel asked. "You have demons emerging from the Crags left and right."

Falmagon's eyes widened, uncertain how to respond.

"You should be thanking me. I have kept your precious Anshedar safe for years while you Half-bloods hide away in your castle. You would certainly be dead if I had not come along to save you."

"You expect me to thank you? You plan to kill me anyway, don't you?" Falmagon asked.

Kindel shrugged, resting his chin on the end of the crooked staff. "I will not kill you today."

The answer was all Falmagon needed. With a growl, he reached for Koldovstvo, intent on burning through his bindings and Kindel, wiping the smirk from his face. He was surprised to find his connection to the source of magic was strangely broken. Since adolescence, Koldovstvo was always a thought away, waiting to be molded with his thoughts. Now he found nothing but an empty void.

His jaw trembled as Kindel's smile widened. The man's teeth were as white as the snow. Falmagon tried again. And again.

His mind was a blank canvas. Nothing existed. Emptiness overwhelmed him. He was as simple—and useless—as any common Anshedar.

He panicked. "What have you done?"

"Are you trying to reach for Koldovstvo, Half-blood? I am afraid you may never taste magic again. I have carved the *znaki* above your head." With a grin, he used the staff to point at a board above Falmagon. "Right there, Half-blood. I told you we were enemies."

Falmagon blew his long hair from his mouth again, twisting his head to see an eye carved with a moon and a cross in the wood. "What is that?"

Kindel hummed with delight, balancing his weight on the staff. "Ah! The Highborn do not know how to make the znaki? Very interesting. I am eager to discover what else you will share about your sect."

He looked up to the sky and exhaled. "For now, we best keep moving. Enjoy your ride."

He turned and hopped off the cart.

"It is foolish to keep me alive," Falmagon called after him. "You know the Highborn will come looking for me."

"I doubt it," Kindel said as he passed on the outside of the cart. "If your friend makes it back alive, he will likely say you are dead. The gods know you should be."

The silence that filled the next several hours bled into days as Kindel hauled Falmagon across Kalamaar. Falmagon fell in and out of consciousness, finding difficulty in tracking the time he spent lying on his back. But from the bearing of the wind and sun, he eventually concluded they were heading northeast, which meant they were heading either to Jh'terin or farther north to Jh'tutat. If Maelili told the truth about their farm in the far north, Falmagon wondered if they were going to the shared homestead.

Would he see Maelili again?

Madness prodded at his senses. He never felt fully awake with the blue sky spinning above him one moment and the stars the next. His mind skipped from one thought to another, jumbling his emotions to the point that a knot formed in his stomach. He faintly remembered uttering prayers to the Lightbringer, only to think of Andrik, who abandoned him in the underground caves. Nedezhda's pretty face with her small nose and red hair flashed in his mind's eye several times. He could not shake the feeling that she could be his mother. Jhar's voice, or possibly Kindel, or even the boatman from Narthwich disturbed him with reminders of his purpose.

He was a Kadari; he was chosen.

When his mind calmed, Falmagon considered Kindel's subtle threats and his familial relationship to Maelili, the woman he loved. He knew he loved her. Yet she left him at Arkaim with little explanation, except the desire to find Kindel.

Several times, Falmagon contemplated whether he should speak to Kindel about Maelili, but he worried how he might react when learning how Falmagon felt about her. If someone as daft as Andrik could see his true feelings, he would not be able to hide them from Kindel. Falmagon hated to admit he feared Kindel, but without his magic, he was helpless in the back of the wagon.

He did not know what Kindel knew of Koldovstvo, but he believed the man had some untapped ability. The memory of him disappearing from sight on the beach of Folkmar had not been forgotten. Besides, Kindel's clear distrust of the Highborn did not bode well for Falmagon. The strange vendetta was unnerving at best. He feared sharing anything about Maelili would incite additional suspicion or even paranoia, likely resulting in certain death for Falmagon.

He could not risk it.

Over the passing days, Kindel roused him many times to give him water or a meat-flavored broth from whatever game he boiled over the evening campfires. He seemed intent on not giving Falmagon enough to keep his stomach from growling. Undeniably, Falmagon's fever heightened from his injuries, which made him believe Kindel wanted him weak. Nevertheless, he was willing to change Falmagon's bandages and even layered healing herbs on his wounds each day. Though if given the option, Falmagon would have preferred to have the knotted ropes loosened to give his muscles rest rather than having his wounds treated.

He mentioned slackening his bindings once, which resulted in a throaty laugh from Kindel followed by more silence.

By and by, snow clung to the earth day after day in the frigid temperatures. He supposed he should have been thankful Kindel brought his pack and blanket to help keep him warm, otherwise he would have frozen to death in the cart. All the same, when Falmagon was awake, he spent his time shivering, his teeth chattering until his head and bones ached in equal measure to his wounds. He knew his wounds were slowly improving, simply from hearing the few brief comments Kindel offered or the occasional hum of satisfaction when admiring his own handiwork. The pain did not lessen much, but considering he did not die in the first few days, he imagined he would survive.

About the time Falmagon's fever broke, he realized Kindel was leading them directly north. Although the light of Dahz was hidden behind the clouds, he could see the faint light rising in the east. Before long, he suspected they would reach the outskirts of Jh'tutat, if the northern city was truly their destination. He reassured himself they could be heading to no other place. From his vantage point, he had not caught wind of another human passing them, suggesting how far they had roamed from civilization.

They were traversing the far north.

When the cart suddenly came to halt, Falmagon's first impulse was to look through the gaps between the side boards. Instead, he kept his head flat against the baseboards and shut his eyes, pretending to sleep. He listened to Kindel rustle around on the seat before stepping down into the snow and walking around to the back of the wagon. A moment later, the cart wobbled and creaked as Kindel hoisted himself up next to Falmagon. The butt of the staff hit against the cart twice, and then all was quiet.

Falmagon could almost hear the snow falling.

He could not guess at how much time passed while Kindel stood over him, grumbling to himself. Eventually, he nudged Falmagon with his foot. "Falmagon."

He remained still.

To his surprise, the ropes holding his legs and arms were unexpectedly split, falling away with a dull thud. He hadn't heard anything. Perhaps they were cut with magic. He bit his tongue, almost moaning with relief.

The cart faintly swayed as Kindel returned to the ground, clearing his throat. Falmagon dared to peek for a moment, seeing the back of Kindel's head, his red hair ragged against the back of his cloak. Beyond him, he saw a rugged cottage with a thatched roof standing twenty paces away. He hurriedly closed his eyes as Kindel turned around again.

Falmagon was ready to fight Kindel with or without magic. What he was not prepared for was magical bands of air wrapping him up as tight as the ropes had been and carrying him into the air. He grew rigid, his teeth grinding, floating off the cart and presumably toward the cottage. As he blinked open his eyes, the sides of the cart disappeared; only the white sky above him remained in his vision. Knowing he could not swing or kick, he desperately reached out for Koldovstvo.

The magic came without restraint, buzzing in his eardrums, tickling at the back of his skull. Being drawn away from the znaki opened the gate to Koldovstvo once more.

He did not hesitate, pulling his head upright to see Kindel standing near the open door of the cottage.

Roaring with fury, Falmagon threw Kindel to the left with Koldovstvo. He barely saw him flip across the snow before the magic around Falmagon evaporated. His roar turned to a shout as he fell several feet to the ground. He landed on his elbows and tailbone and yelped; the soreness shot through his muscles, probably reopening the wound in his chest.

He did not have time to examine himself. The horse squealed behind him, rearing up with terror then jerking the cart forward, tearing off across the terrain.

Snow stirred around Falmagon, blocking his view of the plot of land. He twisted around to look for Kindel, only to see the staff materialize in front of his face. He dropped to his back and dodged the blow, the staff slicing over him a breath from his nose. He quickly rolled sideways and shuffled into a crouched position.

He did not wait to see Kindel. He focused on the spiraling snowflakes and swiftly turned them into bladed icicles. With a twist of his wrist, he flung them into the open space ahead.

"By Mulafell! Come on!" he yelled with frustration when his attack vaporized before his eyes, and still he could not see Kindel anywhere. He could not sustain magic for long or he would lose years of his life. The brown strands of hair hanging over the corner of his eye told him he still had time to spare.

Falmagon hollered as magic pulled him through the open door of the cottage against his will. He pulled his arms to his chest to keep them from smacking into the door frame just in time to see Kindel's crooked staff appear across the doorway at the last minute.

The staff caught him under the chin, seemingly crushing his throat, flipping him heels over head. He landed with a crash on the wooden planks, slamming his face into the ground. His mouth filled with the taste of copper; blood shot from his nose. He coughed and gagged, fighting for air, and immediately he felt himself being dragged by strands of air toward the back of the cabin.

He did not have the strength to breathe let alone to look at his surroundings or to reach for Koldovstvo.

Kindel jeered. "Let this be a lesson to you, Falmagon. I am not a fool, nor one with whom you should trifle."

Without warning, Falmagon dropped through an unseen trapdoor in the floor and down a small flight of stairs. His head and shoulder cracked against several steps before he ended up sprawled out on the dirt floor.

He snorted, bursting a cloud of dust over his eyes and bloodied face. If his wounds were not open before, they were now.

The stairs creaked behind him. He blinked, fighting to stay conscious. He could fight. He had to fight.

Drops of crimson, his own blood, hovered in front of him. Kindel's words boomed in the darkened cellar.

Forbid flesh, forbid soul,
Blood-father, Earth-mother.

Falmagon's body went rigid, being pulled from the ground by Koldovstvo. A lantern he could not see suddenly colored the small room with yellow light. The softened layer of dirt on the floor blended with his blood before his eyes. Kindel continued, spinning Falmagon around.

Forbid body, forbid blood,
Fire-drinker, Sky-weaver.

Wisps of air fed into the mixture of blood and dirt, forming the emblem of the znaki in front of Falmagon. He winced at the small etching of the eye, moon, and cross. Kindel kept his distance, moving Falmagon to the back wall. Ropes already fastened over the banister magically entwined over his arms. He struggled weakly, seeing the flash of fire sear the emblem.

Be done thy will; Be done thy will,
Be done thy will; Be done thy will.

The magical symbol smashed into the dirt wall behind Falmagon, blocking him from the source of Koldovstvo, sealing his fate.

He was Kindel the Red's prisoner.

Chapter XVIII
FALMAGON

A chest-ripping scream tore through Falmagon. He pitched his body backward, missing the solid dirt wall by inches. The wooden floor of the cottage above him rattled in the wake of his echoing tenor, the din reverberating off the other three walls, a testament to his continued torment.

He strained for air, his throat dry, and dropped his head to see an arrow's wooden point nestled in the meat of his thigh. Blood flowed down his bare leg like a river, diverging over his ankle and dribbling off his curled toes.

"Look how strong you are," Kindel remarked with amusement as Falmagon bit his tongue to keep from crying out again. He forced his chin up, observing as Kindel placed the strung bow down on the wooden table next to him, a step away from his crooked staff. Through his untamed hair, he saw the lantern light flicker at the rear of the room, causing the shadows on the walls to dance. Kindel gritted his teeth, wiping the sweat from his brow as though he were the one under duress. "No doubt your friend would not have survived. I made the right decision in choosing you." He wrung his hands, returning his gaze to Falmagon. "You know this will end when you tell me the truth."

Falmagon fought back tears.

More than a week had lapsed since he woke up in the back of Kindel's horse-drawn cart, half dead and bleeding. He was no better off now.

Yet he refused to be broken by this man.

For days, he hung naked from the rafters with his hands bound over his head and his feet dangling over the dry earth. The symbol of the znaki, as Kindel called it, remained in the dirt behind him, keeping him from Koldovstvo. In his mind, over and over again he played the magic and the words Kindel had used to create the znaki. If he got the chance to break away again, he would use the same tactic on Kindel.

"Tell me the truth, Falmagon."

"By Mulafell!" he moaned, sounding weaker than he intended. He ineffectively wriggled on the ropes as though he were bait on a hook. He supposed he should be thankful to have some feeling in his leg, though he would rather be numb than experience this torment. The arrow seemed to dig deeper into his flesh with every movement.

Kindel had repeatedly patched the wounds on his shoulder and chest—as well as the new injuries he acquired during these routine inquisitions—but the pain never faded from his senses. He swallowed, keeping his eyes off the multiple holes on his other leg from yesterday's interrogation. The gashes were swollen with pinkish fluid oozing through the pus. When he did break free, he was unsure whether he would be able to walk.

He breathed heavily, grimacing, and tried to sound tougher. By the Lightbringer, he hoped he sounded stronger than he felt. "I told you everything. I do not know anything more."

"I truly doubt that," Kindel said, lifting the bow again, along with a second arrow. He put his forefinger on the end and rubbed the tip against the table as though he might sharpen the edge a bit more. He then rotated the projectile, pressing harder to further tune the edge to a finer point. "You are resilient. Strong-willed. Intelligent. I bet the Spearhead—as you called him—knows your worth as well as I. He would be prudent to keep you close at hand, to teach you his secrets."

Falmagon coughed, watching Kindel line the arrow on the bowstring. The man was determined to kill him in this filthy room.

"I am surprised I did not come across you and your kind sooner while traversing over Kalamaar these past decades. Sure, I heard whispers of the Highborn on their southern islands, but with people speaking of you like gods, I assumed you were more myth than anything," Kindel said. "I should have known better. Nothing is myth."

Falmagon trembled. Neither Kindel nor Maelili had heard of the Highborn before they met Falmagon. He could not understand how any Northmen, even those residing in the far north, could be unaware of the Highborn.

"The Highborn will come for me," Falmagon said, doubting his own words. He could almost see Kindel rolling his eyes in the darkened room.

"Maybe they will come looking for you when spring comes. Alas, winter has only started, and the cold lasts awfully long in the north. Save yourself from suffering and tell me where the Highborn came from. The magic is not yours to wield. Someone gave it to you. Who created you wretched, soiled Half-bloods?" he asked. He jerked his head to knock his hair from his eyes and lifted his weapon, aiming the arrow at Falmagon's leg again.

"I already told you. Why do you ask me the same questions?" Falmagon groaned.

Kindel pulled the string back on the bow.

Falmagon sputtered, "No other could be the first Highborn except my master, Kinhar Sayan. If there is another, I know nothing of him! We were given the gift of Koldovstvo by Dahz the Ligh—"

The twang of the bow sounded, the arrow zipping through the air. Falmagon snarled, throwing his head back as the arrow sank inches above the first.

"Nine Lands!" His brown strands stuck to the perspiration coating his forehead and cheeks.

"The Lightbringer did not give you the power of Koldovstvo." Kindel squinted at him. "Stop lying to me."

"It's the truth!" he screamed. He pulled at the ropes. His muscles flexed, the bindings burning against his skin. His eyes watered. His voice fell to a whisper. "Why are you doing this?"

"You do not deserve to have this power." Kindel dropped the bow to the table with a thud, grabbing his crooked staff. He slammed the butt against the ground and approached Falmagon. "Now, how many of you guard the castle? How many roam Kalamaar? The Seven Islands? Aenar? Answer me, Half-blood!"

Falmagon growled, clinging to whatever strength he could find. He looked at Kindel with blurred vision. His leg throbbed, the muscle twitching against the two long arrows embedded in his flesh. "Why do you keep calling me that?"

"Stop wasting your breath with trivial questions and answer me. We are not playing a game you can win. What must I do to make you speak? Should I beat you with Habermani?" Kindel said, wobbling his staff in the air.

Falmagon eyed the staff, curious as to what might give a stick a name.

The red-haired man flared his nostrils, standing tall to face him. With Falmagon hanging from the ropes that bound him, the top of Kindel's head only reached Falmagon's chin. "Once you tell me everything, I will finally let you die."

"Then kill me," Falmagon spoke through clenched teeth, then shouted at Kindel, "because I cannot tell you what I do not know! If you let me live, I will escape. And I will not hesitate to…to…" His voice drifted off as pain shot up his leg and into the base of his spine.

"Please. You fight like a hare missing its hind legs. You think you could kill me? I seriously doubt you have ever killed a man." Kindel shook his head, eerily calm compared to the storm raging inside Falmagon. He waved him off. "We will unearth what you know and what you do not."

He interlaced his fingers between the two arrows in Falmagon's thigh, causing Falmagon to cringe, and then tore them free.

Falmagon howled, rocking forward, saliva flying from his lips. This would be the death of him!

Kindel grunted, unblinking. "My father would have liked you." He tossed one of the arrows behind him while clinging to the other. Falmagon did not have time to think of a response. Kindel moved as fast as streaming rain, spearing Falmagon's left eye with the second arrow.

The movement was so quick, Falmagon's scream seemed delayed. His body thrashed, kicking at nothing, while his right eye darted to the spine of wood jutting from his socket. The arrow bobbled on the opposite side of his nose; his lashes were pulled by small, unseen splinters of wood lining the stick.

Blood coursed down his face, dripped off his chin, and trickled onto his chest.

He kicked wildly at Kindel, yelling until he thought he would lose his voice completely. He watched as the bastard stepped away, leaning on Habermani, watching him as though he were a hog hung for slaughter. He fought against the shadows pulling at the corner of his good eye, determined to stay awake and alert.

He would not be beaten. He would kill Kindel! He swore to the Lightbringer he would kill him.

He had nearly gained his wits again when Kindel used Koldovstvo to pull the arrow back to his hand, taking Falmagon's eye with it.

His body instantly numbed. His breaths grew faint. He could not fight it any longer; darkness shrouded him like a moonless night.

Dreams swept away any sensible thought. He swayed in and out of consciousness, torn between images of Kindel's cruel mien and Maelili's soft gaze. He could not tell what was real and what was not, although Maelili's smile held so much kindness and concern, he eventually pushed Kindel from his mind; only the faint image of Maelili remained. The shadows in the room enveloped her, leaving everything to the imagination except her green eyes and flowing brown hair.

Her long strands shifted shades and were suddenly painted as bright as an angry sunset.

She did not say a word. She only looked upon him and he upon her. For what felt like days, he did not look away. Even when he realized he was trapped in a dream, he fought to stay in its confines.

His heart yearned for Maelili.

Yet reality gently drew him back to the hollow prison. He could not say how much time had passed when he finally woke, surrounded by the color of charcoal. His first thought was his desire to see the light of the sun, to look upon the face of the Lightbringer, but even the yellow hue of the lantern light had gone out.

He strained his one eye to no avail in the pitch, sensing the goosebumps dancing over his flesh. His hands tingled and ached in the bindings above his head. Holding back a cough, he twisted about slightly, hoping to alleviate some pressure on his wrists. The ropes creaked with his movements, but the pain surging through his body did not subside.

After a moment, the residue of smashed herbs and moistened leaves pressing over his flesh from his chest to his back caused his skin to itch. Obviously still intent on keeping him alive for a while longer, Kindel had patched him up again before retreating upstairs.

The faint smell of rabbit stew drifted through the floorboards, telling him Kindel was likely eating and would leave him alone for the night.

With a snort, Falmagon felt a bandage rubbing against the outside of his nose and forehead. Soon he realized a piece of fabric had been tied over his eye like a patch. He grimaced as he thought of the Kras at Melkorka whose eye he helped Kinhar cut out months ago. Images of the little red brood squirming on the table under his superior might flashed across his vision.

In his heart, he knew some men—weaker-minded men—might consider his current quandary as some type of justice inflicted by the gods, possibly to teach him lessons in humility or mercy. Though unlike him, those men were not chosen by the Lightbringer and, therefore, they were mistaken about his plight.

His empty eye socket burned in his skull, and his body was bloodied and weakened beyond what the mortal body should be capable of weathering. Yet Falmagon was not dead. In the same way he did not die in the wake of the demons, he had faith that he would not meet his end here. He prayed the Lightbringer would give him the courage, the strength, and the sight to survive. He admittedly did not know all, but he knew that neither Dahz nor any other god was responsible for the harm inflicted on him. Kindel would surely tell him that men who abandoned gods were cast aside with equal measure. Falmagon would not lose faith.

No. He would not blame the gods for black-hearted men like Kindel or the wrath they wrought.

Falmagon curled his lip. Not long ago, he vowed to be the hand of the Lightbringer. If Dahz the White-Clad willed it, Falmagon would rid the world of men like Kindel. Unlike the slave Kras, Falmagon would not blubber and beg for clemency. He was not weak like the red broods, and Kindel would know it before they were through.

The creak of footsteps sounded above him. The trapdoor creaked open, spilling light into the basement.

Falmagon froze. The light stung at his good eye, reminding him of the blood palpitating in his empty socket. He could feel it resonating into the back of his skull; he could hear the pulse in his ears.

"Have you woken, Half-blood?" Kindel said, stepping down the wooden rungs. The curved staff, Habermani, stayed in his hand.

The lantern ignited in the corner, more fully illuminating the small room. For the first time in what felt like forever, Falmagon could make out the few grey wisps layered in Kindel's hair. He wondered if he had any grey in his own hair from his casting. The few brown strands hanging over his eyes suggested not.

Kindel's blue eyes were cold as ice as he shuffled across the ground, using Habermani like he was climbing the side of a mountain. His huffed, locking his gaze on Falmagon. His sneer was unmistakeable. "If you favor your other eye, you are going to start speaking right now."

Falmagon swallowed, his tongue feeling swollen. "Speak about what?"

Kindel's hand clutched the top of Habermani until his knuckles whitened. "How in the Nine Lands do you know

Maelili?" When Falmagon did not immediately answer, he roared, "Why would you scream my sister's name in your sleep?"

Chapter XIX
MAELILI

Large snowflakes floated from the grey sky and stuck to Maelili's eyelashes. She blinked them away, stumbling north alongside the frozen riverbed. Her toes were numb, but she was determined to keep moving. She adjusted her cowl, wrapping it tightly around her face, and eyed the failing light.

Ten paces ahead, Brigita and Velkan spoke in shivering whispers. Velkan clutched at Brigita's shoulder, almost consolingly, before turning to face Maelili. She could not read his expression through the red hair that covered his face, but she sensed aggravation. He pushed his lips together, touching beard to mustache, and shifted his eyes back forward, grunting at Brigita. As the weeks dragged on, Maelili could not help but notice Velkan offering additional reassurances to the younger woman. She could not tell if Brigita was growing on him or if he was attempting to keep her from becoming too petulant.

Without saying a word, Maelili looked to the southwest, where Velkan's eyes may have roamed. Any sign of the cities Jh'terin and Farmas were long behind them. For the past several weeks, the three of them traveled from the southern

Crags to the eastern woodlands, and then eventually north again. She was not certain where else they could search without heading to the Seven Islands, but she hoped to find her brother in the far north near the town of Jh'tutat.

"Nothing is out here. Not one lily-livered person," Brigita complained loudly, her shrill tone floating on the air. "Only grasslands and trees and snow. It is no wonder the people at Arkaim looked at us like we lost our minds when we said we came from the north."

"Someone must live this way. Jh'tutat is positioned somewhere along this river," Velkan said. "We cannot lose faith."

Maelili wondered if Velkan spoke loud enough for her own comfort. She saw his light eyes dart back in her direction again.

"We cannot spend the rest of our lives drifting across Kalamaar," Brigita growled, her feet crunching in the snow as though she might stomp through the very earth.

"We will if our Arkhon commands it," Velkan said.

Brigita stopped, faced Velkan, and dropped her pack to the snow. Like Velkan and Maelili, the dye had faded from her hair completely. Her red locks spiraled out from under her hooded cloak like coiled tentacles striking out against the frigid cold. Whether from frustration or winter's cruel chill, her face was almost as red as her hair.

Velkan dropped his bags too and sighed heavily. Maelili watched their breath paint the air as they paused to eye one another.

Although she heard the back and forth, she was unwilling to entertain Brigita. "I did not give the order to stop." She eased forward, swinging her arms at her sides. Her voice was muffled through the wrapped cloth. "We have another hour of daylight at least."

"We do," Velkan agreed, turning from Brigita's heated gaze to Maelili. He spoke in his typical singsong tone. "Yet the farther north we travel, the colder the weather will become and the quicker night will fall. We need to set up camp while we have the light and feeling left in our fingers."

"I have not felt my toes or fingers for miles," Brigita muttered, keeping her eyes from Maelili.

"We are Stuhia," Maelili said, curling her lip behind her makeshift mask. Velkan likely expected her to see the benefit in stopping for Brigita's sake, but Maelili was not in the mood to offer compassion. "If you are cold, warm yourself with your magic. When we stop for the night and need fire, we will make it. If it grows too dark and we have need of light, we will make it. Right now, we keep moving."

"Since when do we use our magic fruitlessly?" Brigita snapped, twisting to Maelili so fast she nearly slipped in the snow. The young woman firmly planted her foot and grabbed Velkan's arm to keep from falling. "How about food? Do you know how to use Koldovstvo to create food too? Because we're nearly out!"

Brigita's words faded in the snowy haze, leaving them in momentary silence.

Maelili closed her eyes, taking her time to answer. She could not keep the scowl off her face, thankful it remained hidden behind her wrapped cowl.

She understood that she might have pushed Velkan and Brigita too hard. Maybe she asked too much. She took them from their homes and families on a quest to the opposite end of the world. While she wanted to find Kindel, she was not blind or stupid. In truth, she recognized that they had walked across Kalamaar for months and had nothing to show for it. Anyone would lose faith after so many failings. Even she was ready to stomp her feet and curse at the flurries.

As an Arkhon, she did not have the luxury to scream at the heavens. She was expected to maintain poise, even when her subject yelled at her like a disorderly child. Keeping calm seemed impossible, especially with the cold prickling at her frozen skin and a headache rising from the base of her neck. If she was honest with herself, her instinct was to beat the life out of Brigita for her impudence, and then to march toward Jh'tutat with as much haste as she could muster. She had the power as Arkhon. Velkan would not say a word. But Maelili was not like the Kaligulas. She would not lead with cruelty. She was a Kluk. She would exercise a calm mind and a gentle hand, as her father did before her.

"My Arkhon…" Velkan cleared his throat when she did not say anything.

"What?" she retorted with more bitterness than she intended.

He took a step closer, keeping his hands in the folds of his cloak. "We need rest, food, and warmth if we are going to survive the north. This foreign land is as treacherous as our own. We can still scout ahead in Klukas."

Maelili dipped her head, considering his words.

The shadow realm called Klukas was not a realm in which Maelili particularly enjoyed traveling. To her knowledge, every Stuhian knew how to enter into the fabric of space between this world and the next. The realm was like pulling a thin veil over the eyes, walking in the shadows between here and there. While she was aware the soldiers of the Stuhian armies often used this skill to scout ahead, she had met few who willingly leaped at the chance to enter Klukas. Disengaging the spirit from the body was not magic but a mastered skill among the Stuhia, one which left the physical body vulnerable.

She did not know what would happen if the body died, but she knew the spirit could not return.

Maelili yielded, dropping her pack. "We will rest for a few hours and then continue. Let us hope we find something in Klukas."

Darkness set quicker than Maelili anticipated with Velkan volunteering to use Koldovstvo to burrow a hole through the ice to fish. In the meantime, Brigita prepped a fire while Maelili ventured to the adjacent forest to find additional wood. Upon returning, she and Brigita worked in silence, sharpening the ends of several sticks to cook whatever fish Velkan caught.

Her mind reeled with self-doubt, taking full notice of Brigita's curt actions and loud sighs while they steadily worked. Maelili told herself that she would not engage with the girl. She did not have time to argue about what she could not change or, more accurately, what she refused to change. They were on Kalamaar to find Kindel, and she was not returning back home until the deed was finished.

Brigita could huff all she wanted.

The flames were crackling by the time Velkan returned.

"The good news is we won't starve," he said, tossing several small fish to the snow, "but we won't be full either."

Maelili lowered herself into a cross-legged position in the soft snow, feeling the cold against her bottom. The fish wriggled helplessly, threatening to flop into the flames of the fire. Brigita walked by Maelili, grabbing a pointed skewer and impaled one of the fish through the side. It twitched on the end as she moved away; eyes wide, she shoved it over the fire.

Velkan mimicked the movement and lifted the stick to Maelili. "My Arkhon."

"You eat," she said with a shake of her head, her white-red hair bouncing on either side of her frozen cheeks, "and watch over me."

Velkan's concerned gaze disappeared from her sight as she folded her hands in her lap and closed her eyes. For a moment she could feel his eyes on her, and perhaps even Brigita's from across the fire. She ignored them. She heard him grumble under his breath and step away.

Tension among the three of them had grown in the past weeks, but Velkan could handle a bit more of her boorishness. The quest was losing its appeal, giving her urgency to see it finished. She did not dare believe Velkan or even Brigita would defy her beyond simple words. And while mutiny may have been far from possible, Maelili risked losing their respect, which would haunt her the rest of their journey and upon returning to Lairhein. Whether among their people or in the wilderness, she had a duty to lead them, and she was determined to do better than she had.

She would push herself. Even though she hated the place, she would go to Klukas.

To enter Klukas, she had to block out the world and remain mindful. Brigita and Velkan rummaging around the fire distracted her for a moment, along with the wood snapping in the open flame. She swallowed a mouthful of cold air and used the sound to ease her mind, to steady her thoughts.

She could almost see the fire dancing, the light flickering on the reverse side of her eyelids. She isolated the sound of the fire, hearing the spitting flames in her right ear and then her left. The fish hissed and sizzled; the smell of the cooking meat filled her nostrils. Her stomach growled, pulling her away from the meditative state.

Unmoving, she regulated her breathing and again let the sound of the fire dance between her ears. Soon she noticed her shoulders slump and a heavy weight adhere to her muscles from her skull to the base of her spine. Her legs and feet numbed, nearly vanishing completely from her awareness, along with the droning of Brigita and Velkan.

She must remain mindful. The task had always been hard for her.

Energy vibrated between her temples, zapping at her senses in attempt to pull her into the shadow world of Klukas. Maelili attempted to pull her spiritual body from her physical frame but instantly failed. Obscure thoughts without any real substance railed against her, keeping her grounded to the physical plane of existence. Maelili could not say she was surprised, conscious of what anguish was hidden away at her core. If she could not push her emotions aside, she would be incapable of ascending beyond her body. She should have known the distress was bound to emerge before entering Klukas. She tried to disregard her uneasiness as images came at her in a whirlwind before dissolving like dust.

Maelili first saw the bouncing red curls of her son, Eisliev, as he ran from the door of their home in Lairhein. While her love for her boy was unquestionable, the grief of being gone from him swept over her. Her husband, Nevyn, came next with his thin frame and affectionate smile. Regret touched her heart, knowing how she betrayed him. He was weak but loyal, which was more than she could say for most Stuhians. Of course, the thought of her unfaithfulness swiftly brought Falmagon's face to her mind's eye. His dimpled smile and long, flowing hair warmed her in ways meant for inexperienced lovers. She feared she would never be absent of this internal desire for his company and his touch.

Maelili watched Falmagon fade while the calling of dreams soothingly pulled her deeper into the trance. A heaviness held her eyes shut, though the rest of her body felt absolutely weightlessness, threatening to topple her body over to the snow. She no longer could feel all of her body, and with exhaustion from their journey seeping into her bones, she knew sleep would come too easily. She refused to succumb; she needed to enter Klukas.

Energy pulsed again between her ears as the emotions subsided, a roar like a dragon enveloping her, and then her spirit was propelled from her physical form with a sudden earnestness.

As always, the hush that followed in the realm of Klukas shocked Maelili. One moment she was fighting against the prison of her flesh, and now she was hovering over the snow feet away from Velkan and Brigita. The reverberation of an endless breeze filled the hollow of her ear before her spirit form fully adjusted to the shadow plane. In Klukas, Maelili was absent of most of her mortal senses, including taste, touch, and smell.

She was but a silent watchman, a ghost among the living.

"Do you think she has made the transition yet?" Brigita asked from across the fire. Her voice sounded miles away, despite the close distance. Maelili watched the young woman brush her hair back with her fingers. Her meal was already finished, the remains burning among the embers.

"I would think so," Velkan said. He looked at the few fish on the ground, lifeless and unmoving.

Brigita rubbed her small nose, unknowingly looking through Maelili's ethereal form to her body, which remained sitting upright with legs crossed. "I cannot remember the last time I entered Klukas."

Velkan narrowed his gaze, leaning forward. "Have you not gone to Lairhein to see your kin? As much as you speak of returning, I would have thought—"

"I will wait until we step back through the red walls of Lairhein to see them," Brigita interrupted. "I have no interest in seeing them and not being able to touch them. Tell me, have you gone to see your husband?"

"Of course I have," Velkan said. "Many times."

Velkan's words stung Maelili, prompting her to remember how she also refused to visit her own husband in Klukas while away. Of course, her own reasoning was due chiefly to her discomfort with the shadow world. Klukas demanded a Stuhian remain void of emotion, which her father said—too often—would lead to long-term, insufferable consequences. Those who learned to ignore their own emotions would forego empathy and, instead, be consumed by their own selfish aspirations. Such characteristics were unfit for a leader and incompatible with what it meant to be a Kluk.

Even now, with the lingering thought of her husband, Maelili struggled against her mortal body, which attempted to tug her back inside its folds. Hiding her emotions was strenuous, taking constant effort. She hurried to suppress her feelings, ignoring whatever more was being said around the campfire. Velkan and Brigita would only incite more emotion with their discussion. She needed to get away, cover ground, and see if Kindel could be found.

She flew northward.

Darkness was not without color in Klukas. Instead, the black of night resembled broken twilight with faint greys hued with canary yellow and cornflower blue. Maelili could make out the speckled snowfall, the silvery ice of the frozen river, and the small trees that multiplied to the east. She could see farther than she might with her human eyes, but not by much.

For miles she kept her thoughts on the landscape and off anything that might cause her to feel. She searched for any sign of civilization hoping Jh'tutat was not far from their current camp, but nothing stirred on the horizon. She lost track of time and distance, flitting along, knowing she could slingshot back to her body at any given time. As long as

Brigita and Velkan guarded over her, she would remain safe in both Klukas and in the material world.

When the skeleton of a wooden cabin emerged adjacent to the forest's edge, she scarcely believed the structure was real. Drawing closer, she thought it might have been abandoned, but a weak glow of lantern light glistened in the cracks outlining the door.

Elation paused her movement. She hovered for a moment above the ice, regaining tranquility, and then advanced.

Her ethereal form passed through the solid door to enter the empty one-room cabin, taking in her surroundings. To her left, a cot was pushed up against the wall and covered in pelts. Next to the bed was a small table with a mortar and pestle, dried herbs, and several pouches filled with different ingredients. She guessed the occupant could not have gone far, seeing that a hearthfire burned with some vigor to her right. Near the fire sat a table and chair. The table had a plate of half-eaten food and a copper mug brimming with what might have been water. Scattered arrows, a few stained with blood, were dispersed on the table. A strung longbow was angled against the chair.

Maelili listened expectantly beyond the door she just entered but heard nothing. The denizen must have stepped outside but a moment ago, yet she recalled seeing no one. She considered leaving to continue her search.

"Lightbringer, save me," a man lamented from somewhere inside. The sound was so faint Maelili barely heard it, but the weeping that followed undoubtedly came from beneath her. "Please."

The shock almost sent Maelili reeling back to her corporeal form.

Stomaching her distress, she searched for the source of the sound. As the sobbing intensified, she drifted downward through the floorboards into the secreted basement beneath. The darkness had no effect on her vision in Klukas.

The dusty ground and dirt walls were ignored at the sight of the lone figure against the wall. Unclothed and bloodied, the shivering man could not hope to see Maelili on the other side of the veil looking back at him. His body convulsed, weeping uncontrollably in the darkness. Tangled strands of brown hair hung over the left side of his face, obscuring it from view.

She only preserved her ethereal form long enough for his name to catch on the edge of her tongue.

"Falmagon."

Chapter XX
MAELILI

"Falma—gon!" Maelili choked on the name, jolting back into consciousness. Her head spun with confusion, trying to make sense of what she had seen. He had been hanging in the dark, bleeding. She fell forward, catching herself on the snow. The cold stung her fingertips.

Velkan raced around the fire in a heartbeat, steadying her with his hands. "My Arkhon."

Brigita was slower to respond, rising from where she sat hunched over. The fire whipped against the night breeze, causing her shadow to flicker against the pale snow. "What did you say?"

Maelili stifled a cough and lifted her chin. Velkan looked back at her with gentle green eyes. His red hair was vivid against the fire light, tucked back on either side of his hood. "I saw Falmagon," Maelili said, twisting her neck to face Brigita. "He is being held north of here. He is hurt."

"The Highborn we saw at Arkaim? He is here?" Brigita angled her brow, looking over her shoulder.

"Yes," Maelili said. "We must go to him. I think he is dying." She scrambled clumsily to her feet while Velkan attempted to help her, standing to his full height. She staggered out of his grasp and reached for her pack lying in the snow.

"Arkhon, please take a moment and tell us exactly what you saw. You have not rested. You have not eaten," Velkan tried, his hands hovering in front of his chest as though he were still steadying her movements. "The haze of Klukas can be misleading when you first return. Gather yourself."

"You may have slipped into a dream," Brigita said.

Maelili threw her pack over her shoulder impatiently. "It was no dream! And we do not have a moment. He is being held in a cottage." She jabbed her finger to the north. "He is strung up and bleeding with arrow wounds in his legs."

"I mean no disrespect, my Arkhon, but I do not understand," Brigita said. "Why would he be this far north? Why would he be tortured? The Highborn are respected in these lands, practically treated like the gods themselves."

"I don't know. I only know what I saw." Maelili locked her jaw to keep her chin from quivering. "Now grab your things!"

She did not wait for their reply and began trudging off with as much strength as she could muster. After a few steps, the light of the fire extinguished behind her, suggesting one of them smothered the flames with Koldovstvo. Without a moon, the pitch of night blocked her vision. She cast an orb of light with Koldovstvo without slowing her pace. Moments later, she could hear Brigita and Velkan's quickened footsteps attempting to catch up with her.

"How far, Arkhon?" Velkan called after her.

"Not far. A couple leagues," she said over her shoulder, "maybe three."

"Nine Lands," she heard Brigita mumble.

Maelili stopped, throwing her bag to the ground. Her orb of light brightened as she turned around to face Brigita. "Do you have something you want to say?"

Brigita froze, eyes widening slightly, staring back. Her hand gripped the strap of her own pack slung over her shoulder. "What?"

Maelili flared her nostrils and stomped back across the snow, ignoring Velkan, who scooted to the side in time to move from her path. She pulled her shoulders back, realizing she was screaming at the other woman. "I hardly need to give you permission to speak your mind! You tell us every thought bouncing between your ears whether we have interest in hearing it or not. So out with it! What do you want to say?"

Brigita's mouth moved mechanically for a moment as Maelili stood toe to toe with her, less than an arm's length away.

"Arkhon—"

"Out with it!" Maelili screamed.

"We came here to find your brother, not—"

Maelili slapped Brigita across the cheek with enough force to knock her clean off her feet. The young woman yelped, snaking sideways and crashing to the snow in a heap. Brigita did not attempt to stand again, trembling as she regained her senses. Her hand momentarily touched her flesh under the wild strands of her red hair.

Ignoring the pain zipping through her frozen hand, Maelili towered over Brigita. "I will not hear another word from your lips unless I ask for it! Not for the remainder of our journey. Hear me now. If you say one word without my blessing, I will bury you on Kalamaar. You will never see Lairhein again. Am I understood?"

Brigita stooped beneath Maelili, submissively placing her hands in front of her. "Yes, my Arkhon. I understand." Her voice did not waver.

Maelili balled her hand into a fist, though it numbed from the pain. She growled under her breath and moved to retrieve her bag. She could feel Velkan's judgmental eyes on her as she passed by him. He certainly would not approve of her outburst.

She could not look at him. She left him to help Brigita to her feet while she started back off into the night.

The confrontation with Brigita was over in a blink of an eye, but Maelili's internal rage stayed with her for miles. She supposed the anger kept her warm or, if anything, kept her moving. Without any sustenance or sleep, she should have collapsed long ago, but she did not slow. Even with her leg muscles burning, her hands numbing, or her eyes burning from the cold wind, Maelili forced herself along the unseen path.

In time her heartbeat slowed, and she was able to think a bit more clearly. She could not say she was upset with Brigita as much as she was with herself. As the pieces began to come together, she could only assume how Falmagon ended up in the far north.

Maelili could only blame herself.

She ran away from him. She used him to gain information about her brother and then deserted him. His falling in love with her was not her intent, but it happened, and whether or not she would admit it aloud, the feeling was mutual. She did not mean to fall in love or *want* to, but such were the circumstances. She had to make things right before returning to her own family. Even if she never found Kindel as a result of pursuing Falmagon, she could not leave him to die alone screaming to the gods for mercy.

Maelili promised once she saw him freed, she would leave him to her memory. She would never speak his name again.

She steered them east of the river running north, following the same path she took while in Klukas. The nights grew longer with the coming days of winter but could not outlast the trek to the mysterious cottage. Morning's light eventually blushed behind a bulwark of clouds, so Maelili dispelled her orb of light.

About the same time, Velkan gained the courage to walk alongside her again. "Arkhon," he started.

"I don't want to talk about it, Velkan," she whispered with a shudder.

Velkan kept his eyes forward, his feet crunching heavily against the snow. "We need to discuss this. We are but three in a land of strangers. If you break, we all fall. Brigita is loyal to you, Arkhon."

"I know," Maelili said. "I would not have brought her along if she was not. You do not need to defend her."

Velkan was patient, walking alongside her for several more strides. The breaking light illuminated the grey-clad countryside. He allowed silence to pull the truth from her lips.

"I love him," Maelili admitted. "By the gods, I don't want to, but I do. I cannot allow him to die."

Velkan hummed to himself as though she only confirmed what he already knew. He glanced over his shoulder briefly at Brigita trudging behind them at a distance, and then rubbed the frost from his beard. He did not push the matter of her feelings or the morality of them and instead asked, "Are you sure he is being held?"

"I was not dreaming," she said softly, catching sight of a brown speck against the skyline. She lifted her finger and exhaled. "The cottage."

With a burst of energy, she shoved her pack into Velkan's fumbling hands as he tried to make out the homestead on the horizon. Maelili could not run on the snow, but she could move quicker without the added weight. Velkan shouted at Brigita as Maelili hurried across the flat land. He scrambled to keep up with her to no avail.

Old snow created a thin veil over impressions in the dirt. Maelili noticed marks indicating a horse's hooves, cart wheels, and possibly the outline of a footprint or two, but for the most part, the ground looked recently untouched.

Her thoughts were on Falmagon entombed in the grisly basement as she closed the distance to the cottage. Velkan had the power of sacred magic and, at her command, would heal whatever injuries Falmagon endured with Koldovstvo.

She was not concerned about restoring his health as much as she was about his reaction to her presence. Almost a month had come and gone since she spoke to him at Arkaim; she wondered how much of that time he'd spent in this hole. *Would he blame her?*

The question echoed in her head as she approached the outside of the lodging. As anticipated, a wagon of sorts sat unattended near the cottage. Beyond the cart was a small makeshift barn built against the side of the cottage. A horse snorted and stuck its head out over a wooden fence, which kept it from coming any closer.

Maelili turned to eye the entryway to the cabin she saw in Klukas hours earlier. She paused for only a moment; unwilling to wait for Velkan and Brigita, she stepped forward and pulled the wooden door open.

A wave of cooked venison mixed with the scent of crushed herbs hit her immediately. Not knowing what to expect, she held Koldovstvo at the forefront of her mind, ready to burn the cottage to the ground if needed. Yet nothing stirred inside the homestead. In fact, nothing looked to have been touched since she scouted the premise in Klukas. The bloodied arrows, the bow, and the food remained untouched on the table. Even the mug was still filled with water. She scanned the cot and herbs nearby moments before catching sight of a trapdoor positioned at the back of the cottage.

Footsteps crunched behind her.

She spun around, ready to unleash magic.

"Arkhon!" Velkan cried with surprise, lifting his hands defensively in the doorway.

She instantly pulled back, seeing him and Brigita rearing back in the snow. Brigita's cheek looked bruised and reddened in the pale light. Maelili grimaced. "Sorry." She could not say if she was apologizing to Brigita directly or to both of them. She rotated around to continue examining the inside of the building. "Whoever lives here is not home. We must hurry."

"Where is the Highborn?" Brigita dared to ask. She did not meet Maelili's eyes.

Maelili surveyed Brigita. Her tone was not condescending; the question was honest. She pointed at the hatch. "This way."

Her footsteps thudded in the closed space. She listened intently, thinking she might hear Falmagon beneath the floorboards. She creaked open the small door and gazed into the dark hole. A fixed wooden ladder descended into the basement.

Fear gripped her. She hoped she was not too late.

"Wait here," she said.

"Arkhon," Velkan protested. "We need to stay together."

Maelili eased herself down onto the first rung. "No. I need you to stay here."

Brigita made a sound as though she wanted to say something, but she kept her lips pursed. She turned around to look out the front door.

Velkan sighed.

A few more rungs and Maelili dropped beneath the floorboards, landing softly on the hardened dirt floor. She immediately heard raspy breathing; at the same time, the smell of urine, feces, and sweat hit her nostrils. Maelili gulped and formed an orb of light with Koldovstvo. The dank room was no more welcoming in person than it had been in Klukas.

Despite her accelerating heartbeat, she steadied her breaths and enhanced the light. The room brightened from the rafters to the swirling specks of dust floating over the floor.

She disregarded the rickety table shoved up against the wall to her right, fastening her eyes on Falmagon, who hung from the creaking ropes by his hands. He made no movement to acknowledge her presence, his head sagging toward the floor. His hands were swollen and red, his arms taut against his weight. The ground beneath his unmoving body was stained red.

Maelili covered her mouth at the sight of the wounds in either of his legs as well as the bruises up and down his midsection. She now saw what his hair had been hiding when she saw him in Klukas—a bandage covered the left side of his face. She inched forward.

"Falmagon." Her unsteady voice did not have enough strength to echo off the walls, but the Highborn still stirred.

He moaned, sputtering awake. His fingers flexed and curled above the knots of his bindings. Slowly, his chin lifted and one blue eye fluttered open to look at her.

"Maelili—" he croaked, wriggling back with obvious apprehension. "He found you...your hair..."

Her hand trembled, her fingers moving from her lips to her red locks and finally resting on Falmagon's chest. His skin was burning hot, feverish. "I am going to get you out of here."

"He won't let you," Falmagon said, his eye watering beneath his straggled strands of hair. His single eye dashed between Maelili's face and her bright hair. "He wants to kill me."

"Falmagon." She searched his face. "No one is going to kill you. Velkan is upstairs. He will heal your wounds. You are going to go home. You—" She looked past him to see an eye carved with a moon and a cross into the wall. "A znaki? Nine Lands, who has you held here?"

Falmagon wheezed between his clenched teeth. "Your brother."

"Kindel," she said with disbelief. "Where is he?"

"I do not know where he went." The fatigue and agony etched across Falmagon's face did little to shield his suspicion. His questions flew from his tongue. "How could you not know your brother did this? How else did you come here?"

"I came on my own," she offered.

"He knows everything about us. He made me tell him. He can use magic," Falmagon stammered. "Your brother is like me, like the Highborn but with more power. He—" His single eye shot to the orb of light above her head and then back to Maelili. "How did—wait—you can, too."

She pressed her hand against his chest, fighting back tears. She could not find any words to soothe him. She could not explain the Stuhia. She did not have time. "I am getting you out of here."

With a quick thought, she used Koldovstvo to cut his bindings. He dropped to the floor with a husky cry, his hands immediately falling to the wounds on his thighs. He winced, and the bandage slid off his head.

He looked up to her, his face wrought with pain. She knelt and cupped his face in her hands.

"Gods," she said, looking into the gooey pit where his eye once was. The wounds on his legs would be simple for Velkan to mend, but to fully restore Falmagon's sight would drain too many years. Her tongue felt swollen in her mouth as she reached for his arm. "Can you walk?"

Falmagon leaned into her, gracelessly pulling his legs under himself. He delayed, studying her. "I will never make it up the ladder."

Maelili shouted over her shoulder. "Velkan!"

Chapter XXI
Falmagon

He dragged his hands back from Maelili slowly and clasped them together. Falmagon could not make sense of what was happening. Clearing his dry throat, he hoped to work up some moisture in his mouth as though that would grant him clarity.

Maelili shouted again with more fervency, causing the soft ache building in his head to throb. "Velkan! Come quick!"

Falmagon groaned, touching his temple. Energy reverberated in the back of his skull. The instant he'd crumpled to the floor, he sensed the power of Koldovstvo return to the edge of his mind. The magic was distant, but he knew he could reach out to it if he wanted. With the znaki scratched into the wall several feet above him, he had escaped the range of the magical ward.

He eyed the magical emblem, repeating the words in his head that Kindel used to create the shielding symbol. He dared not say them out loud. Not yet.

Forbid flesh, forbid soul,
Blood-father, Earth-mother.

Forbid body, forbid blood,
Fire-drinker, Sky-weaver.
Be done thy will; Be done thy will,
Be done thy will; Be done thy will.

For a moment he considered embracing Koldovstvo if only to have a simple taste, as though he were parched for power and not water, but the thought faded as he struggled to keep his eyes open.

Again Maelili promised to see him to safety. He barely heard her.

He stared at her with confusion, pondering what illusions Kindel was capable of with his magic. He had watched Kindel disappear from sight like a Kras twice now.

Was it possible he could change himself into the appearance of Maelili?

He tried to make sense of what had happened since she came down the ladder. He remembered speaking to her, telling her of her brother's power. She freed him. She too had cast magic. She promised him home—Melkorka.

"Are you real?" He shuddered, almost forgetting his nakedness. He dreamed of her too often while hanging in this prison. He was a fool to believe she had really come.

How much had he said that could be used against him? If Kindel were tricking him, how much more would he be punished?

"I am real," she reassured him, reaching for his withdrawn hands.

Her touch was real enough. "I want you to be real," he admitted.

"Arkhon!" A man answered Maelili's call, his voice higher than Kindel's and unfamiliar to Falmagon in his dream-like daze. The sound jostled him. He wondered what *Arkhon* might refer to when the man yelled again. "Are you okay down there?"

"Yes, of course, but I need you," she answered.

Falmagon found the strength to study the redheaded man who hurried down through the trapdoor. He resembled Kindel with his long red hair and wide frame. Falmagon again thought about calling on Koldovstvo; maybe he could burn his captor alive along with the long red hair that haunted his peppered thoughts. However, when Velkan came closer and stepped into the orb of light, Falmagon recognized him as one of Maelili's friends from Kal'bane.

But Velkan did not have red hair before. At least Falmagon did not remember the fire color. He peered closer at Velkan. The man certainly was not Kindel.

"Why are you all different? What trick is this?" Falmagon managed to say, twisting to reach weakly for Maelili's white-red hair. She traced his arms and pulled his hands gently from her locks into her lap. His eye fluttered toward the orb of light, similar to what he could cast. "How are you using Koldovstvo?"

He sucked in a mouthful of air through his narrowly parted lips waiting for a response. For days, he had imagined running his hand through her brown locks, but her hair was no longer colored like the sands of Folkmar. Her white-red hair, although brighter, reminded him of Nedezhda the Longwalker back home.

Was Maelili a Red? Was he meant to kill her? Was Nedezhda his mother? Had he gone mad?

He shook the thought away. He did not want to think of killing Maelili or Nedezhda. Kindel the Red deserved death. Only Kindel.

"I don't have time to explain," Maelili said. "We need to get you fixed up. You must go home."

"I cannot leave," he replied with a grunt, touching his tender leg. "These will take months to heal."

"Velkan," Maelili directed.

Pushing the frayed wisps from his eyes, Velkan neared Falmagon and gulped with hesitation. He scratched at his beard before kneeling. "If you wish it, my Arkhon, I will give my life for his. Though I would like to see my home again."

Maelili shook her head. "I only ask you restore him enough strength to escape this place. Keep what youth you can." She moved Falmagon's hair to the side, revealing his gravest injury. "I am afraid the eye will stay gone."

Velkan hovered his hands over Falmagon's legs, a red and yellow radiance immediately flushing under his hands as he manipulated Koldovstvo. Falmagon tensed, realizing what was happening before his legs began to tingle under the magical energy. A memory surfaced, one he hadn't thought of in a long time. When he was younger, he watched Dorofej mend Andrik's fragmented bone after he stupidly fell from a tower at Melkorka. The injury would have otherwise left Andrik crippled, tearing through his leg at a terrible angle. Healing Andrik cost Dorofej years of his life and likely prevented the old mage from ever healing again.

Falmagon's legs prickled and burned as magic seared through him. He cringed, grinding his teeth as the fibrous tissue and skin stitched back together. As the spell went on, Velkan's hair peppered with grey. Additional wrinkles formed in the corners of his eyes and over his cheeks. Falmagon looked back and forth between Velkan and his healing legs. The affliction in his muscles and bones, the weariness that settled on his mind, disappeared entirely.

Once the bloodied lesions from the arrows became nothing more than sores, Falmagon touched Velkan's outstretched hands with his own. He knew too well the irreversible aging effects of Koldovstvo. He searched for words. "Please stop."

Velkan pulled away.

"Thank you." Falmagon was suddenly speechless, overwhelmed with emotion as life returned to him. Breath. Vitality. Strength. He could have slept for a week uninterrupted and not felt so alive. He breathed deeply and searched Velkan's blue eyes. The man, gifted with the ability to give years of his life for another, averted his gaze. Falmagon was unsure how to speak to him.

What power did Maelili have to command a man to heal him? Was she like Kinhar? Was an Arkhon like a Spearhead?

"I owe you so much," Falmagon said. His immediate thought was to thank the Lightbringer, but the words were forgotten in his confusion.

"You owe Maelili," Velkan said, "and no other. She has stepped aside from her onus to see you free. Go home, Highborn."

"I do not understand," Falmagon said, staring at his exposed blotched skin once more before meeting Maelili's gaze. Her eyes were as green as the deepest waters. "How is this possible? How are you here?"

"Velkan," Maelili rose to her feet, ignoring his pointed questions, "go see if you can find him some clothes."

"Yes, my Arkhon," Velkan said, dipping his chin.

Falmagon watched Velkan retreat to the ladder and ascend to the cottage. A conversation between him and another—a female who Falmagon surmised was Maelili's second companion at Arkaim—immediately echoed down the hatch. They may have been arguing in heated whispers; he could not be certain. He ignored the rustling above and stood to face Maelili. "Please speak to me. Tell me how you found me. How are you able to cast Koldovstvo? Why did you not say anything before? Why does he call you Arkhon? What does it mean?"

Maelili stared hard at him, lifting her chin slightly as though she held a station above all others in the world. Her visage was of nobility and strength. "I am not going to answer your questions, Falmagon. I—I have my reasons. We do not have the time and I do not have the mind. We will find you clothes and we will send you home where you belong," she replied. She blinked, trembling with her next words. "You must forget about me."

Falmagon stepped closer, her eyes level with the bottom of his chin. He took in a breath, noting that she mentioned only herself and not her friends. "How could I forget about you? I have not stopped thinking of you since the moment we met."

"Falmagon."

"Do you love me?" he blurted.

"I—" she stammered. She lowered her eyes, the light orb twinkling from existence. As darkness fell around them, she whispered shakily. "I do."

He did not let her say any more. To forever remember her face, he crafted his own orb of light over them. Falmagon gently lifted Maelili's chin and pressed his lips to hers. They were cold, chapped, and perfect. Her hot breath flooded from her nose, pushing back against him. He pulled her body against his own, wrapping his arm around the middle of her body.

She settled into his embrace, breathing heavily, and pressed her forehead against his chest. "We cannot, Falmagon. You must leave."

"And you will come with me."

"No," she said, pulling his arm from her waist and stepping back. He did not fight her, swallowing hard under the weakening light. "You will go home. Alone."

He shivered, suddenly feeling colder than he ever had before in the forsaken hole in the earth. "Why?"

"I must take my brother home," Maelili said.

"By Mulafell! Your brother is insane!" Falmagon reached for Maelili. When she stepped outside of his reach, he pointed at his missing eye. "Look what he did to me!"

"I know."

"If I see him, I will kill him!" Falmagon screamed.

Maelili's eyes went cold. "You will not. Kindel is all the family I have left." She bit her lip and stepped aside. "You will go home. Now."

"You are not—"

"Go," she said decisively, looking at the wall across the makeshift dungeon. "I don't want to see you again. Ever."

Her words hurt him. Even in the moment, he knew the violence inside him that begged for release was born from his heartache and not anything righteous.

He wanted something equally painful to say in return, but nothing suitable came to mind. His hand scratched at his chest as though it might tear his heart through his flesh in a single swipe. If he were capable of surviving it, he would lay it at her feet. His first footstep came with the knowledge that he would have to live with her rejecting him a second time. His wrath, his fire, emerged in a single hushed word, like smoke on the wind. "Fine."

Falmagon walked past Maelili and grabbed a ladder rung. Every slow step took effort. He waited for her to say something more, anything to stop him. When the silence became too deafening to bear, he climbed out.

Velkan waited for him at the top, holding an armful of clothes. The gods only knew how much he had heard of their conversation. He offered Falmagon a hand. "I found these stuffed under the cot. I sent Brigita outside so you could dress without an audience." He pointed to a worn pack sitting by a cot. "Take my gear. You should have enough rations to last you until Jh'terin."

Falmagon bit his inner cheek, steadying himself and taking the clothes. He looked at the inside of the cottage for the first time, having to twist his head back and forth to see with his one eye. A messy cot, a cold meal, and too-familiar herbs were strewn about. Falmagon swallowed. "Where is he?"

"Who?" Velkan wrinkled his brow. "If you mean your captor, I cannot say. No one has been here since we arrived. I suspect the Arkhon will make short work of him when he returns."

Falmagon grimaced. Either Velkan did not hear his conversation with Maelili or he was playing stupid, though he looked innocent enough. "I doubt it. Why do you call her Arkhon?"

It was Velkan's turn to scrunch his face. "If she did not tell you, I will not either. Why are you so far away from home?"

"I will answer your question if you answer mine," Falmagon said.

Velkan gestured to the clothes. "Best get dressed and be on your way."

"I suppose you will not tell me how you have wielded Koldovstvo either? Are you Highborn?" Falmagon asked, studying the larger man. The red hair hanging over Velkan's face still made him uneasy. "By Mulafell. How many of you are in the far north? Why are you not at Melkorka with the rest of us?"

"We are not like you, Highborn," Velkan said. "I am sorry, but you will leave this cottage disappointed."

Falmagon looked down at his feet, heat building behind his eyelids, helpless in the wake of the situation. He was freed and then discarded as swiftly as food caught between the teeth. He gave Velkan a flinty gaze, not having the words to argue with the man who was better described as Maelili's sentinel. The woman he loved remained beneath the surface, apparently refusing to come out from the pit until he was gone. He held no power.

He cleared his throat. "Well—that's that, then." He fumbled with the clothes. With haste, he awkwardly pulled the white tunic over his head, then slipped on the brown trousers and brown cloak. Afterward, he pulled on the stockings, slipped his feet into the leather boots, and put on the wool gloves provided for him. The clothes were not his own, but they fit him well enough.

Velkan caught his attention, reaching for a bandage near the herbs and layering something green on the inside. "I know this is not how you wanted to go, Highborn." He stepped forward and wrapped the bandage over Falmagon's missing eye, assuring the herbs were pressed over the wound. Falmagon flinched but did not stop him. "I wish you safe travels. Take care of your people."

Falmagon stood to his full height to meet the redhead's gaze. He took note of how Velkan put the emphasis on his people being different. Somehow, he did not think he was speaking of the Highborn but instead referred to the Anshedar. "I will return."

"It will do you no good. You will not find us."

Falmagon felt a lump form in his throat. He walked past Velkan and out the front door. He was not surprised to see Brigita waiting outside, her red hair flowing, her arms crossed under her breasts.

"I hope you said your goodbyes," she snipped.

His thoughts spun, and he pinched his lips together to keep them from trembling.

"Take care of her," he said. "By Mulafell, take care of her."

Chapter XXII
Maelili

"Best get dressed and be on your way." Velkan's light tone carried down into the hole behind Maelili. His and Falmagon's muffled voices and footsteps sounded above her. She trusted Velkan or Brigita would be quick to escort Falmagon away from the cottage. For herself, she'd rather be ignorant as to how he was convinced to leave.

She dawdled beneath the floorboards, unwilling to face him again. She sucked in the stale smell of the underearth and blew it out between her teeth. The sour air left a decayed taste on the tip of her tongue. She focused on the tang as though it might distract her from the ache in her chest.

She pinched her forearms in an attempt to keep herself grounded, but her thoughts were unmanageable despite her disinterest in daydreaming about what could or should be. Falmagon's voice distracted her from delving too deep, though she would have preferred not to hear him speak.

"Well—that's that, then."

"Gods." She cringed, eyes burning at the sound of his uneven tone.

Even in rescuing him, she hurt him *again*.

She kept her back turned from the light flooding through the hatch, studying the table pushed against the wall. In the yellow haze, she could see little except that the tabletop was barren. She did not want to imagine what tools may have lined its surface. She gradually twisted to gawk at the space where she'd found Falmagon hanging. Strands of rope dangled from the wooden planks above her. With a closer look, she realized several loops of rope circled the wooden beam, suggesting Falmagon was not the first prisoner to be held here. She gulped, refusing to look too closely. She did not want to know whether blood stained the knotted threads.

Her mind reeled, trying to understand what torture Falmagon underwent. *What was Kindel doing here?*

Her insides were tangled. She should be excited at the possibility of reuniting with her brother. She did not want to think about whether or not he was Falmagon's captor. Maelili never knew Kindel to be violent or cruel, yet with almost a century gone, she would be foolish to claim she knew her brother. She spent league after league hoping Falmagon met her brother on the shores of Melkorka, and even now, hoped Falmagon told the truth. Maybe the thought was blind optimism, but she wanted the search for Kindel to come to an end.

"He is gone," Velkan interrupted her thoughts, calling down from the ladder.

Maelili cleared her throat. "I am coming," she said loud enough for him to hear her. "Give me a moment."

Her chin quivered. She tucked a strand of hair back behind her ear and twisted away from the splintered ropes hanging from the rafters. She could not deny her feelings for Falmagon; she loved him. She knew she would regret not looking on him again, but she was also glad he had gone. She did not want him here when Kindel returned to the cottage. She could not fault Falmagon for wanting to revenge. If she were captured and tortured, she would vow to avenge the wrongs against her. Nine Lands, she planned to ultimately locate her own enemy, the Kaligulas, and separate their heads from their shoulders, but she did not come to the ends of Aenar to watch her brother die.

It was only now she realized the extent of her impulsiveness in freeing Falmagon. This land called Kalamaar, the Highborn, and everything in between were all unfamiliar to her. Perhaps Kindel was defending himself or responding to something about which Maelili was completely unaware.

She hoped Kindel would forgive her.

"No! Maelili!" Velkan's scream chilled Maelili's spine, springing gooseflesh across her arms. Something crashed against the floorboards as he stomped across the floor above. The cottage creaked and cracked under some unseen pressure. "He is killing Brigita!"

"Gods…Falmagon," Maelili mouthed the name, her mind reeling with how she might have made a mistake in releasing him. She rushed to exit the basement just as the door slammed in the cottage above. Her hands shook as she scaled the ladder and pulled herself through the hatch. She took in just enough of the inner room to bound over a fallen chair and strewn remnants of herbs, pushing the door wide against a sudden strong wind. Outside she witnessed a horrific scene reminiscent of the old wars between the Stuhia and the skin-switchers.

Lightning and fire zipped back and forth fifty paces ahead, rustling and crackling. The horse whinnied somewhere behind her. Maelili lifted a hand protectively, the bolts and flames zigzagging in every direction, vaulting into the open wilderness. She first spotted Velkan rushing toward the battering elements. His red-gold hair bounced over his shoulders as he unhooked his heavy cloak with a single hand, letting the wind take it.

"Stop!" he cried. With a wave of his hand, Velkan manipulated stone magic to sprout the earth toward the heavens in columns. Seven-foot pillars of rock checkered the landscape, engulfing Brigita in a fortified stronghold, protecting her from the energy sprouting from the attacker's hands.

Maelili noticed Brigita fall to a knee behind the rock, seemingly thankful for Velkan's protection from the onslaught. Half of Brigita's face was covered in armor fashioned from thick bark through magic, blackened and smoldering from the multiple attacks she had already endured. She turned her chin in time to make eye contact with Velkan before the fortification fully surrounded her.

Ice and frozen chunks of dirt flew in all directions as Brigita vanished behind the wall of earth. The attacker beyond hit the structure a couple more times with Koldovstvo, but Velkan forged a new pillar for every one that fissured. The storm of elements created a wafting, brown-hued cloud of filth filling the area, almost hiding the assailant's identity from Maelili. But she still recognized him.

Her instinct was to cry out joyously that the enemy was not Falmagon standing in the residue. Yet her chest tightened seeing familiar red strands of hair as the man, her brother, clutched Habermani and moved his attention from Brigita to Velkan.

Maelili swallowed the knot forming in her throat seeing her father's staff. Habermani diluted the amount of Koldovstvo channeling through it, increasing the amount of magic Kindel could wield at any given time. He could fight longer and sling more powerful spells with little worry about growing old. She needed to stop him.

"Kindel!"

The sound was swept away by a gust of wind and masked by Kindel shouting over her, furiously pointing Habermani at Velkan. She barely heard him. "All you Half-bloods will die! You do not deserve this magic!"

"Kindel!" Maelili shrieked again, sliding away from the door. The sound of her voice was carried off as she heightened her scream. "Kindel!"

The house behind her creaked again as the earth rumbled under her feet.

Kindel was oblivious to her standing by the quaking cottage. He embraced Koldovstvo, touching the void magic of their bloodline, and skipped through the empty space between him and Velkan in a breath's time. The end of Habermani crushed into Velkan's ribcage. His eyes bulged, mechanically looking toward the center of his body, only to be hit with the other end of the staff under the chin. His head snapped back, stretching his neck and knocking him back.

Kindel was not finished with him. He flitted through the snow in a flash of color to crouch under Velkan before he could fall. Scowling with hate, he snapped the end of the Habermani against the back of Velkan's skull. The resounding pop turned Maelili's stomach.

Velkan slid against the broken ground with a grunt, his large hand gripping at the snow.

Maelili embraced Koldovstvo to move like Kindel and intercept them. She had scarcely taken two steps before Velkan used sky magic to push himself off the ground. Anger—a rare emotion for the man—lined his facial features. He rotated, the full of his hand and half of his arm glowing with a golden hue. With a shout, he punched her brother in the chest. The magical energy exploded, sending Kindel skidding and rolling across the terrain while clinging to the staff. The aftershock of the powerful strike knocked Maelili back into the corner of the cottage.

The pillars surrounding Brigita cracked.

Maelili crumpled to the ground with a heavy groan, feeling pain shoot through a rib. She coughed and tried to stand, only to have darkness invade her vision. She rarely witnessed wielders of sacred magic like Velkan use their power as weapons. They were meant to be healers on the battlefield.

A disorienting, gurgled cry urged her to get to her feet. Her body flooded with heat; her heartbeat sounded in her ears. Shoving herself up, she angled her head toward Velkan and Kindel, calling out again.

"Kind—" she croaked, her word morphing into a primal scream. Velkan stood limp with Kindel at his side and the end of Habermani shoved through his neck. Blood jetted from the ripped flesh before pouring down Velkan's shoulder and broad chest. With his head oddly tilted, Velkan blinked once, his body twitching in shock. Finally, Kindel pulled the weapon free.

Velkan dropped. Dead.

Maelili's gut knotted. "No!"

Koldovstvo filled her as she sprang across the distance to Velkan. Kneeling by his body, she cupped the wound on either side of his neck. His lifeblood spilled between her fingers. His empty green eyes stared wide open at nothing. The speed with which Kindel had moved and the power he'd put into his attack nauseated her.

"You…killed him." Over the years, she had thought of hundreds of different scenarios for her reunion with Kindel. She expected warm embraces and gentle words, fireside chats and joined laughter. Never this.

"Mae—lili?" Her brother's hollow voice was swept away in her misery. He dropped his staff to the ground by her.

She ignored Habermani, tears flooding her eyes. The northern wind only seemed to increase in its strength, roaring in her ears as it swept over the terrain.

Any other time, even despite the circumstances, she thought she might be strong enough to ignore the sting in her heart, but without food or rest—with her recent heartbreak—she was sapped of self-control. "Why?" she growled, her voice gravelly. She struggled to meet Kindel's blue eyes. "Why would you kill your brethren? We came here to bring you home."

Kindel blinked rapidly, suspending his breath for a moment. His entire body went rigid, looking back at Maelili with a dumbfounded expression. "Are you sure he is not one of the Highborn? One—one of the Half-bloods?"

"This is Velkan Amaria! He served our family since our father's reign. He has traveled the length of Aenar to find you at my command. He was a friend!" The rock pillars behind Kindel crumbled to the ground. Maelili lifted a hand at Brigita, who staggered from the wrecked earth, her fresh bark-like armor fading from her skin. She covered her mouth at the sight of Velkan. Maelili rattled with rage. "And that is Brigita Mather."

"By the gods," Brigita whispered. "Velkan."

"Amaria. Mather," Kindel said, clearly recognizing the names. "I am sorry, my sister. I did not know him. I thought he came to free my prisoner." He gestured off into the distance.

Brigita approached as Kindel's voice faded. "My Arkhon..." She knelt to Maelili's side, placing a hand on her leg. The left side of her face was burned. The first signs of age touched her cheeks and forehead from her use of Koldovstvo.

"Arkhon?" Kindel's eyes widened.

Maelili could not look back at Velkan's body as she wiped the tears from her eyes. They continued to roll down her cheeks despite her attempt to steady her breath. She could feel the flush in her face as she stood to face him. "Yes, Kindel. Your brothers—Ghanimer, Simon, Peter—and your sister, Elena, are all dead at the hand of the Kaligulas. I buried them one by one alongside Father."

Maelili sucked air through her nose and held it for a moment. She hated speaking of her deceased siblings, especially Ghanimer, who she willingly abandoned to save herself when threatened by Drast Kaligula.

She breathed deeply, hardly believing she was explaining this over Velkan's corpse. "Years ago, we reclaimed our home from the Kaligulas. I have been searching to bring you home." She swallowed hard, looking at her brother's confused expression. She could not guess what he must have thought over the past seventy-five years. "Sadly, your return will no longer be one of celebration. You will be tried by the Ninth Council for your murder of Velkan. I will speak mercifully for you, but their ruling will stand. If you are not put to death, you will forever be indentured to his husband."

Kindel tensed his jaw so tightly that his cheekbones became visible. "Why would I return? Take Father's staff if you must, but I cannot go back to Lairhein."

"Why would you not?" Maelili asked. "You fear judgment well deserved?"

"I do not fear judgment, Maelili. I have my charge to fulfill here on Kalamaar." Kindel pushed his red-grey hair from his eyes. "Demons are bleeding out from under the mountains. The alleged Highborn—half-blooded offspring forged between the Stuhia and the Anshedar—are taking control of the Northmen while wielding Koldovstvo— our magic! The magic gifted to the Stuhian people! They wrongly pay homage to the Lightbringer. Yet they do nothing to stop the looming threat of devils springing from the Netherworld."

"How do you know they are half-bloods and without their own gifts?" Maelili asked. "Who is to say only the Stuhia can wield Koldovstvo?"

"Our people walked with the gods in the ancient days, Maelili. The Anshedar were nearly wiped from existence because of their destructive nature. You know the histories," Kindel hissed. "The Highborn are born from those Stuhia with the profane bloodline, those who left Lairhein after the Carian Council was put to rest."

Brigita, despite her young age, seemed to understand the significance of Kindel's revelation. She formed a fist, clutching Velkan's bloodied clothes. "Nine Lands. That was more than a thousand years ago."

"We should have executed them. Our stupidity has created these monstrous humans. They have not the foresight of the Stuhia, bound to live their short lives. The Anshedar blood makes them age like any human but the bastards control the elements as well as any Stuhian soldier. Come with me and destroy them, and then I will return with you to Lairhein. I do not fear judgment, I promise you. I will take my punishment, but not before I cleanse the East of these half-bloods."

"Kindel—" Maelili tried.

"I know you loved one of these monsters. I suspect you could not have known what he truly was," Kindel said with an air of urgency. He reached down and grabbed Habermani, pushing it into Maelili's hands. His eyes brightened as though he could tell his secret at last. "He is my prisoner in the cottage behind you. Come and see him. Kill him with me and then we will march on Melkorka."

Maelili gripped her family's heirloom in her hand, looking to Brigita, who touched Velkan's dead body in sustained disbelief. From the corner of her eye, she caught sight of the blood staining the edge of the staff.

Brigita may have been right all along. Her brother had gone mad while away from Lairhein.

"We are not murderers," she said.

"The Highborn are no better than the Kaligulas, Maelili. You must see that," Kindel said. "They are power-hungry and dangerous. You will feel better once we kill him. I promise you."

"No one is in your cottage, Kindel," Maelili said.

Kindel, seemingly forgetting about Velkan, accidentally kicked the dead man's legs as he stepped forward. He smiled at her. "He is beneath the floorboards, hidden away in the basement. I have him—"

"I saw," Maelili said. "No one is down there."

"What?" Kindel's head flinched back slightly. "You mean to say he escaped…or you freed him?"

"We did not free anyone." Her hands shook. She hoped she might keep her murderous brother from pursuing Falmagon. "I have seen a znaki broken before, Kindel. Leave it alone. He is gone." As soon as the words sprang from her mouth, Maelili wished she had told the truth instead.

She met Brigita's speechless look.

"Broke a znaki?" Kindel's eyes widened, twisting to look for prints in the snow. "By the gods, he is more powerful than I thought. He could not have gone far."

Chapter XXIII
Falmagon

"Lightbringer, my Lord, see me home," Falmagon murmured, trudging south along the treeline. A harsh, never-ending airstream pressed at his back, flapping his cloak against the back of his knees and thrashing his hair about in every direction.

For a moment, he thought he heard a scream in the far distance but could distinguish nothing in the steadfast gale. Still, he looked over his shoulder to see the flakes weaving through the air forming a white blanket of flying snow. His vision was completely obstructed.

With the freezing wind stinging his eyes, he faced south once more, his hands clenched into fists. He was glad Velkan gave him gloves to fight the cold. No doubt the weather would worsen between here and the Seven Islands.

Mile after mile he plodded on, away from the desolate cottage, hoping each step would push Maelili farther from his mind. He could not imagine a life without her, but he could think of no words to convince her to stay with him. Twice she had pushed him away. He wondered if any Highborn could truly have love. Nedezhda may have been right—the Highborn were destined to be unloved; maybe he was unlovable.

Perchance the Lightbringer could not allow him to love, lest it interfere with his onus to the Highborn and the Kadari. His parents abandoned him. Andrik deserted him. Maelili rejected him.

Were Maelili and his final farewell a matter of fate?

He frowned at his plight.

With the aim of distracting himself, Falmagon looked for the sun's glow behind the clouds. He found the light hanging low above the birch trees. The days were much shorter than they had been before Kindel brought him so far north. He swore these lands were always overcast, but in truth, the Season of Frost was ruled by gods unlike his patron, the White-Clad. He prayed he would survive until spring.

"Deliver me safely to Melkorka. By Mulafell, guide my feet away from demons and enemies alike. I just want to go home," Falmagon said. Creaks and cracks echoed in the wintry forest to his left as the branches fought against the weight of the snow and the heedless wind. He had no desire to enter the forest, even if he was meant to seek shelter from the storm. He recalled the old maps at Melkorka that marked the many marshlands within the forest's belly. Ice-covered or not, he would not risk traipsing over them.

His foot slipped on the ice, but he regained his balance and adjusted the pack on his back. "Give me strength, Lightbringer, and I will bring you glory. I will never love again. I swear it."

As though his prayer went unheard, heavier snowflakes began drifting down from the heavens, threatening to further block his already limited vision, pelting against him on all sides. The cold sting of each crystal of snow was like a pinprick to his head, face, and neck.

"Stay the light, Dahz! I am yours to mold as you see fit. Hear me!" he said louder to both bolster himself and remind himself not to lose courage.

In his heart, Falmagon knew he was facing his final test. He would have to find his own way home without divine intervention. If he had been chosen as Kinhar indicated or was worthy to be called Longwalker—or even blessed enough to be among the Kadari—he would have to trek to Melkorka without the aid of any gods.

Despite all that had happened, he held faith that he could see it done. He was not at his full strength, but the trek home was not impossible. His duty demanded he speak with Kinhar about the demons and tell him of Erzebeth's wisdom. A Red needed killing. Nedezhda—mother or not— meddled in death magic, yet the true concern was Maelili's brother. Falmagon was confident that he was the one meant to be slain.

With the aid of the Highborn, he vowed to come back and see it done.

He adjusted the bandage over his missing eye, feeling the herbs pressing against the wound. It was not so much painful as it was uncomfortable.

A tumult of shouting and screaming resounded behind Falmagon, halting his struggle against the wrath of wintertime. He stopped and twisted around to see three dark figures advancing through the snow. He lifted a hand to his forehead in attempt to block Dahz's yellow radiance reflecting off the glistening landscape. With his limited eyesight and the inhospitable weather conditions, he could barely make out the red hair on each figure.

He bit down on a smile. It looked like Maelili changed her mind and was coming to be with him. She truly loved him. Maybe he was not forsaken to a life of emptiness after all. And yet a moment ago, he had sworn to the Lightbringer that he would lead a loveless life.

He began walking toward her to embrace her return. He waved his hand over his head in a wide gesture.

Maelili howled something unintelligible, frantically waving a familiar staff over her head. He took a few more steps, allowing him to get a better look at her and her two companions. Brigita stomped along in a half-run, a good distance behind, trying to keep up. Maelili's panicked expression ultimately came into view as she skidded closer. She hollered again. "Run, Falmagon!"

He squinted at the male figure trailing a step behind her. Kindel—not Velkan—suddenly embraced his magic and darted by her in a blur.

Maelili cried out in desperation reaching out for her brother. Unseen magic struck Kindel in the side knocking him from his feet and into the snow. She advanced on Kindel, shouting at him to stop.

Falmagon dropped his arm and clambered backwards, realizing the danger. Kindel had come to kill him before he could return. He knew he could not win one-on-one, and who knew which side Maelili or Brigita would take in the end.

He cursed and turned to flee.

He took only a few steps before realizing he could never escape Kindel in the open countryside and looked to the forest with dread.

Falmagon sped in between the white and black trees, stamping by the closely grown vegetation. Snowberries and shrubs with wide-brimmed leaves were but splotches to him as he hurdled through the woods. With every step, Falmagon feared he might land on the thin ice of an unseen fen. He gritted his teeth and pressed onward, weaving east and south. The snow-laden trees and heavy snowfall caused the already faint light of the sun to dull all the more.

"Run!" Maelili screamed from somewhere in the distance, telling him he had not gone far enough and she could not hold back her brother.

For all he knew, Kindel could be right over his shoulder.

He picked up his pace, pushing off the trees as he scampered through the woods. Before long, Falmagon no longer could see the wide-open plains, finding himself lost among the seemingly identical trees. The spindly stalks with thinning bark stretched in every direction. It looked as though the gods had one design and repeated it throughout the length of the woodland.

He halted to catch his breath with a snort, his lungs burning and wheezing. He hoped he had not become hopelessly lost—Kindel might kill him, but so could the wilderness.

The tree next to him splintered across the middle, the fibers of wood wrenching apart as the tree began leaning toward him. Falmagon had not the time to look for the cause. He stumbled forward ten paces or more and dived into a wet bank of snow, growling to himself as the slush enveloped him.

The tree went down behind him, clipping the branches of several others around it before the trunk finally snapped. It hit the ground with a deep thud, the impact vibrating through his frame.

Its collision with the ground caused snow to spew into the air. Just as Falmagon pried himself out of the soggy snow bank, Kindel appeared on the opposite side of the tree. Kindel lifted his hand and sneered. "Time for you to die, Half-blood."

The bulk of the tree shifted, groaning and cracking as it lifted into the air at Kinhar's command. Veering back like a sideways battering ram, Kinhar drove the full of the fallen tree at him. Falmagon gasped, moving from a half-crouch to a sprint, pushing his legs hard in an effort to avoid being crushed. He faltered through the snow, cringing as additional trees behind him either fragmented from the force or were ripped from the ground by their roots. Snow and ice misted the air from the canopy overhead. With a snarl, Falmagon lunged to the side amid more trees. By a hair's breadth, he dodged the oversized log crashing at his back.

Staying on the tips of his toes, Falmagon twisted around to see Kindel's distorted figure coming at him. The enemy snaked through the trees at the speed of the wind.

Falmagon elevated his hands to cast a spell but could not move quickly enough. Kindel's blue eyes flashed in front of his own, fiery hair blazing against the pale backdrop, and then a fist pounded his empty eye socket.

He bawled, blood gushing into his bandage and down the bridge of his nose. He raised his hands only to have them swiped to the side. Kindel's elbow cracked against his jaw, and another jab hit him in the gut.

By some miracle, Falmagon kept his wits about him, unleashing a torrent of fire from his hands with more intensity than he had against the Witiko. He could feel his life draining from his body. The arc of fire lashed out at Kindel, striking him in his left side. He yelped, hurrying from his vantage point, his clothes smoldering and smoking along with his burnt flesh.

"You will be the one who dies!" Falmagon cried, trying to follow Kindel's quick movements.

Kindel leapt back several feet where the shards of broken trees lay. He loosed a handful of fire bolts at Falmagon, who responded by raising shields of ice to catch each one, fizzling from existence harmlessly.

Falmagon roared, glaring at Kindel through the increasing snowfall. Knowing he would age years from the effort, Falmagon twisted the snowflakes into daggers of ice and shot hundreds in Kindel's direction. The targeted spread left Kindel standing in the unavoidable shade of inevitable death.

Frantically, his enemy attempted to use Koldovstvo to offset the ice daggers' trajectory, but Falmagon pushed them forward with more effort, sending a second wave behind the first. He could sense the power of his magic burning from the top of his forehead to the center of his chest.

Through his strain, he saw something more move from the corner of his eye.

Another haze of color tore through the trees toward his quarry. Quick as lightning, Maelili appeared next to her brother, holding Habermani in her hand. She cried out, her other arm extended with the intent of pushing Kindel clear of the attack.

"No!" Her distorted shout bounced off the remaining trees, piercing through the northern windstorm like a knife. The sound would haunt him for eternity.

Falmagon watched, horrified, as the countless projectiles pierced through Maelili and Kindel. The sharpened shards impaled their flesh, sending them staggering backwards through the falling snow. Stains of bright blood followed their descent until each body bent and dropped in the earth.

"Gods!" Falmagon blubbered. "No, no, no."

The race to reach them seemed like an eternity. As loud as his shouts were, his footfalls sounded like war drums, every branch and clump of ice crushing beneath his weight.

The watery, fetid discharge continued oozing from his missing eye. He wiped his nose and cheek, smearing the gore down his face, and then ran his fingers through his hair. He passed by Kindel's sprawled, unmoving figure. Blood spilled from Kindel's jugular and chest, pooling around his scorched left arm and the side of his stomach. His hair had less color than when Falmagon was held prisoner at the cottage; deep wrinkles lined his cheeks, indicating his advanced age. He had expended himself greatly without Habermani in his hands.

Without a doubt, the man was dead before he hit the ground. His body did not even twitch.

The *Red* was dead.

A knot formed in Falmagon's throat as he looked to Maelili several feet away. Her chest heaved above a swelling in the earth. He inched closer, seeing her white-red hair draped over the sludge and dirt. Her legs convulsed, awkwardly bowed underneath her as though she wanted to stand. Her green eyes sheened with tears looking at him, and then her eyes fluttered shut. Her cough turned into a gurgle, spurting a mouthful of spit and blood over her lips.

"Ark—hon!" Falmagon heard Brigita's distant yell from somewhere in the woods.

Maelili's eyes popped back open. She tilted her head toward the sound and tried to shout. "Brigita."

Falmagon barely heard her burbled cry.

His eyes raked over her body. Several dozen pin-sized holes were scattered from her throat to her knees, crimson barely noticeable in the dark greens and greys of her attire. Her insides were likely mush. She would soon be dead like her brother.

He dropped to his knees next to Maelili, reaching for her cheek. "Gods, I—"

She used what strength she had to recoil from his touch. Falmagon pulled his hand back, gripping his shirt until his knuckles hurt. Her look was fierce. He could not recall ever being looked upon with such hate. Her tone was tart. "Leave me, Highborn."

"Arkhon!" Brigita had gotten closer. Falmagon hastily scanned the forest; she was still nowhere to be seen.

"I did not want this," Falmagon tried, fighting the scratch in the back of his throat. His shoulders curved forward, shaking his head with disbelief. His fingers rubbed against his full-grown mustache.

"Leave me!" she croaked.

"I—I don't want to leave you like this." He searched for something more to say. "I loved you, Maelili."

Snow crunched to his right. He lifted his head to see Brigita stall at the edge of a birchwood. She shouted again, "My Arkhon!"

Maelili just barely lifted her head from the ground. "You disgust me."

Falmagon drew back, seeing Habermani lying beyond Maelili's reach. He glowered at her hatefully and then reached for the weapon. He gripped the solid staff in his hand, feeling a strange power tingle in the back of his skull.

"What have you done to her?" Brigita screeched. The sound of her footsteps amplified as she rushed through the forest. "What have you done, Highborn?"

Falmagon did not respond. He knew the answer—he'd made the mistake of giving Maelili his heart when he was truly unlovable.

A gust of wind, powered by Koldovstvo, lifted him from the ground and flung him from Maelili's side. He spiraled once through the air and slammed into the ground.

With a groan, he stood to face Brigita, who was muttering something under her breath. The trees on either side of him tremored, the roots sprouting from the ground by some strange magic.

He screamed in defiance and extended his hand that held Habermani, throwing Brigita backwards into a tree to break her concentration. She flipped around the base, crashing into the snow with a thump.

Falmagon did not wait to see whether she climbed back to her feet. He ran.

Chapter XXIV
Maelili

Her breath caught in her swollen chest as she gasped for air, her torso and arms tensed. She strained against the uneven woodland floor, the tempest thundering behind her through the trees. She balled her hands into fists to contend with a nonstop shiver rocking through her. She needed to manage a bit longer.

She was not ready to die.

All of a sudden, her lungs emptied, a burst of white mist expelling from her trembling lips. As though her craving for life overcame death's call, she immediately inhaled, frantically speaking a single word with the breath given to her. "Brigita," she uttered with what strength she could muster.

Only the relentless wind answered her call.

She could not move to see where Brigita might have gone. Maelili had lost feeling in her legs while Falmagon still hovered over her, and she had not the strength to shift her head. She feared her upper body was frozen solid and was surprised to be able to move her lips at all. She was so very cold. And thirsty.

The short exchange between Brigita and Falmagon could have happened a lifetime ago and she would know no different. She hoped he had not killed her too.

She tried to squirm one way or another to no avail.

"Brigita," she tried again.

Nothing.

Her aching eyes, helplessly frozen open in the frigid far north temperatures, were as dry as her throat was parched. She had no choice but to stare at the enlarged snowflakes spiraling down from the sky. She knew the heavens were not the home of the gods; her spirit would not float from her body and ascend into any land beyond the sky. She would be ripped free from this flesh and steered into the Netherworld to be judged by Wolos. If she met her charge in life, she could be taken beyond Thrice Nine Lands to Thrice Ten Kingdom and rewarded for her valor. If not, she would be twisted into a ghost, demon, or devil to roam the frozen wasteland of the cursed Netherworld forevermore.

Maelili believed her charge was to bring her brother home and to have her revenge on the dishonorable Kaligulas. Yet Falmagon robbed her of her calling. He also robbed her son of a mother, her husband of a wife, and her nation of their Arkhon.

Falmagon killed her.

She hated him for it. Her ire may have very well empowered her to remain conscious for a few final moments. She was without peace, filled with uncertainty and fear, but she was breathing.

She was so thirsty.

"Arkhon." Brigita appeared over her. The woman was no longer young, wrinkles lining the edges of her mouth and wide eyes. She placed her hand on Maelili's forehead; her touch was hot like a flame. Her voice quivered. "By the gods, why did you run ahead? My bloodline does not allow me to move as fast as you or your brother."

Maelili's voice grew weaker. "It's not your…fault. I was reckless."

"He killed you, Arkhon. You freed him, and he killed you!" Brigita cried.

"He did," Maelili admitted. The taste of copper filled her mouth. She could taste nothing else.

Brigita wept. For how long they sat there, Maelili could not say. Darkness pulled at the corners of her eyes, and she fought against it. Once or twice, she attempted to soothe Brigita but could not be certain her own words came out as anything more than sobs.

Brigita coughed and sputtered over her, tears streaming down her face. Her discolored cheeks looked worse in the cold, blue and bruised, where Maelili had wrongly struck her half a day ago. Bloodied scratches lined the girl's exposed flesh as well as the burn marks from combat.

The world above Maelili flashed white. She could see little else besides Brigita's distraught features. "You fought well," Maelili finally said.

She softly shook her head in reply and looked away to the south. "Velkan is dead. Kindel, too. Habermani is gone." She lifted her hands to wipe her tears away. "I will get your father's staff back. I will give it to your husband and son. I will rip Falmagon's heart out."

"No," Maelili choked. "No, Brigita. Go home."

"Arkhon…" Brigita leaned in. Maelili could feel pressure on her hands, and she knew Brigita was holding on to her.

"Go home," she repeated. "Protect my son. Guide him to greatness." The blood filling her mouth gushed out.

Her vision darkened as she thought of Eisliev back in Lairhein. She could see his childish red curls bouncing as he bounded down the road. She imagined her husband—her powerless husband, Nevyn—scooping him up and squeezing him tight. Maelili longed to hold her child again.

Her heart ached.

"As you wish, my Arkhon," Brigita said reassuringly, using the words Maelili so often heard from Velkan. She wondered if she would meet him, her siblings, or her dear father on the other side. Brigita's voice pulled her away from her musing. "Tell me, Arkhon. What more can I do?"

Maelili hoped she had the strength to speak her final request. "Tell Eisliev to beware—of the Kaligulas—"

Month of Melting
Sixth of Frost
119 CE

Epilogue
Falmagon

Falmagon Sej stepped down from the stirrup hanging off the black mare he acquired from a stable master at Narthwich and unstrapped Habermani from behind the saddle. The buzz in the back of his skull returned, the power of the artifact surging through him. He had not learned how Kindel or Maelili had moved so swiftly or disappeared from sight, but he discovered Habermani gave him the ability to wield Koldovstvo smoother than he ever had before.

He kept the crooked staff close and smiled, quickly reiterating the words to make the znaki in his mind. He would need to tell Kinhar word for word.

Forbid flesh, forbid soul,
Blood-father, Earth-mother.
Forbid body, forbid blood,
Fire-drinker, Sky-weaver.
Be done thy will; Be done thy will,
Be done thy will; Be done thy will.

He pulled on the reins to lead the horse up the short incline to Melkorka's rickety gate, using the staff as a walking stick. The memorable tower and elevated keep had his knees feeling weak since he began his climb from the adjacent shoreline. After months, he was finally home.

The horse whickered near his ear, blowing hot air from its wide nostrils. He nudged the horse away with his hand and caught his breath. He could see quick movement behind the split wooden planks as he approached.

"Open the gates!" Nedezhda's imposing voice was unmistakeable. The wooden doorway began opening at her command, creaking in the ancient pivots.

She waited for him in the courtyard as several Kras pushed at the doors with all their might. Falmagon looked to the red broods—for no other reason than to avoid Nedezhda's set gaze. He recognized Branimir Baran and Mojmir Nok, the one-eyed Kras. He scowled seeing how he and Mojmir were missing the same eye.

The Kras gawked at him like he was a ghost. He pulled back his shoulders and strode by them, handing his reins off to another Kras he did not recognize.

"The boy is alive after all," Jhar said in his deep tone, taking strides across the courtyard to reach Nedezhda's side. His black cloak swayed over his brown boots.

"I am not a boy," Falmagon growled, his words flooding out in a single breath and sounding angrier than he intended.

"Clearly," Jhar said, pointing at Falmagon's grown beard and mustache. He nudged Nedezhda at his side, causing her to recoil. "You always held faith he survived, didn't you? You and Dorofej?"

At the mention of the old Highborn, Falmagon squinted his lone eye at Dorofej's cottage in time to catch a glimpse of the black mage, wrapped in his murky robes, disappear inside and shut the door behind him.

Nedezhda straightened her back and lifted her chin at Falmagon without any real expression. Her red hair rested against her cheek. "I did not have a doubt. Falmagon may be the most resolute among us. I suppose this means you have earned the title of Longwalker?"

Falmagon came to a halt, balancing his weight on Habermani. His words came with more authority than he anticipated. "That is for the Spearhead to decide."

Jhar grunted, ogling at the staff. "You have the stranger's crooked staff." He ran a hand through his black hair and blinked several times as though he were just taking a first look at Falmagon. With a snort, Jhar stepped back and dipped his head down as though he could see under the wrapping over Falmagon's face. He said, "And you lost your eye. By the gods, what happened out there?"

"My report is for the Spearhead," Falmagon said, meeting Nedezhda's eyes. *Was she his mother?* Her countenance was as cold as stone, giving him no clue to her true relationship with him. He did not think he would ever look at her the same; in the end, however, his loyalty was to the Kadari and the Lightbringer.

She dipped her chin with respect. "Welcome home."

Jhar whipped his head sideways to look at Nedezhda with astoundment. "Welcome home?" He blew air from between his lips. "Never mind that. What in the Nine Lands happened?"

He did not give Jhar an answer. Stroking the long hairs of his mustache, he walked around them both with his eyes on the keep. His eyes flashed to the open window that marked Kinhar's study.

"Falmagon!" He stopped, taking notice of Andrik racing toward him with wide eyes. The man nearly tripped over his own feet, his fat lips flapping faster than Falmagon could blink. "It really is you! I thought you were dead for sure. Dorofej said time and again that you were alive, but no one had any way of knowing. I cannot believe you have returned! Are you okay?"

Falmagon hesitated, thinking about how he wanted to respond to the other Highborn who abandoned him to the demons beneath the mountain. On the road, he thought he might reprimand Andrik, refusing to speak to him again as long as they lived. But since reaching Folkmar—through prayer—he reflected on how Andrik's cowardice gave him the opportunity to defeat Kindel the Red, thus saving the Highborn from Erzebeth's warning of doom.

"Falmagon?" Andrik scrunched up his ugly face, mouth gaping open. Falmagon noticed the Highborn staring at the dressing covering his missing eye.

"I am well," Falmagon said, clamping Andrik on the shoulder.

Andrik paled, horrified by the bandage. Falmagon was glad the wrapping was fresh. After leaving Maelili and fleeing from Brigita, he spent several weeks in Farmas before making his way to Valishul. For almost a month he stayed in the small village waiting for a boat to take him across the channel to the Seven Islands. He had plenty of time to clean his wounds and gather his strength.

He may have enjoyed himself more if he had not been looking over his shoulder for Brigita. After a month, however, he determined she was not coming for him. Maybe he'd killed her when throwing her into the tree.

"I—I did not tell the Spearhead of your woman at Arkaim," Andrik blurted out under his breath. "I know I said I would, but I decided against it. I—I thought you were dead in those tunnels, fighting those devils. I did not want your memory to be tarnished. I wanted you to be remembered as a hero."

Falmagon lifted his eyebrows at the admission. He was glad he chose to embrace Andrik instead of rebuking him, yet he saw no reason to thank the Highborn. "What did you say, exactly?"

Andrik darted his eyes around the courtyard. "I told it exactly like it happened. I said we saw a Northman dragged away by a demon, and we pursued it at your command. After defeating the creature, you went farther into the cave to determine the extent of the threat. When you did not return, I thought you were dead and I returned to Melkorka."

He frowned. Andrik certainly did not include his own cowardice in the tale. "Thank you, Andrik. I must speak with Kinhar now."

"It is good to see you again. We are better off having you with us."

Falmagon grunted in agreement and started up the stone staircase into the keep. His thoughts reeled, wondering if Andrik told him the truth. If Andrik truly felt as he suggested, Falmagon guessed that guilt had plagued Andrik on his own trek back to Melkorka; his words in the depths of the mountainside were not nearly as favorable.

He stepped through the door and climbed the stairs toward Kinhar's study. When he reached the door, he did not hesitate to push through.

The hearthfire burnt hot in the center of the room contending against the cold outside; its white smoke spiraled out of the window. Behind his desk sat Kinhar Sayan, the Spearhead, who set a book down the moment the door swung open. His knotted hair stretched down the side of his head, the ends coiled into a pile on the floor.

"Kinhar," Falmagon said.

"My son," Kinhar said weakly, the gap between his lips barely visible among the white hair of his beard and mustache. He cocked his head to ascertain no one had followed Falmagon into the room. "It is true. You are alive. The Lightbringer would not let you die."

"He could not shield me from the hatred of men, but he strengthened my spirit when it would have otherwise dwindled," Falmagon agreed, closing the door behind him. He strode across the room, Habermani clicking against the floorboards with every step. Kinhar visibly took notice of the staff as Falmagon declared, "I prayed to Him for deliverance to bring me home."

"And so He has." Kinhar bobbed his head. "You are chosen; you will lead the Kadari. I knew it without a doubt. Now tell me, did you do as you were instructed?"

Falmagon stopped at the head of the desk. "I have done all you asked and more, Spearhead."

"Sit and speak." Kinhar gestured to a chair behind Falmagon.

"If it is all right, I'd rather stand," Falmagon replied, gripping the staff. "I have learned to think better on my feet."

"Very well." Kinhar cleared his throat. "What did you learn from Erzebeth?"

"Andrik and I learned her threat of demons returning to Aenar was true, although Andrik does not know the full scale of the threat. Hundreds, if not thousands of demons have burrowed beneath the Crags of Kazimir. A war is coming, Kinhar." He scratched at his head, thinking of how much time passed since he spoke to the dark-haired, pale-skinned woman in Arkaim.

Kinhar's blue eyes dimmed at his ominous words.

Falmagon hurried to say more. "Erzebeth told me a Red would destroy the Highborn. I believe this was Kindel, the stranger from the beach, who once owned this staff called Habermani." Falmagon lifted the staff but kept it from Kinhar's twitching hands. "I killed him, Kinhar."

"The staff is your prize to keep," Kinhar said. "Do you know its power?"

"Not fully, but I am learning," Falmagon answered.

"Good," Kinhar said.

A cool wind swept through the window, spiraling Falmagon's hair. He gripped the crooked staff between his fingers and finally asked the long-awaited question. "Am I a Longwalker, then?"

"Yes, Falmagon Sej. You are the Highborn Longwalker," Kinhar declared. He shifted in his chair, the wooden legs beneath him creaking as he leaned forward. "Now, tell me about Nedezhda."

"What of her?" Falmagon asked.

"While Erzebeth's advice cannot be ignored, the Lightbringer said the evil lurked within the walls of Melkorka," Kinhar said, then pointed toward the window. "Not roaming in the wilds of Kalamaar."

"I—I—" Falmagon gulped. *Was she his mother? Could he betray her? If she had given birth to him, she also abandoned him.*

"Remember, Falmagon. You are a Kadari," Kinhar cooed.

Falmagon met Kinhar's eyes, the truth spilling from his lips. "She is not to be trusted, Spearhead. She wields death magic unlike anything the Highborn have ever known. Andrik knows it. He is loyal to her."

"Praise the Lightbringer that this truth has been unearthed." Kinhar stood up, reaching for his own walking stick that leaned against his desk. His hair unraveled, hanging to his ankles as his flimsy beard bobbled against his chest. He looked to his books and stood. "She will be executed. And we cannot be too careful of Andrik either. We will need a weapon. A dagger."

"Executed?" Falmagon gulped. "A dagger?"

The Highborn never made weapons.

Kinhar spoke with grit. "Yes. We must be ready to protect the Highborn, the Anshedar, and all Aenar. It is our eternal duty."

Falmagon considered the znaki and swelled his chest. "It will take some time to master but I know how to ward her from Koldovstvo. We will not be defeated."

"Excellent, my son." Kinhar flashed his teeth. "Her death will bring about the age of the Kadari. You will be at the forefront. You will lead us to glory."

MELKORKA

BOOK 1
The Kaelandur Series

THRICE NINE LEGENDS

Joshua Robertson

Month of High Grass
Third of Warmth
124 CE

Chapter I

Branimir Baran cowered away from the copper ore heating in the open hearth. He could not keep his heart from beating in his chest, knowing this would be the first weapon to ever have been crafted at Melkorka. His masters, the Highborn, had never needed a corporal weapon before this day. Even a hundred years ago when they had defended against the demonic Bukavac that bled from the Crags of Kazimir, not a single Highborn had held a weapon. Then again, there was not an *Eretik*, or an evil magus, living among them a hundred years ago.

Even at a distance, the warmth of the hearth touched Branimir's cheeks. "Why does the law say to cut off *their* heads?"

He scarcely noticed he had actually said the words until Jhar Gurov responded with a throaty growl, "It says to decapitate them, crush their skull, and blacken their carcass! The law of men is clear enough about Eretiks! You would not understand, Kras. You are not like us."

Branimir, standing at half the height of the man, turned his head away. The words struck him. It was true he was not the same as the Highborn. Many would think he had demon blood running through his veins, considering his red skin, pointed ears, and pale eyes.

He absentmindedly grinded his crooked teeth and pulled at his long, hooked nose. He supposed he was considered grotesque by human standards.

Regardless, Jhar's next words implied the man did not fully understand why they were crafting the copper blade either. "The real question is why we have to fulfill the law of the Northmen. This is not what it means to be a Highborn!"

A timeworn man, shrouded in murky robes, swayed in a wooden chair behind Branimir. The rockers of the chair creaked at every incline. The man's grey mane bobbed, including the braided tassels of the beard hanging from his pointed chin. He spoke smoothly in a strange accent, "A proper weapon for a proper beheading, so we are told, yes?"

"Weapon or not, we are not blacksmiths, Dorofej," Jhar said firmly grasping his waistband. Branimir took a slight step back toward Dorofej, as though the wrinkled Highborn could protect him. Jhar had an expression that suggested he was on the verge of strangling something.

"We are never the things we ought to be, yes?"

Jhar gained momentum with his discourse, his voice drowning out Dorofej. "How does Kinhar expect us to make a dagger by hand? The Highborn do not make daggers! Never have!" The dark-headed man snorted hard enough to suck the layered soot from the wooden floor to his nostrils.

"And yet here we are, yes?"

"Yes. Here we are!" Jhar slurred in mocking tone. "We should at least be allowed to use magic to hurry things along!"

Dorofej looked to the fire as though he might have been measuring the weight of the suggestion. The old Highborn hovered over Branimir even when sitting hunched over in his rocking chair. Branimir scooted closer to him, his own heartbeat thumping loud enough to ring his ears. With a gulp, Branimir followed Dorofej's gaze to the hearth, hoping to find whatever calm the Highborn had suddenly found.

Branimir had to admit that there was something hypnotic about the copper softening under the intense temperature of the kiln. Its glow was a cherry red with a black coating that slowly formed around its surface. It helped him breathe a bit easier.

Jhar paced around the room. He scrunched his face up, persisting in his rant. "If we must do this, would it have been that hard to find copper nuggets? Do we really have to sit here like fools watching the slag separate?"

"Found on the Seven Islands or Kalamaar, copper is not," Dorofej said. "Kinhar was lucky that he found it in Arkaim at all."

"He did not find anything! It was that new convert—that young woman—who he had fetch it for him like an inept hound."

Dorofej nodded again, his knees bending and extending, keeping rhythm with the chair. "Katerina, her name is, yes? Katerina Gajic from Arkaim. It was likely she would be sent, with her father being in the merchant trade and—"

"I don't need a story, Dorofej. It doesn't matter. He should have sent a Kras. Those little, red broods are the pawns, not the Highborn!"

"Too far a journey for a Kras, I would think. In the wake of the Crags, beyond the hills and the sea—"

"Dorofej!" Jhar said the man's name as though he were casting it into the fire with the burning copper.

The older man innocently raised his bushy eyebrows, his blue eyes widening momentarily at the younger Highborn. He seemed to finally take the hint of Jhar's irritation and mused, "Do not let my reasoning mind disturb your senseless repartee. By all means, let your tongue continue to twitch."

Jhar scowled.

Branimir watched and listened, finding a hint of hilarity in the situation. Any fear he had a moment ago finally fled as he covered his mouth to stop himself from cackling out loud.

He swallowed hard to stomach the laughter. Branimir had been brought up like every other Kras that served at Melkorka. It was their duty to serve the Highborn from birth to death, following directions without question. It was a simple way to live. In fact, it had guided his bloodline for at least the past millennium. He was smart enough to not be caught with a fit of the giggles.

Again, Branimir focused on the copper in the fire. The residue from the ore separated to be collected from the natural element and then disposed. Soon, the metal would be ready to be crafted into a blade and then delicately sharpened.

"Kras," Jhar mumbled, "tell Kinhar that *Kaelandur* will be ready by nightfall. He can have his execution then, if that is his wish."

Branimir stood up from the fire. Apparently, the Highborn had named the copper dagger to be formed. It would be called Kaelandur.

He dipped his head slightly. "At once, Lord," Branimir wheezed between his crooked teeth and cracked lips.

"Killing one of our own and with a weapon. It is madness," Jhar blathered, his fingers twisting to fists, turning white.

Branimir made no comment. The statement was not directed toward him.

Instead, Branimir straightened his wool jacket and pulled the cuffs over his crimson-colored hands. Adjusting his black cloak, he headed toward the rickety door leading to the courtyard. Rays of sunlight pierced through cracks in the wood. The fresh smell of spring pressed against his nostrils.

He grinned behind his closed lips, knowing the Season of Frost was still a quarter of a year away. He still had time to enjoy the sun. The cold was the worst.

He had just taken hold of the latch when Dorofej whispered his name.

"Branimir."

He turned on command. Dorofej was the only Highborn who ever called him by name. "Yes, my Lord."

Dorofej leaned forward in his rocker, clearing his throat while turning his head to observe the younger Highborn. Jhar paid him no attention as usual. Dorofej took a slow breath before speaking in a soft tone. "It has been many years that you have served the Highborn at Melkorka, has it not?"

"Yes, Lord. Over five decades."

With the flames dancing behind him, Dorofej's blue eyes looked like stones frozen in ice. He peered toward the slave as if weighing his next words carefully.

Branimir waited. His time was not his to measure.

"You have never known of an Eretik being beheaded here at Melkorka prior to Nedezhda, yes?"

Branimir kept himself from gasping at the sound of the Eretik's name. No one at Melkorka had said Nedezhda Mager's name in two days. Chained in the dungeons, she was already forgotten by the Highborn.

Branimir had not questioned her fate. She was considered a traitor the moment she was found meddling with death magic and worshipping dark gods. Laws about such things were for the humans, not him.

Branimir shuddered, his hand quivered against the latch with each word. "I do not understand, my Lord. Do you ask whether I have known of Eretiks among the Highborn, or whether I have known of Eretiks who have come to Melkorka, or simply knowing of Eretiks losing their head altogether?" The penalty for questioning the Highborn was not pleasant and ranged from a firm beating to missing appendages. The Highborn were not considered violent as humans were concerned, but the Kras were not regarded much more than a filthy throw rug. Beating out the crud was not only believed to be necessary, but commonplace.

The handle clicked noisily against the planks of the door. The fear churning in his belly practically bubbled.

"I mean what I ask and nothing more," Dorofej replied.

"No, Lord." Branimir gulped, choosing his words carefully. "In my lifetime, or the lifetime of my lineage, there has never been an Eretik who has lost their head at Melkorka. My father would have told me."

Dorofej harrumphed, returning to his private thoughts. Branimir waited, frozen under the gaze of the Highborn.

Several moments passed before Dorofej turned back to the fire.

"Odd for it to happen this day, it is."

The statement seemed to reflect Dorofej's conversation with himself, not meant to be heard by others. It was surely not directed toward Branimir, a lowly Kras.

The Highborn did have a funny way of constantly talking to themselves.

"Do as Jhar told you, Branimir," Dorofej said.

"Yes, my Lord." Branimir dipped his head again and squeezed through the narrow door into the morning sunbeams. He sighed with a sense of relief.

The sun was high for it being only a few hours after morning meal. As was common in the Season of Warmth, the sun brightened the stronghold called Melkorka. The castle was considered great in ancient times, as well as now, even when compared to modern day manors in the cities on the mainland. Branimir had never been to the mainland, but he had overheard stories from the Highborn. He was quite sure nothing could ever be greater than Melkorka.

It was not an exceedingly large castle. In fact, it could easily be overlooked if not sought out. Melkorka did not oversee any city, village or hamlet. No monuments pinpointed its exact location. Melkorka stood alone, hidden and forlorn, like a lone warrior, dauntless and diligent.

Branimir had heard the stone structure was crafted from chiseled boulders nearly two thousand years ago. The massive rocks, the size of faerings, or long boats, were stacked in such a way that they almost appeared to have grown straight out of the hilltop. It was said that the heavy stones had been carried by an unknown means from the Crags of Kazimir to the south and east to build Melkorka. Although it was likely that the Highborn had used their magic, Branimir preferred the stories that suggested that giants had moved the chunks of rock. There was something thrilling about creatures who towered over humans.

His gaze drifted, seeing the few Highborn and fewer Kras. Of course, most of the Highborn would be in the keep, and there were not many Kras left at Melkorka. Not many at all.

The flapping tapestries atop the towers of the stronghold stole Branimir's attention. The symbol was circular with thick golden, dancing swirls strewn throughout. Such a sign was meant to represent the god, Dahz, the ruler of the golden sun and Protector of Men.

"Bran!" A comforting voice resounded as he made his way across the courtyard toward the keep. "Bran!"

Branimir turned to see another Kras come running from the guardhouse just inside the main gate. Mojmir Nok rushed across the worn path inside the walls, barely making a sound. His scarlet skin glistened against the sun rays, a head of thin, black hair bouncing over his offset mouth. Mojmir was an odd creature to look at. Not because of his traits of being a Kras, but because he was missing his left eye. This gave more attention to his right eye. Its color was dark as pitch.

Mojmir squeaked again in his shrill voice. "Bran!"

Branimir raised his hand to quiet his friend. "What is the hubbub, Mojmir?"

"Andrik sent me. Kinhar is in the dungeon with … her … he wants you."

Branimir chewed the inside of his lip. Obviously, *her* could only be Nedezhda Mager, the Eretik. "Why me?"

Mojmir shrugged his shoulders.

Branimir turned to look at the housing unit he had just exited, holding Dorofej and Jhar. Similar stone houses with thatched roofs lined the inner side of the wall. They had just replaced the straw at the beginning of the season and would have to change it again in a few months before the cold came.

He scratched his head. Being sent to Kinhar was one thing but being summoned by him was another matter entirely. "I needed to speak with Kinhar anyhow."

Branimir turned from Mojmir without a farewell and quickly climbed the stone staircase that stood adjacent to the keep. He did not hesitate and entered through the sturdy wooden door. Mojmir had gone his own way after delivering the message. Even if Branimir had the option, he would not have asked Mojmir to join him. A Kras always had their orders to attend to and could not be distracted by idle chitchat.

Branimir stepped within the hall of the keep. It gave suggestion to the skeleton of the building's framework. The walls were the same stone as most of Melkorka, but the main flooring was made of beaten earth laid between the stone walls. There were two upper floors that had planks of timber covered with light layers of dirt in many areas. He tiptoed to the dungeon to the left and then right, following no more than a dirt trail that led at a harsh angle into the depths of the earth beneath the castle. The single path to the dungeon was much like the others, smooth and even from ages of being walked upon.

Branimir glided his hand along the smooth stone as he crept down into the dungeon, careful not to slip down the crevice. He cautiously placed each of his small feet in front of one another and inched twenty feet deep toward the dilapidated door that was supposed to hold prisoners securely beneath Melkorka.

Branimir approached the poor excuse for a door. He had been enslaved to the Highborn for his entire life. Never once had he tried to make an escape, nor had any Kras within Melkorka. It was likely that the Highborn would have their heads before they could dream up a scheme for escape. Branimir could as easily claim that no prisoner had ever runaway either, but then again, there had never been a prisoner at Melkorka in his lifetime.

Nedezhda was the first.

Branimir pushed open the door, afraid that it might crumble beneath his touch. When it did not, the Kras scooted inside the narrow opening.

Kinhar Sayan's voice was easily recognizable in a hollowed wheeze, "It pains me to have to sentence you to death, but there is no other way. You know the penalty of being an Eretik. I do not have to explain the law to you, Nedezhda."

Kinhar's coarse cloth outlined his frail frame. He was easily aged beyond that of the ancient Dorofej. Kinhar stood, stooped with his hand against the stone wall for support. His white hair fell to his heels, tied in knots to keep him from tripping over it. His upper lips and chin had flimsy hair of the same color that hung wildly over his mouth and chest.

He appeared to be more hair than man.

"I know your schemes, Kinhar. Taking my head this night will not silence your wickedness."

Nedezhda was sprightly, despite the chains that bound her body to the stone wall. A small etching of an eye scraped with a moon and a cross was engraved over her head. Branimir could only guess that the symbol prevented her from touching the craft, *Koldovstvo*. There was no evidence of torture to her flesh or mind, as she stared defiantly at Kinhar. Her light blue eyes were alarming, shining in the darkness, with a hint of knowing that made Branimir shiver and turn his head away momentarily.

"The evil traces of Koldovstvo flow deep in your veins, my poor girl. Madness has enveloped your mind and has led you to paranoia and delusion and—"

"I know what was said!" The woman's nose was small, but her nostrils flared with the intensity of a horrendous beast. "You spoke of the Kadari!"

Kinhar was poised as though her shouts were the quietest of whispers. "Such faith I had in you, Nedezhda. The Highborn are the hand of the Lightbringer. We will be the deliverers of hope even when there is none to be had."

"The Highborn are to have no allegiance," she began.

"And yet, you have allied yourself with the heart of darkness, embracing its futility and uniting eternally with its acidic breath," Kinhar continued.

Nedezhda gave no sign of wavering to her elder. "Cut me down this night or the next, Kinhar Sayan, but know that my innocence will be avenged. The Highborn do not kill their own."

"The law must be upheld. It has been decreed that your actions extend beyond the privilege of breath. Dahz demands that Strega's breath be breathed by His brethren and not those that spit on righteousness."

"You speak of the gods as if they speak to you. You speak of good and evil as though it is defined by the divine. Any delusion that runs rampant in Melkorka is in your mind, Kinhar!"

"Bah!" The old man turned his crumpled face from the younger woman, taking notice of Branimir standing idly behind him.

Branimir recoiled at the man's sudden attention.

"Alas, you have come, Kras," Kinhar spoke steadily, turning his attention back to the Eretik with a snort. "See how the Kras knows their function without question, ever vigilant in their loyalty to those of exceptional power. The Kras to the Highborn is the Highborn to the Lightbringer, Nedezhda. Such simple logic you should have recognized early in your apprenticeship."

"Such loose connections are contrived by men absorbed with entitlement, taking advantage of the less fortunate," she flung back at him.

Kinhar shook his head in disbelief at the woman, returning focus to the Kras. "What news do you bring from Jhar and Dorofej?"

"My Lord, Kaelandur will be ready by nightfall."

"So, it is this night that justice will run its course in Melkorka?"

Branimir hesitated, uncertain if the question was meant for him. It was awfully difficult to know when the Highborn were speaking to one of their gods or themselves entirely. "Yes, my Lord."

Kinhar looked at Branimir, with a hint of surprise that he had spoken and then continued, "I have a task for you and the one-eyed one."

Branimir recognized the reference to Mojmir. "Speak it and consider it done, my Lord."

"Take this," Kinhar grabbed a hand full of Nedezhda's hair and tore it from her head. She screamed, blood immediately surfacing on her scalp.

Branimir winced, holding his small, red hand out to take the strands of hair from his Lord with as much eagerness as he could muster. "Yes, my Lord."

"Take this inland toward the Crags and set fire to it so that when the evening gale blows, the ashes are swept toward the shores of Strega's Deep. Make haste and do not let any Highborn go with you."

"You will bring death to the world," Nedezhda hissed.

Kinhar frowned at her.

Branimir winced at her words. He was inclined to ask Kinhar of the true purpose of the task, but he knew better than to question the Highborn.

He bowed his head in submission. "As you wish, my Lord. It will be done at once."

"By the time you return," Kinhar said with more ferocity than Branimir had ever witnessed from the old man, "the

Eretik will have her neck severed and body bloodied in flame."

With the hesitation of a raindrop falling from a thatch roof, Branimir raised his pale eyes slowly to look at Nedezhda and quickly wished he had refrained. Her cold eyes were ignited with equal rage, stained with the shadow of an inescapable death, and were frozen to his own with timeless hatred.

ABOUT THE AUTHOR

Joshua Robertson was born in Kingman, Kansas on May 23, 1984. A graduate of Norwich High School, Robertson attended Wichita State University where he received his master's in social work with minors in psychology and sociology. His bestselling novel, *Melkorka*, the first in *The Kaelandur* Series, was released in 2015. Known most for his Thrice Nine Legends Saga, Robertson enjoys an ever-expanding and extremely loyal following of readers. He counts R.A. Salvatore and J.R.R. Tolkien among his literary influences.

www.ingramcontent.com/pod-product-compliance
Lightning Source LLC
Chambersburg PA
CBHW050545190726
48283CB00007B/2015